KU-624-262

About the Author

Stephanie Butland lives near the sea in the north-east of England. She writes in a studio at the bottom of her garden. Researching her novels has turned her into an occasional performance poet and tango dancer.

 @under_blue_sky

 @StephanieButlandAuthor

Also by Stephanie Butland

Novels
Letters to My Husband
The Other Half of My Heart
Lost for Words
The Curious Heart of Ailsa Rae
The Woman in the Photograph

Non-fiction
How I Said Bah! to cancer
Thrive: The Bah! Guide to Wellness After cancer

Nobody's
Perfect

4 4 0140550 8

Stephanie
Butland

Nobody's
Perfect

ZAFFRE

First published in the UK in 2021 by
ZAFFRE
An imprint of Bonnier Books UK
4th Floor, Victoria House, Bloomsbury Square,
London WC1B 4DA
Owned by Bonnier Books
Sveavägen 56, Stockholm, Sweden

Copyright © Stephanie Butland, 2021

All rights reserved.
No part of this publication may be reproduced,
stored or transmitted in any form by any means, electronic,
mechanical, photocopying or otherwise, without the
prior written permission of the publisher.

The right of Stephanie Butland to be identified as Author of this
work has been asserted by her in accordance with the
Copyright, Designs and Patents Act, 1988.

This is a work of fiction. Names, places, events and
incidents are either the products of the author's
imagination or used fictitiously. Any resemblance to
actual persons, living or dead, or actual
events is purely coincidental.

A CIP catalogue record for this book is
available from the British Library.

ISBN: 978-1-83877-322-9

Also available as an ebook and an audiobook

1 3 5 7 9 10 8 6 4 2

Typeset by IDSUK (Data Connection) Ltd
Printed and bound in Great Britain by Clays Ltd, Elcograf S.p.A.

Zaffre is an imprint of Bonnier Books UK
www.bonnierbooks.co.uk

For Auntie Susan

Chapter 1

Early September

TODAY IS AN IMPORTANT day for Kate and Daisy. If Kate doesn't get this right, the consequences are huge. If Kate doesn't make sure that her daughter's teacher understands precisely what Daisy needs, then her life will be at risk.

The man who is to be Daisy's teacher walks down the school corridor towards Kate. Her stomach tightens; her heartbeat flits up by the tiniest of wingbeats. This meeting is critical for Daisy, Kate reminds herself, no wonder she's uncomfortable. That, and the tiredness, and the late summer heat.

Kate breathes deep, but that only makes her agitation worse, because every time she takes a deliberate breath like this, pushing air into every last bronchiole, it's a physical reminder of all the capacity that she has, and Daisy lacks. And that makes Kate think of the responsibility she has – so much more than a parent of a well child. (Though heaven help anyone who says, in

Kate's presence, that Daisy is unwell.) So much more weight on her shoulders, too, because she has no one to parent with.

'Hello. You must be Ms Micklethwaite, and Daisy?' When Kate untwines her fingers from Daisy's in order to shake the proffered hand, she feels how her own hand is clammy; when Daisy's teacher smiles, she knows her own smile to be too wide, too long, in response. Only then does she recognise that, however stressful this might be, there's something else going on. It's a long time since she felt this particular hum of nerves and adrenaline. She had forgotten what attraction is. She wills her body to forget again.

'I'm sorry to have kept you waiting.' His smile is straight, but his eye-teeth are crooked. His eyes are a steady, dark brown, set deep, his matching brown hair short and neat. He is shaved so smooth that Kate imagines his skin cool to her fingertips, like the pear she took out of the fridge this morning.

'We were early,' Kate says, taking back her hand, pulling herself together. 'Please, call me Kate. As you know, Daisy is going to be in your class and there are a few things I want to discuss.'

Mr Swanson squats to make eye contact with Daisy. His shoes, Kate notices, are polished to the bright black of a robin's eye. Her boots are scuffed. Well, she doesn't have time for everything.

'Daisy, I'm Mr Swanson, and I'm going to be your new teacher.'

He puts out his hand and shakes Daisy's. Daisy nods, solemn, then examines her hand, front and back, as though this touch might have left a mark. 'Spencer Swanson,' he says, glancing at Kate. She savours his name, and the fact that he offered it as an equal to her own. But he misreads the look on her face, imagining a suppressed laugh, perhaps, and smiles. 'I know, I know, I should be starring in a musical.'

Kate laughs, too loud, and Daisy giggles at the sound. Kate tells her body not to do this. When she speaks, her voice is the steady, serious one she recognises as her own, these days, when she has no choice but to be a steady, serious adult. Though she'd rather not have to be. Or at least, not always. She imagines, briefly, how it would be if she met this man somewhere else. In a bar, late. Though Kate is lucky if she gets to a bar twice a year. 'It's not that,' she says, smiling nonetheless, 'it's just that we parents don't usually get to use first names.' She remembers being introduced to the Head – 'I'm Miss Hillier' – and trying to remember the last time she was given no option but to use a title. She is on first-name terms with her Open University tutors; even the hospital consultants introduce themselves as Sam or Humzah or Janice, despite having worked so hard for so many years to move to Dr and back to Mr, Mrs or Ms again.

'Well, I'm all modern.' Spencer is still smiling. 'You need to watch out for me. Shall we go along to the classroom to talk?'

Kate assumes he's already been briefed. This both pleases and aggravates her. She is glad, of course, that the school is taking Daisy's needs seriously. But she wishes that she could have been the one to tell him everything. That way she'd know that he had it straight. She knows how easily the d-word – disabled – can be used when she isn't around, because once, when she had picked Daisy up from playgroup, Daisy had asked her what it meant.

The classroom is empty, and it feels to Kate as though it's waiting. The walls are bare and the display boards clear, the tables too neatly organised, the books arranged by size. The parquet floor is bright and unscuffed, and the not-quite-pine smell of cleaning fluids is everywhere. At a sink in the corner stands a shortish, stoutish, fiftyish woman, washing out plastic containers and stacking them on a draining board. She looks round when the classroom door opens. She smiles politely when she sees Spencer and Kate, and her eyes brighten at the sight of Daisy.

'This is Wendy Orr, who I'm pleased to say is going to be our teaching assistant in reception class this year,' Spencer says. 'Wendy, this is Daisy Micklethwaite, who's joining us tomorrow, and her mother, Kate.'

'We know each other.' Kate smiles. 'Wendy used to be my parents' neighbour. When they first moved here, before I was born. When did we last see each other? It must have been at my mum's wedding, I think?'

'Is it that long?' Wendy asks, shaking her head in a way that signals, 'time flies'. 'I suppose it must be. Tell her I'll be in touch soon, won't you?'

'Of course.'

Spencer shakes his head. 'Small towns,' he says, almost to himself. Wendy dries her hands and turns to Daisy, who's been standing at Kate's side, quiet, throughout.

'Hello, Daisy. Shall I remind you where we're going to hang your coat when you start school tomorrow? I know you've been to see us already, but there's a lot to remember.'

Daisy nods and holds out a hand. Sometimes Kate's heart breaks at her daughter's easy trust in others. Just as she's never yet known she is on the heavy end of the seesaw, she's never had reason to distrust an adult, apart from maybe the ones who try to tell her that needles won't hurt, or wake her to listen to her chest in the middle of the night when she is in hospital. But it is easy to see that Wendy is someone as happy in the company of children as adults, and Daisy has a fine instinct for the people who will do the same jigsaw puzzle with her over and over again, and recognises Miss Orr as one of them.

'Actually,' Kate says, 'I wonder if you could join us? I'd really like to talk to you both.' Wendy will share the school-day responsibility for Daisy, so she should be involved in these discussions, too. The fact that Kate can't bear the thought of being alone with

5

this man who is making her body both crave and panic is irrelevant. Totally irrelevant.

'Shall we sit down?' Spencer offers a too-small orange chair to her and then folds himself down onto another one with more grace than Kate can manage. Wendy joins them, sitting with ease and a smile. 'We're all ears,' Spencer says.

'Yes. Right.' What Kate is here to do is just a more formal version of what she does, in some small way, most days. She's shifting the world to accommodate Daisy. She is prepared, with her own notes and leaflets from the hospital. What she wasn't prepared for was Spencer. Well, she's just going to have to get on with it.

But then Kate looks at his hands, resting on the table next to a pen and notebook, and despite herself, she notices that he isn't wearing a wedding ring. That his hands are handsome hands, his nails clean, his knuckles round. He has been watching her face, waiting; she can feel the places where his gaze rested as surely as if he'd touched her. She wiggles her toes to stop herself blushing. She's twenty-four years old, not thirteen. She's a mother.

Kate launches herself into the familiar. 'Please don't think of cystic fibrosis as a disability. It's a condition that means that Daisy's pancreas doesn't function properly, and her lungs produce mucus that is especially thick.' On cue, Daisy coughs, a throaty, full sound that Kate's mother calls her pit-pony cough. The three adults turn to look at Daisy. The cough hasn't even

6

interrupted her drawing. 'The coughing,' Kate says, 'is a fact of life.' Spencer and Wendy smile at her. *Please*, she thinks, *don't anyone say that I'm brave or Daisy's brave. Please don't either of you put your heads on one side.*

But Spencer keeps smiling and says, 'That's a cough that belongs in a working men's club, not a reception class.'

'Exactly.' Kate feels that too-wide smile again. Tells her body to stop. Again.

Daisy starts to cough again, and this time, she gets up and comes towards Kate. 'Do you need to spit, Daisy?' Kate asks, and when her little girl nods, she takes her to the sink, where Daisy hacks up mucus that Kate washes away with hot water. They both wash their hands, then Daisy returns to her colouring, and Kate to her chair.

'Daisy's been taught to cough up mucus when it's loose,' she explains, 'in sinks or bins or drains. That won't be a problem?' Kate makes it sound like a question for the sake of politeness. What's best for Daisy has to happen.

'Not at all,' Spencer says.

Wendy offers, 'I've worked with a little boy with CF before, in another school,' then adds, quickly, as though she might have somehow caused offence, 'although I know that Daisy will be different. And it was a long time ago. I just meant that I've had some experience. Of the coughing, and the supplements, and . . .' Her voice falters away, and she looks at Daisy and then, less sure, back to Kate, who smiles.

'I'm glad to know that. Thank you for telling me.'

'This is all new to me,' Spencer says. 'In practice, if not in theory.' He drops his voice, raises his eyebrows, a theatrical confidence. 'It's six years since I qualified, which a lot of people will tell you is no time at all.'

Kate smiles, thinking of her role as The Youngest: youngest mother at the clinic and the toddler groups, youngest student at her Open University exams. There she had sat amongst rows of people who, she imagined, were doing just what she was doing: making sure they had the learning, although life had stopped them from going to university the way that Kate's sixth-form friends had. She had got together with the old school crowd the first Christmas after Daisy was born, encouraged by her mother to 'go and enjoy herself'. She'd dressed up; she'd been delighted to see her old friends. But after an hour and a half of stories about the drunken stealing of traffic cones and midnight drives to Brighton beach, she'd felt lonelier than she had at any point since Daisy's birth, less than four months before. None of her friends were interested in Daisy, not really; they said things like 'Oh, my God, I still can't believe you have an actual baby, Kate,' and then asked what else she had been doing. There had been no understanding of how all-encompassing a newborn was, or acknowledgement that she was grieving for Daisy's father still. Kate had gone home early, and has turned down invitations from everyone, except her kind, funny friend Melissa, ever since. But even Melissa drives Kate crazy, sometimes, with the way she assumes Kate is waiting for her own life to start. It's as if she thinks keeping a tiny, vulnerable human alive and well is the time-and-energy equivalent of having a vegetable patch.

Kate, cramped on her orange chair in the reception classroom, resolves to tell Melissa about this afternoon properly, instead of mentioning it as though it's a haircut. She smiles at Spencer, almost meets his gaze. 'We all have to start somewhere,' she says.

He nods. 'Exactly. So please, if you wouldn't mind, assume I know nothing, and tell me everything, from the beginning.' Spencer moves his arm and in doing so touches the sleeve of Kate's jacket, just above her wrist. It's as though her arm can feel his fingertips despite the two layers of fabric between their skin. 'I want to do a good job here. I'd appreciate your help.'

And so Kate begins. She explains the need for Daisy to have a high-calorie diet, and that she needs to take enzymes and supplements to help her to get enough nutrition and to grow, although living next door to a bakery usually makes it easy enough to get calories into her.

'What does Granny call you, Daisy?' she asks, and Daisy, without looking up from the complex curlicues she is adding to the wings of the butterfly she is drawing, says, 'The croissant queen!' The three adults

9

laugh, and Kate feels the beginnings of how she feels with the few people who already make up Daisy's family. It isn't just that she trusts them to take care of her, it's that they understand that Daisy is more than the sum of a malfunctioning pancreas and gummed-up lungs and a life expectancy of forty-one. Kate has her mother, her stepfather, and her father, though he's working away for a year. Daisy's paternal grand-mother, Patricia, died a year ago and it's only since then that Kate realised how much she did for them – the babysitting, the old-fashioned Sunday lunches, the trips to the library with Daisy that allowed Kate to get her Open University assignments done during the day, instead of after Daisy's bedtime. Then there's Melissa, and she's great, she really is, but she's busy with her own life. The life that Kate, in her darkest moments, knows that she herself should have had. How won-derful it would be if the – well, the sheer pressure of Daisy, the weight of her, could be spread a little fur-ther, distributed in part to these two serious-looking people who are concentrating on Kate's every word.

As Kate talks, Wendy makes small agreeing nods and noises, and Spencer writes notes in a black A4 notebook with a silver pen, his eyes moving from the page to Kate's face to Daisy. Daisy draws and colours and coughs, apparently oblivious as her mother talks about the absences for clinic visits and the almost-constant need for antibiotics and which tablets have to be given when.

The conversation is exactly the one that Kate wants to have; apart from the way her mouth dries every time she is about to speak to Spencer directly, and her gaze keeps moving from her own hands to his, to the plump knot of the tie at his throat and his Adam's apple moving up and down above it. But she does what she needs to do, because she is a mother, and a role model for her daughter, or at least that is what she intends to be, every morning, even if it doesn't always go as well as it should. She certainly has no time for this – whatever this is that is in the air between her and Spencer. Plus, it didn't exactly go well last time.

As they are about to leave, Daisy solemnly presents her butterfly picture to Wendy, with the words, 'It's a Red Admirable.'

'I can see that.' Wendy smiles. 'I get Red Admirals in my garden sometimes. Thank you. I'm going to take this home and put it on my wall.' Kate has no doubt that this is exactly what will happen. And then Wendy says, 'I didn't show you where we're going to hang your coat, Daisy.' Then, looking to Kate, 'Have we got time?'

'Of course.' And Kate is left alone with Spencer. They are both standing, in readiness for saying goodbye. Although Kate is tall, her line of sight is equal to the top of Spencer's shoulder. The top of her head would probably sit just under his chin. She blushes at the thought, and looks at the tips of her boots, conker-brown leather and two winters old. She's tossing up whether to ask Spencer about his last school, or whether he likes Throckton, when Spencer speaks. His voice has a faint Scottish accent, but there's something else, too, a barely perceptible softness: the sound of a place where people are kind.

'May I ask you one more thing?'

'Of course.' Kate's mind flips through what she might have forgotten to mention.

'Is it just you and Daisy? Or will we be seeing Daisy's father as well?'

'Daisy's father died before she was born,' Kate says, hearing defensiveness in her own voice. 'As you probably know.' His question has made her flinch. He was entitled to ask it, she will suppose, later.

Spencer flinches, too; a visible, if tiny, twitch of the muscles round his eyes, the air sharp between them. 'I didn't know,' he says. 'I'm sorry to hear that.'

There is a spiked pause, while Kate tries to find the ground again, and Spencer stands, unmoving, while she feels herself sway. 'Well, if you haven't heard the story, someone will tell you soon enough. It's all Throckton had to talk about for a while.' How Kate would love to lose herself, somewhere bigger than this small-minded town, somewhere where she was all new, and no one could talk about her past as though it was their own property. When she goes to stay with Melissa in London, the anonymity of it is a slightly frightening high.

'I don't listen to gossip,' Spencer says, a little formally.

And then Kate hears how she must have sounded: sharp, shrill, a woman defined by her past. A woman that she doesn't want to be. She makes the effort; after all, she is going to have to talk to this man most days for the next school year. Her stomach capsizes a little as she looks up into Spencer's face.

'I don't get asked the question very much. It threw me, a bit. Everybody round here knows that it's just me and Daisy.'

'It's fine,' Spencer says, and his eyes are bright as he looks at her, although his smile is muted. 'But like I said, I really don't listen to gossip. It's – it's a point of honour, if you like. So if there's anything else you want me to know, you'll have to tell me yourself.'

Daisy rushes in – 'I can reach my peg and I don't even have to stand on my tibbytoes!' – and they leave, with Kate in a different kind of rush: mixed feelings and bitter tastes and high hormones. On the walk home, she tries to focus on the most important thing: she has no doubt that her daughter is going to be in safe hands with Spencer Swanson and Wendy Orr.

Getting ready to take Daisy to school the next morning, Kate puts on her usual lick of mascara, to make her pale eyelashes less eerie and her pale eyes stand out; she picks up a lipstick, but puts it down again. She's a mother, a student, a feminist. She is raising Daisy to be as independent as she can possibly be. And she will never again be the girl she was, who thought only of a man, and sacrificed so much of her own life and others' happiness for him.

She persuades Daisy to stand still for long enough to take a photo of her in her school uniform, then bundles her into her coat. Daisy adds her butterfly wings; Kate cannot help but pick her up and take a selfie, which she sends to her mother, her father, and Melissa. Then she catches sight of the time – 'Come on, Daisy,' she calls, picking up the rucksack full of high-calorie snacks, carefully labelled medication, and a tube of hand sanitiser that Daisy is well-drilled in using. 'It's time to go.'

Daisy-as-butterfly flutters through the town and into the playground, where, freed from her mother's hand, she runs round the playground, laughing and jumping, chasing and being chased. Kate's heart lifts as she watches. Around her, other parents, skittish and peaked, are making an occasion of First Day At School. There's the twitter and grumble of conversation about time flying and getting to eat your lunch uninterrupted and how sad it is that they're growing up and hahahaha perhaps we'll have to have another one. Kate doesn't join in.

If she reminisced, it would be about the last time she stood in a school yard, when she was one of the brightest students in the sixth form, not so many years ago. Throughout her school days she had been marked out because she was clever and quiet and not one for the rough-and-tumble, shouting, chaos. She remembers

14

standing apart with her small group of friends, or sitting on the steps reading a book. The university open days she went to when she was a sixth former thrilled her with the feeling that here, at last, was a place where she would thrive. Then came Daisy, and Kate went nowhere. But she cannot regret this path, not with her beloved butterfly-girl laughing and running around the school playground. Not when the sun is bright, and the day is new, anyway. It was different, last night, as she lay in the bath, having given up on her dissertation because she couldn't get to the end of a thought, let alone a sentence. Then, she had felt tired, lonely, cold. Her great bid for independence – moving into her father's flat while he worked abroad for a year – was not all that she had hoped for. At least her childhood bed in her mother's home had been familiar. At least there had been the sound of the TV, her mother's and stepfather's voices rumbling companionably away downstairs. So last night Kate had gone to bed early, and lain awake listening to the laughter and music from the Italian restaurant below, wondering if this was the sum total of her life. Yes, this morning is better. She turns her face to the low September sun, closes her eyes.

'Can you believe we're here?' Amelia's mother Jo says, quietly, next to Kate. Jo and Kate met at a playgroup and have struck up a sort of play date-friendship, although their conversation seldom strays beyond their girls and Jo's son, Jack, who is two years older than Daisy. Jo has at least a decade on Kate, and a lot of the things she talks about mean nothing to Kate, who has no responses to the tiresomeness of sisters-in-law, the problems of what to give as eight-year anniversary gifts, the bickering over whose turn it is to change the duvet cover. And, of course, Jo with her two healthy children and her kind husband, cannot understand what Kate's life is really like. Jo does not need to worry about Jake and Amelia's health the way Kate worries about Daisy's. Jo doesn't shy away from thoughts of her future, and the swallowing loneliness that she hardly dares name. But Kate and Jo listen to each other; they like each others' children; they are kind. It's something. 'It seems like yesterday that she was born,' Jo adds after a moment, but Kate can see that Jo is talking to herself, so she says nothing. Now Daisy and Amelia are studying the hopscotch pitch painted on the tarmac as though they are forensic scientists at a crime scene.

The only thing that seems like yesterday to Kate is yesterday. Her stomach is still roiling at the thought of Spencer; the way she felt when she was close to him, how he became cold when she mentioned gossip, as though she had accused him of something. Perhaps she had. Sometimes, Kate's mother reminds her – mildly, gently – that the world has moved on since Daisy was born, and Kate might not be the hot topic she once was. It's certainly true that silence no longer washes before her; the whispers in her wake seem to have stopped. But she is still a little to one side in the world. And whatever her mother says, she knows that if someone was describing her, it would be as 'Kate who was supposed to go to Oxford but then she got pregnant and it turned out the father was that policeman who died. And the little girl has cystic fibrosis.' She tries not to care. She knows there are things she could add, if this is to be her biography: that she still dreams about drowning in a freezing January lake, that she is determined that her degree will start to turn her into the woman she was always meant to be, that she loves her daughter beyond all that she thought was possible, and that there are times when she would do almost anything for a heed-less afternoon with no one to think about but herself. That she was not ready to be the adult she is; when she wakes in the post-drowning-nightmare darkness she sometimes wishes she could go back to being seventeen, and do things differently.

And then the bell rings, and Daisy rushes towards Kate to be de-winged and cuddled and to tolerate a kiss. As Kate watches her go – an unexpected catch in the hollow of her throat, an emptiness in her stomach more significant than she had ever thought it would be – she thinks she feels herself being watched. She doesn't look, because she doesn't know whether she will be more disappointed if Spencer Swanson is look-ing at her, or if he isn't.

Chapter 2

Mid-September

'THANK YOU SO MUCH, Mum,' Kate says to Daisy's beloved granny as she lets her into the flat, one Saturday two weeks into term time. 'I have no idea how I let myself get so spectacularly behind on this dissertation.'

'Always a pleasure to spend time with Daisy,' Richenda says, and then she strokes her hand down Kate's arm, looks at her in a way that makes Kate want to ask if she can pack up the flat and come home. 'Is it just the dissertation?'

For a moment, Kate wonders if her mother somehow knows that her daydreams about Spencer Swanson can stretch what should be a fifteen-minute dash around the supermarket into a dazed half-hour of wondering what it's like to sit down to a meal every evening with someone whose main topic of conversation isn't butterflies or mermaids. But then Richenda adds, 'I know Daisy's birthday is a strange time.'

Kate nods. The anniversary of Daisy's birth is also the anniversary of her cystic fibrosis diagnosis, of Kate's shock and fear as she discovered exactly how wrong her fantasies about birth and motherhood were, and how much more than love and care Daisy was going to need to allow her to grow up safe and strong.

'Yes,' she says, and she looks away, remembering how naive she was, how quietly and solidly her mother had been at her side. The flat has got itself untidy again, clothes clumping the radiators and mugs on the coffee table, a messy pile of half-unpacked shopping on the kitchen counter. Kate never thought about all the care she got from her mother and Blake when she lived with them. Not just the housekeeping, the bills being paid, the magical replenishment of tea-bags, toothpaste and printer ink, but the feeling of not being alone. She laughs, touches her mother's arm in return. 'And having my own place takes a lot of time.'

Richenda tilts an eyebrow, smiles back. 'I'm saying nothing. How are you getting on?'

'I think I'm nearly there,' Kate says, 'but it's the last bits, the references and the notes and the pagination and it all just seems to take so much longer than you think.'

Richenda nods. 'Yes, things like that always do, don't they? I was setting up a spreadsheet yesterday. Two hours, just vanished.'

'Daisy, Granny's here,' Kate calls, and Daisy rushes out of her bedroom, and is up and in Richenda's arms in a heartbeat.

'Hello, sweetheart. How's school?'

'Good!' Daisy says. Kate wonders how the other parents – the ones who aren't in receipt of a daily briefing from Wendy Orr – cope with knowing as little as she would know if Daisy was her only source of information about school. But although Daisy doesn't give much away in answer to questions about her day, she is keen to pour her own drinks, all of a sudden, and has explained to Kate why it's important to let someone else finish talking. Daisy often sings a song about a butterfly that Kate has never heard before, and spends time at bedtime telling her mother about the story Miss Orr is reading at school. It fills Kate with an optimistic melancholy. What she wants is for her daughter to have a good life independent of her mother. What she hadn't realised is how empty that would make her feel.

'You can see how school is.' Kate nods towards the fridge covered in pictures and paintings. Richenda laughs.

'I was thinking I'd take her swimming?'

'Sure. She's been a bit tired, but nothing worse.' The people who love Daisy live in dread of chest infections, coughs and colds, which will render Daisy pale and peaky, with a line in her arm to deliver antibiotics more efficiently.

'Good. Could you go and get your swimming bag, Daisy?' Richenda puts the little girl down as Kate organises supplements and tablets into the sections of a container. 'I'll take her to the spa at the hotel. I can give her tea, too, if that helps.'

'That would be a massive help,' Kate says, 'thank you. I can't thank you enough, Mum, really.'

Daisy lands with a jump and a bounce at her grandmother's feet. 'I'm ready!' she says. And just like that, Kate is alone.

It ought to be a pleasure. Or at least a relief. Her degree, begun when Daisy was eleven months old, had at first felt like a lifeline: an escape from the small and often frightening world of caring for her daughter, and permission to herself to start living her life, in part, for herself. Then it became a refuge from the loneliness and isolation she felt as her friends started to graduate and go out into the world and her own life shrank. Kate studied, and she remembered how she loved to learn; how once, she was the most hard-working, the most promising in her class, and no one doubted how well she would do. But lately, she's lost interest. It all feels pointless.

Kate has been too tired to work in the evenings when Daisy's gone to bed, instead spending too much time in the CF chatrooms that she moderates, or sending Instagram posts to Melissa, both ways of distracting herself. The six hours when Daisy is at school seem to drain away like bathwater. She had intended to fill them with work and walks and reading, and forging a new version of herself that was more than a wrung-out mother. Often she walks back to school at

3 p.m., trying to add up the time she has spent, always seeming to have an hour spare after she has subtracted going to the supermarket, researching jobs and postgraduate training on the internet, sorting washing, updating Daisy's food diary, messaging with Melissa. All things she would normally do around Daisy's day. Plus, she's planning for Daisy's birthday next weekend. She's allowing her mum to fuss about food and games, but she's still been spending way too much time on presents and procrastinating over what kind of cake to order from the bakery and café next door. And now, the deadline for her dissertation is looming, waiting. It's her final piece of degree work, and it's on the portrayal of disability in print media. She's already had one extension for it. She'll get comments on this draft, rewrite it as necessary – she hopes that not much will be necessary – and then that will be it.

Kate knows she should be proud. But she isn't. It all feels like an anticlimax. And she's angry with herself, too, at how much time she spends thinking about Spencer. She's always aware of him at pick-up time. He is sometimes moving around the classroom, tidying and sorting, but more often talking to parents. Often it looks as though he is being besieged by two or three flirting mothers, clamouring for his attention like ducks chasing bread. These women are all married: Kate assumes they are doing it for the thrill rather than with any serious intent. Not that it's any of her business. And she isn't one to throw stones.

And anyway, she knows that she made a terrible impression on Spencer when they first met. She still cringes when she thinks of it. And she thinks of it a lot. And then she is annoyed with herself, because she is not going to be this woman. She will not define herself in relation to a man; she will not make it seem to Daisy that everything she does is a way of killing time until Love Comes Along. What's the point of being a mother who seeks to show her daughter that it's possible to be complete and equal in the world on her own terms, if she starts mooning around like one of Disney's pre-liberation efforts at the first sight of a single man?

After fifteen minutes of half-hearted work in the flat, Kate picks up her laptop and bag and heads for the neighbouring café. Her favourite place to work, a table tucked around a corner from the main shop and communal table, is free. Kate likes the background noise of the café better than she likes the silence of her flat. Her sandwich – brie and bacon on walnut bread – is better than anything that she would, or could, be bothered to make herself. She has only so many hours, only so much energy. After Daisy, and studying, there is little to give to the kitchen. On most Sundays they have lunch with Granny and her husband, Blake. Mondays are for pasta followed by whatever leftover pudding they brought home the day before. Tuesday, Wednesday and Thursday are a rotation of baked potatoes, stir-fries, things with oven chips, and Daisy's favourite food in the world:

24

macaroni cheese. Friday night is pizza and movie night, which at the moment means Margherita and *Moana*. Kate's fridge and cupboard are mainly snack storage systems, full of dried fruit and cereals and peanut butter and cheese and loaves of bread from the bakery – anything that will get enough calories into Daisy to help her grow. She has gold-top milk delivered by the local dairy, and buys comb honey whenever she finds it at the farmer's market, as Daisy will eat it in cut-up squares on a fork.

Kate soon settles to work, checking footnotes and making a list of what's missing to add later. She's so absorbed that it takes a moment to become aware of someone standing over her. When she does notice, she assumes that Angie has come to take her plate, or to deliver another coffee, which panics her because when she placed her order she had asked for a coffee in an hour and she can't believe that time is passing so quickly. But when Kate looks up from her laptop she sees Spencer Swanson, and her stomach has a mild convulsion and her panic, brought on by being confronted by the man who's fast become her idle fantasy, must show in her face because he holds up the hand that doesn't have a coffee cup and saucer in it, and says, 'I'm sorry to disturb you, I just saw you here and it seemed rude not to say hello.'

'Hello,' Kate says. She wonders about explaining the one-hour coffee thing, but decides it will make her sound a bit odd, although not as odd as something along the lines of how she thinks she has probably dreamed about him every night since she met him, which is the other option her brain is offering. So, she says nothing else. She smiles, though. It looks as though Spencer is going to move past Kate to an empty table behind, but then, 'It's your hair,' he says, unexpectedly.

Kate looks up at him again.

'There are so many people I've met that I can half-recognise, or that I'm ninety per cent sure of who they are when I see them outside school, but I'm not quite confident enough to talk to them. But that hair of yours. It could only be you.'

Kate says, 'I know. Daisy and I could never have a life of crime.' The two of them have the same pale, fine, silver-cream-blonde hair that makes people look twice. Daisy likes to wear hers in two bunches high on her head; Kate lets hers swing straight to her shoulders, or tucks it behind her ears, where it doesn't stay, slithering forwards again when she moves. 'Would you like to join me?'

'You look as though you're busy,' Spencer says, but he doesn't say no, and he doesn't move away. Kate closes her laptop, puts her notebook on top of it, and tries to forget the general attractiveness of Spencer and remember that he is trying to make a home in a new place. According to Jo, who is more plugged into the playground grapevine than she is, he's from Dorset via Scotland and taught at a school in west London before life blew him to Throckton. No one seems to know exactly why or how he came to be here; even the chattiest and most assertive of playground parents have not been able to find a connection with a Throckton resident, a holiday in the area, any kind of reason for Spencer Swanson to have considered moving here. If Kate can figure it out, she'll have something to offer the playground mothers who never quite let her in. And maybe if she talks to him, she will stop thinking about him so much.

'I'm just finishing an assignment. I'm nearly there,' she says. Spencer sits opposite her and puts down his coffee. As he stretches his legs he kicks her ankle, and somewhere in the flurry of I'm-sorry-did-I-hurt-you and really-it's-fine they both relax. For a moment at least.

'Daisy is such a pleasure to have in my class,' Spencer says. 'You must be really proud of her. And—'

'Please don't say something about disabilities,' Kate says, trying to keep her voice light. Spencer looks at her. He seems to contemplate her for a long time.

'I was going to say: and she probably knows more about butterflies than the Natural History Museum.' If Spencer's voice is a colour it's a pale, bruised violet.

'I'm sorry,' Kate says. 'I'm just so used to defending her—'

'I can tell' – Spencer's voice is gentle but it lets the hurt through – 'but maybe you should give me a chance to behave the way that you want me to, before you shout me down for being in the wrong.'

'I really am sorry. You can't imagine what it's like round here sometimes.'

'Well, I'm not from round here,' Spencer says with a smile, and Kate gets a glimpse of those crooked teeth again, and can't help but smile back, especially now that his voice is moving to a warm, rich gold. 'But I am the only male teacher in a primary school, so don't go thinking you've got the monopoly on being gossiped about.'

'I have noticed that,' Kate says, 'but I can assure you that the playground chat about you is all good.'

Spencer half smiles and shifts in his chair. 'You should try the staffroom. That's a different story.'

'I thought you didn't listen to gossip,' Kate says, a little delighted to find herself teasing this – now she comes to get a really close look – undoubtedly handsome man. Not conventionally handsome, maybe – a Colonel Brandon more than a Willoughby – but good-looking nonetheless.

'I don't,' he says, 'and it's all about me, so I know it all anyway.' He smiles as he raises his cup to his mouth; when he puts it down again there's a smudge of froth hanging on the corner of his upper lip. Kate's fingers ache to wipe it away, but she thinks that what would be cute, or a little bit sexy, in a film will be pure mother hen if she attempts it.

And then Spencer laughs, a surprising growl that seems to come out of the middle of his chest rather than his mouth. 'I've got coffee on my lip, haven't I?'

'Yes,' Kate says, and she points to the mirrored place on her own mouth where the foam sits. He rubs it away with his fingertip.

'Got it?'

'Yes.'

'You definitely shouldn't try any kind of espionage, either,' he says. 'Your face is very open.'

'No crime, no espionage,' Kate says. 'My career options are closing down fast here.' She hopes Spencer can't read everything: she doesn't want him to know how fast her heart is beating, the way a disconnected part of her brain is mulling over the fact that this feels more like a date than any of the few official dates she's ever been on. Spencer picks up the biscotti from his saucer. 'Do you think anyone ever eats these?'

'I do.'

'Really?' Spencer reaches over and puts his biscuit on her saucer. 'It's all yours.'

'Thank you,' she says. 'The trick is to dunk them.'

'I think the trick is to give them to you.' He smiles. She smiles back.

'What were you doing?' Spencer nods at Kate's laptop. 'Were you studying when I interrupted you?'

'Yes,' she says. 'I'm finishing my dissertation. It's the last part of my degree.'

He nods. 'What in?'

It's another of the questions Kate doesn't exactly dread but wishes there was a simple answer to. Spencer

29

misreads her face as she is deciding what to say. 'Sorry, Kate, am I getting in your way?' he says, making as if to move. 'I didn't mean to stop you working—'

'It's fine,' she says. 'I was just—'

'And can I call you Kate? Is that OK? I think of you as Kate—'

He's blushing, Kate thinks, *just a little*. And then she feels her own cheeks flame. 'Please,' she says. 'Stay. I'd like the company.'

Then Angie arrives to deliver Kate's hourly coffee, and takes her plate away. When Kate and Spencer settle down again it's with the feeling that they have used a wobbling steppingstone to cross a stream that's just too wide to be taken in a single stride.

'Where were we?' asks Spencer.

'I have no idea,' Kate says. Wants to say: *it doesn't matter, it's just lovely to talk to you.*

'Your degree,' Spencer says, a sudden remembering.

Oh, yes. 'I'm doing an open degree,' Kate says, 'because I was going to go and study geography at uni when I got pregnant with Daisy, and I was determined to keep on studying, but between the CF and all of the other things that were going on at the time, I couldn't make a decision about what I wanted to do. The career choices I thought I had all changed, because everything was always going to be about Daisy from then on. So I wasn't making decisions on my own behalf. I'll have a BA and then I need to decide what to do next.' She looks at her hands. It must be nerves that's making her tell him so much. Especially as he only asked what she was studying.

Spencer nods. 'And what are you thinking of?'

'I'm thinking about physiotherapy, but it's a logistical nightmare.' There's an MSc she could do, at Birmingham, but it would be full-time study for two years; that's assuming that the psychology component of her open degree is enough to get her on it in the first place. She'd have to think about travel, which would mean long days away from Daisy, or moving the two of them, which is unimaginable on almost every level. *But then*, asks the little voice of Kate-before-she-was-a-mother, *are you really going to stay in Throckton forever?*

And Spencer smiles, out of all proportion to what she's said, and says with the thigh-slapping air of someone finally remembering where they left their keys, 'That's what I was going to talk to you about! Wendy and I have been looking at some cystic fibrosis information, and Wendy has started following some blogs' – Kate wants to kiss them both for even bothering to think of such a thing – 'and we were talking about whether we could be doing anything more with Daisy, physio-wise. To support what you already have in place, I mean. If it's not necessary—'

'Well, it all helps,' Kate says. She describes what she already does with Daisy to help keep her lungs clear: going to the park to blow bubbles for the ducks, blowing up a balloon every morning and night before she cleans her teeth, bouncing games, wheelbarrow racing, tickling her to make her giggle, trampolining, how any opportunity to get Daisy using her lungs to capacity should be taken. She explains that they shouldn't be put off by the spitting and the phlegm. When she's finished talking, Spencer nods.

'I'd say how much I admired you if I was sure you wouldn't bite my head off,' he says with half a smile.

'Thank you.' Kate nods with the matching half of the smile. She thinks of saying his name, doesn't quite dare. Their coffee cups are almost empty.

'I would have asked you about this at school,' Spencer says, not looking at her, 'but there are always mothers around, and they never seem to be you.'

'I've noticed that,' Kate says; her turn to not look. There is another conversation going on, far below this one, as though somewhere underwater their hands are reaching out for each other. So when Spencer finishes his coffee and leaves, it seems more like a beginning than an end.

Kate knows that she didn't imagine the blushing. And, when she collects Daisy or drops her off, it seems that Spencer always makes eye contact with her and smiles. He sometimes avoids the other mothers for long enough to have a quick word with her about trampolining, or to warn her that a sore throat is doing the rounds of the children. On the Wednesday after the coffee, he said how much he'd enjoyed talking with her; Kate had said that 'Adventures in Bread' was a great place to live next door to and only afterwards wondered whether he was hinting, or suggesting that they see each other again.

The next day, more than midway through September, Kate submits her dissertation at last, and time runs away as she emails her tutor. She's late enough to be walking against the swelling wave of parents and children heading for the park to make the most of the last of the warm tail-end-of-summer afternoons. Through the window Kate sees Daisy, waiting with her coat on and the slightly reproachful expression that she wears on the mornings when they wake up in hospital. Wendy is at the sink, washing up brushes. Spencer comes over to open the door for her.

'Mummy's here, Daisy,' he says. 'Hello, Kate.'

'Hello.' Kate steps inside. The shadows of the classroom after the bright light of the playground mean she can't read the expression on Spencer's face. But he is close enough to touch; his voice is warm.

'Good day, Daisy?' Kate asks, though her eyes find Spencer's, and look for confirmation there. Not knowing the ins and outs, the coughs and meals of Daisy's life for six hours a day is more difficult than she thought it would be. She'd longed for freedom; it's more like emptiness.

'Yes,' Daisy and Spencer answer. Daisy stands against Kate's legs, resting her head against her mother's hip. Her fingernails are edged with purple paint. Kate thinks about how much she likes this time of day, when Daisy is tired and wants to be cuddled more than she wants to enjoy what an almost-five-year-old considers to be independence. She is about to say so when she reminds herself that Spencer sees parents learning to let their children go every day of his working life. That, in turn, reminds her of the other question she has been thinking about. She still can't decide whether to ask or not. Which probably means that she shouldn't. She starts to smile a goodbye.

Then Wendy, now in the reading corner where she is tidying the books, says, 'There's been a lot of birthday talk.'

'Yes, a lot of birthday talk,' Spencer confirms. He puts out a hand, as though to touch Daisy's hair; brings it back to his side.

'Well, it's not every day that you turn five,' Kate says. Daisy nods, earnest, and Kate and Spencer look at each other again. Kate is finding it harder and harder to look away from him. Maybe that's what makes her ask the question after all.

'Daisy's having a party on Saturday—' she begins.

'Oh, we know all about the party.' Wendy laughs. 'With the balloons and the bouncy castle and the butterfly cake.'

Although the school day is certainly over, with the sound of a hoover from deeper within the school and the quiet air of an empty playground outside, Spencer makes no move towards leaving. His jacket is hanging on a coat hanger on the back of the door; it would be an easy thing for him to go and get it, a signal that this conversation is over. He doesn't. Now that Kate's eyes have grown used to the change in light, she can see that he is looking at her in the same way she imagines she is looking at him: moonstruck, wondering.

'Well, I thought maybe you would like to come?'

'I can't, sorry.' Spencer steps back, sounding anything but sorry, sounding stung. He bends to pick up a pencil from the floor, though Kate can see that really he is doing it to avoid looking at her. 'It wouldn't really be appropriate.'

'Both of you, of course,' she adds, quickly. 'Miss Orr? Mum said to say she would love to see you.'

'Oh, how lovely,' Miss Orr says. 'Could I bring Jilly?'

Kate flips through her memory, remembers that Miss Orr being gay is something that is quietly discussed amongst some parents, as though it's a scandal or a novelty; one day she'll tell them what she thinks of them, but for now she only has the energy to walk away. 'Of course,' Kate says. 'We'd love her to come.'

Miss Orr beams. 'I'll have to check the diary, but if we're free we'd love to come.'

'That's great,' Kate says. 'Isn't it, Daisy? We'll bring an invitation for Miss Orr tomorrow.'

Daisy bounces on her toes. 'I won't forget,' she says, her face earnest. Spencer is putting his jacket on, in slow motion, his back to them.

Kate turns towards the door, the bright September afternoon, hearing how her voice sounds taut as she says, 'Come on, Daisy, let's go and let Miss Orr and Mr Swanson get on.'

Chapter 3

Late September

'T OP-UP?' BLAKE, Kate's stepfather, is holding out a bottle of Prosecco; she tips her glass towards him, and he pours.

'Thanks.'

'How are you doing?' Blake touches her shoulder. 'Your mother and I were saying, we miss you.'

She leans against him, just a little; they don't usually have much contact. It's hard to be physically affectionate with a man who didn't come into your life until you were nineteen, traumatised and pregnant. But she loves Blake, and loves the way her mother has become happy, calm, kind, in the way she never was in the years before. 'I think I'm OK,' she says.

'Good.' He nods. 'Just don't forget we're here. I know you want to be independent, but part of that is knowing when to ask for help.'

Kate laughs. 'Which I am famous for being good at doing.'

Blake cocks an eyebrow at her and laughs back. Oh, Kate feels lucky. She never would have thought her life would be like this, five years ago, when she was lying in a hospital bed, looking at Daisy the way she would have looked at an unexploded bomb. She didn't dare admit it, but she had been frightened – had felt wholly unequal to the task of looking after this baby through the night, let alone for the rest of their lives. It was as though a fog descended and she must fight her way through it, suffocating in dense, cold air with every breath. Richenda had spotted the postnatal depression early on, and the counselling had, in retrospect, helped, though at the time it had felt, to Kate, like just another fog to fight her way through.

And now she is laughing, and Daisy is happy and well. Kate wonders, briefly, what her life would have been if Mike had lived. Perhaps not much different. He was never going to leave his wife; and, Kate can see now, it would have been a disaster for them all if he had. There would have been a different kind of heartbreak, but she would still have been standing here, five years on, feeling the almost-queasy mix of happiness and old, hard memories that this day always brings.

The party is almost over. The afternoon has passed in a hubbub of chat and laughter. Kate found it easier to join in than she'd anticipated. Reception class has given her some common ground with the other parents, so she is easy in herself as she talks about the children's tiredness, how strange it is to not know what they are doing all day, how their houses are full of models made from cereal boxes and string.

There are some mothers she avoids, still, but she's not the only one. Jo refers to Serena, Sarah and Cara as 'the unholy trinity', and Kate, who had invited the whole class to the party, was secretly relieved that none of their children could make it.

But in general, she doesn't often feel like the only child at a dinner party. When the conversations switch to Mr Swanson, though, she has moved to talk to a different group. The humiliation she'd experienced from him two days before still waspish under her skin. Though maybe he was just being professional, like he said. Ramona's mother asked Kate whether she thought he was handsome; she pretended not to hear, but knew that her blush gave her away.

'Look at her,' Kate says. Daisy had changed out of the tasteful, beautiful silver-and-navy party dress that Kate had chosen for her as soon as she'd opened the parcel containing the fairy princess outfit from her granny. ('Sorry,' Richenda had said, but both she and Kate knew that she hadn't meant it. She seems to delight in sequins and sparkles as much as Daisy does. This continually surprises Kate, who is trying to fight the rising tide of pink in her life, and remembers a childhood of navy corduroy coats and shoes chosen by her mother for durability and good sense.)

'I know. She's like a dog with two tails.' Richenda and Blake have also bought Daisy a huge trampoline, installed in their garden for her to come and play on as often as she likes. Daisy is running between that and the bouncy castle that's been the centrepiece of her party. She has always been encouraged to jump, for the sake of her health; Kate sometimes feels bad that her daughter loves it as much as she does. It's as though she's tricking Daisy, and the deception has worked so well that it shames her.

'Or two dogs with two tails each.' Hope, Blake's greyhound, and Beatle, Kate's beagle, who stayed behind when Kate and Daisy moved to the flat, had been shut in the house while the party went on, out of the way of cake and crisps held at tempting heights, and children and parents nervous of dogs. But now, with all of the parents except Jo gone, and Amelia quite happy around dogs, they have been released and are following each other round the lawn, sniffing up crumbs and tolerating Daisy's sticky-handed rubbing of their ears. Daisy, Richenda and Wendy are deep in conversation, pointing at the flowerbeds; Jilly approaches Kate.

'This has been such a lovely afternoon,' she says. 'Thank you for inviting us.'

'Thank you for throwing yourself in,' Kate says. She'd worried about Jilly at first – she'd arrived in a pale dress and heels, and Kate had wondered if she had ever been to a children's party, or indeed, ever met a child – but before long she had shucked her shoes and joined in with pass the parcel as enthusiastically as the five-year-olds.

'It's good to get to know the people Wendy talks about,' Jilly says, and as she does so Wendy looks round at them, and an expression of such love passes between the two of them that Kate feels shy, and lonely, and comforted, all at once. 'Obviously Wendy would never have favourites, but if she did, Daisy would be one of them, for sure.'

Kate smiles; she wants to blurt that she hopes it isn't because of the CF; that she doesn't want Daisy to be treated like some child who must be treasured because her life could be shortened by disease. This is why she doesn't drink much: all the fears she squashes down every day will very easily rise with one glass too many. And Daisy's birthday isn't always easy, anyway, with the wondering of how many birthdays Daisy will see, and Kate's memory of holding her newborn, searching for Mike's face in the face of his squalling daughter, feeling the beginnings of the claustrophobia that her life was about to become.

'We're off.' Jo approaches, saving Kate from herself – she puts her glass down, before she's tempted to drink any more. A tired Amelia is held on Jo's hip. 'Say thank you for a lovely time, Amelia.'

Amelia mumbles something that might be a 'thank you' into Jo's neck, and Kate laughs. 'A pleasure, Amelia. We'll see you at school on Monday.'

She walks to the gate with them, and watches as they head off down the road, tries not to think about how they are going back to the other half of their family, a father/husband and brother/son, when she and Daisy will soon be back in the flat on their own. Kate doesn't mind. Or at least, she would rather be alone than unhappy with someone. But it would be nice to put Daisy to bed and come back into the living room to find another adult she could roll her eyes at, drink wine and look back over the day with. Jilly and Wendy leave, too, full of thanks and embraces, Richenda and Wendy promising that they won't leave it so long next time.

Kate is just about to walk back around to the garden when she hears someone calling her name. 'Kate. Kate! I'm here!'

'Melissa!' Kate's friend is carrying a balloon and a bottle of wine, and wearing a dress that almost touches the pavement. It's unclear whether she's dressed up for this party or is coming from a ball that has overrun. Kate hugs her, tight, and her friend's earrings, great metal stars, press into her cheek. She's the only person Kate knows who smokes. The clinging smell, woven in with perfume and whatever Melissa puts in her hair to keep it so perfectly tumbled, makes Kate feels like a child and an old woman rolled into one. 'I thought you'd forgotten!'

'I wouldn't forget Daisy's big day,' Melissa says. 'I'm not late, am I?'

'Well – it finished at four.'

'What time is it now?'

'Half four.'

Melissa looks as disappointed as Daisy was when she realised the big trampoline couldn't come back to the flat with them. 'God, Kate, I'm sorry. I thought it started at five. I honestly did. I thought I was early.'

Kate laughs. 'How many five-year-olds' parties start at five? Don't worry. Everyone's gone, so it works better this way anyway.'

Ten minutes later, Kate is watching Melissa and Daisy on the trampoline. Melissa has tucked her dress into her knickers, much to Daisy's delight, and the two of them are shrieking as they try to coordinate their bounces. Kate loves that Melissa is here, however tired, however hungover. Melissa's silver block-heeled boots are abandoned at the side of the trampoline, and Kate wonders where she bought them. But then she imagines herself in all the places she goes – school yard, playground, café, hospital, shops, park – and realises that one pair of scuffed brown boots and one pair of black plimsolls are really all she needs. Before she can follow this trail too far, Melissa does a for-ward-roll back onto solid ground and runs barefoot across the lawn to her friend. 'I thought you and me could go out tonight. Are you up for it?'

'Where?'

Melissa shrugs. 'Dunno. Does it matter? Somewhere we can talk properly. It's been ages.'

Kate nods. 'June, I think.'

'No!' Melissa looks shocked, but she's the one who has been travelling for three months, so she shouldn't be. Kate was touched that she sent postcards to Daisy, bright scenes of Eastern cities, parakeets and sun bears, mountain ranges. 'DAISY!' she had scrawled on the back of them. 'LIFE IS AN ADVENTURE!' Or 'AUNTIE LISSA IS BEING VERY NAUGHTY!' 'Then we definitely need to go out. Will your mum babysit?'

'I don't know,' Kate says, by which she means, my mother has turned her pale house and beautiful garden over to five-year-olds and strawberries and chocolate and shouting for the afternoon so she might want a quiet evening. It's probably not fair to even ask.

'God,' Melissa says, five hours later, sprawled on Kate's sofa in Kate's only set of matching pyjamas, 'your own place. I'm never going to manage that in London.'

'It's not really mine,' Kate says. She was tipsy when they left her mother's, at 6.30, having spent a cheerful hour helping to clear up and finishing the Prosecco as they did so. She managed to get to the point where she was floating above her worry, rather than feeling it drown her. Then she and Melissa had shared a bottle of red wine with their meal in the Italian restaurant. The pasta had soaked up some of the wine, but not all. They are now on the only alcohol in the flat – a bottle of Cointreau that her father had left in the

44

cupboard. She wishes she'd made herself tea, instead, but it seemed too late, or too pointless, to stop drinking. 'I've got it while my dad's abroad. I don't know what will happen when he gets back.'

'Come on,' Melissa says, 'you're a trust-fund babe and you know it.'

'Hardly.' Kate has the money her parents had saved for her university years and her future, which they had signed over to her on her twenty-first birthday. She knows she's lucky – knows, too, how easy it would be to fritter it all away. She tries to stick to her monthly budget of benefits and takes a small amount of fun money, less than the annual interest on her savings; she manages it most of the time. If she can ever get a job, a mortgage, then she should be able to afford a flat in Throckton. Yes, she knows she's lucky. It's wrong to envy Melissa her freedom. Wrong to think of how this crazy-feeling night is one of Melissa's tamer evenings. And wrong to resent her friend for that. And yet, it's hard not to.

'Even so,' Melissa says, topping up both of their glasses and opening a sharing-size bag of crisps. 'I'm never going to have a place of my own.'

'Daisy lives here,' Kate says, glancing involuntarily at the bedroom door, even though Daisy will be fast asleep in her bedroom at her granny's.

'You know what I mean though. You're lucky. Well, sort of.'

Kate lets it pass. 'Where's your internship, again?'

45

'Oh!' Melissa sits up straighter, as though her boss is about to walk in. '*Interiors* magazine. Seven hundred people applied. Thirty of us at the selection day. The money's terrible, but—' She shrugs. Kate knows what the shrug means. It means that Melissa can afford this time; that she is investing in her future, making the most of her opportunities, safe in the knowledge that this is the first step on the glittering pathway that leads her out of university to – well, to anywhere she wants to go. She's the opposite of Kate, who has completed her own degree in snatched corners of time, reading in hospital waiting rooms and making notes for essays while listening to the soundtrack of whatever Daisy is watching on Disney Plus. And whose path to anything feels impossible. She wants to cry.

This is why she shouldn't drink.

When Melissa holds out the bottle, Kate reaches her glass to meet it.

'You should come back to London with me tomorrow,' Melissa says. 'Meet the gang. You'd love them. They'll love you. There's—' And she goes off into a rambling description of her housemates. Two of them are in a band; another one is a waiter in a place where he regularly makes two hundred pounds a night in tips; another (or maybe the waiter) has a YouTube channel and might be getting a job as a TV presenter. They've all graduated in the last couple of years. The only rule they have is about everyone who is home in the evening eating together. Kate looks around her flat; thinks about how living away from home might be less lonely if she was part of a chaotic, clever, ambitious group of people who, if Melissa is to be believed, are having the time of their lives, and don't plan to stop any time soon.

'I don't think I could,' Kate says. 'School on Monday.' On Sunday evenings, once Daisy is asleep, Kate has a routine: sorting washing, shopping lists, checking whether she needs to order more medication yet, looking over the diary where she keeps a note of anything relevant to Daisy's health. It's all tedious and necessary admin that means she isn't chasing her tail all week. And Melissa will go back to her place in east London and – well, Kate doesn't quite know what will happen then, but she knows that Melissa will pretty much please herself. Her drunken brain imagines a velvet beanbag, candles in vintage French-jam jars, a dark-eyed man playing a guitar, a selection of bohemian knickers drying on a radiator. *Don't be ridiculous*, she tells herself, *it won't be like that at all. It will smell of old food and they will always be bickering about who puts the wrong things in the recycling. There will be a lightbulb in the hall that has needed changing since they moved in, but no one has remembered, or bothered, or cares enough. When you come home drunk you will fall over someone else's shoes.* She closes her eyes.

The next thing Kate knows, it's 11 a.m. on Sunday. Church bells might have woken her, or it might be the pinging of messages on her phone. She can't focus. Hauling herself to a sitting position on the sofa, she looks around for Melissa, but sees only the tipped-over Cointreau bottle and a cigarette stubbed out on the draining board. Kate told her she couldn't smoke in here. The kitchen window is open and the cool, almost-October air snakes around Kate's ankles.

She closes the window, switches on the kettle, and checks her phone. There are two messages. One, from her mother, reminds her that lunch is going to be at two o'clock today because Blake has worked an overnight shift; and the other is from Melissa, saying she has decided to get an earlier train, because she needs to do some stuff before the gig later, but Kate can come down any time she likes. For a moment, Kate is tempted to follow her to have some fun – her mum could be persuaded into another night of looking after Daisy, and Kate could be home in time to pick her up from school tomorrow – but then her stomach reminds her of how much she had to drink last night, and there's the pull of loneliness that comes when Daisy isn't here. It's Richenda who will be enjoying the post-birthday excitement, the exploring of gifts unopened at the party yesterday. Kate does all the day-to-day drudgery, and all of the worrying (well, most of it). At some point today she'll have to get Daisy's food diary out, and try to remember everything she ate yesterday, and the times she took her medication. And in between looking at presents at her mother's, later, she'll have to make sure she asks what Daisy has eaten. She can't even fully enjoy the good stuff. She's always monitoring, or making sure of one thing or another.

Kate fills a mug with water from the tap and drinks it down. Her head pulses, her throat feels raw. God, was she smoking last night? No, she wouldn't have. It's just the laughing, the talking, the – she checks Spotify on her phone – yes, the singing along to the music they loved when they were in the sixth form: Katy Perry, Mumford & Sons, The Wombats. Well, she's allowed to enjoy herself. She thinks of Daisy's warmth, how there is nothing better. And then she thinks about Melissa, heading back to London, and about how seeing an old friend will probably be forgotten already, while to Kate yesterday evening was the most grown-up fun she's had in months.

There's no point in turning up at her mother's in this state: Kate will only get a disapproving look, and maybe a chat about not taking Richenda for granted (fair enough) and being a responsible parent (not fair at all). She goes to run a bath, texts Melissa to say that she'll come to see her soon, and takes some painkillers. At least the hangover has taken her mind off Spencer Swanson. See? She hasn't thought about him at all today, not until right this minute.

Chapter 4

Early December

THE CYSTIC FIBROSIS CLINIC visit on the first Thursday of December begins like any other of these routine appointments. Richenda drops Kate and Daisy at the main doors of the hospital, and when they get to the CF unit they are greeted and shown to their room by Chantelle, Daisy's favourite nurse.

Daisy immediately lets go of her mother's hand and takes Chantelle's. 'I am a star,' Daisy says. 'A star, Chantelle!'

'You sure are, Daisy.' Chantelle laughs.

'Daisy's the star in the school nativity,' Kate explains. 'We're going to the dress rehearsal, after this.'

'And I thought it was an example of her robust self-esteem.' Chantelle grins as she opens their consulting-room door. Because of the risk of cross-infection between cystic fibrosis patients, each family visiting the clinic has its own room; Daisy and Kate will stay put, while the nurses, physiotherapists, social workers and consultants move from one patient to another as they are needed. Kate thinks of how this has become the norm for her – as normal as clubbing or speed dating is for Melissa. When she last went to see her GP, she had been disorientated by the waiting room full of shared air and shared coughs, something that she rarely experiences these days. When she was pregnant, everyone told her that having a baby would change her life. No one – including her – had known how many tiny differences Daisy would make. Not even a waiting room would seem normal again.

Daisy is unpacking colouring books, pencils and a box of dried fruit from her backpack. She had been tired that morning, and so consented to sit on Kate's lap long enough for Kate to brush her hair properly, to a silvery sheen, rather than only giving her time to get the worst of the tangles out and put her bunches in before wriggling off in search of something more interesting to do. In the small, stuffy room at the clinic, Kate puts her hand on her daughter's crown and knows that a hand on her own head would feel the same dense smoothness beneath it. Oh, how she loves this child. And how she wishes things were different. She is not always sure which things.

'Right, Daisy, I just have to go away for a few minutes, and when I come back we're going to do the usual,' Chantelle says. 'I'm going to weigh you and measure you and we're going to blow into the machine, and spit in a cup, and I'll listen to your chest and feel your tummy.'

Daisy nods, already colouring in. 'Any problems?' Chantelle asks Kate. 'How's school?'

'Fine, I think, but it's such a big change. For both of us. Daisy loves it but she's really tired.' Chantelle nods and touches Kate's elbow. The nod and touch, Kate knows, are meant to convey that Chantelle understands all that Kate isn't saying. Kate tries not cry in front of other people, but she knows that now, if Chantelle asks her how she is, her composure will melt away like snow in salt water. She would soon be sobbing as though she were the child here, over Daisy going to school, about the relief at being able to have some time to be alone, about her loneliness, and how sometimes it feels as though she is only now beginning to understand what parenting this child means.

Kate turns away, looking over Daisy's shoulder as she starts to put a collection of small cuddly toys in a row. 'Schools' is her daughter's new go-to game.

The CF clinic routine begins. Daisy stops playing for long enough to submit to being weighed, measured and examined. She coughs on command and answers Chantelle's questions about what she eats and what she does at school. Chantelle and Kate go through Daisy's supplements and medications, and the diary that Kate keeps of Daisy's food intake, her sleep patterns, her activity and physiotherapy. It all goes along as usual, until Chantelle shows Kate the weight chart with today's data added.

'Her weight gain's dropping off,' Chantelle says. 'Probably nothing to worry about, but I think you need to see Victoria.' She makes what Kate hopes is a better-safe-than-sorry face. 'She's with another patient at the moment, but I don't think she'll be long.'

'If you think that's best,' Kate says.

As they wait for the consultant, Kate looks at Daisy for signs of anything she's missed. The skin below her daughter's eyes looks blue-green under the harsh hospital lighting, her veins showing through; but Kate thinks she probably doesn't look her best in this light, either. Daisy is thinner, certainly, but taller, too: Richenda said only yesterday how she is growing like a weed, and Kate had felt proud that her daughter was thriving, despite everything.

Daisy sits on Kate's lap and dozes while they wait. Getting up to be at the hospital for nine means an early start, and Kate too feels the lack of sleep and the warmth of the room relaxing her. She had learned calmness, the hard way, after Daisy was born. Knowing that she was the only one truly responsible for her baby – although she had caring grandmothers for parentheses, was watched from a safe distance by Kate's father, and by friends like Melissa – she had become the parent Daisy needed. She is the parent who asks questions, rather than the parent who frets and cries. Once, Jo commented on Kate's strength and said she didn't think she could cope the way Kate did. 'You could if you had to,' Kate answered with a shrug. 'I've never had the luxury of falling apart.' *Never had the luxury of other things, either*, she had thought: Jo and her husband's weekends away to spas and European cities make her want to cry with envy. Kate can't imagine ever having the things required to do that: money to be reckless with, headspace to be away from Daisy without worrying about her, someone who she wants to give a weekend to. (She imagines her and Melissa in somewhere like Prague or Milan, Melissa sleeping until noon then trawling markets for vintage fur coats, fuelled by vodka shots. And Kate in her wake, texting her mother and longing for coffee and time to read her book.)

As they wait for Victoria, Kate focuses on the child in front of her, the one she loves without end, despite all the ways she feels her own life has been compromised. She doesn't believe that Daisy has a serious problem: she would know, because since Daisy's birth Kate has watched her for signs of difficulty as though both of their lives depended on it. Because they do. It's second nature. It's habit. It's tiring and it's tiresome, but it's what Kate does. Getting drunk with Melissa after Daisy's party was probably the only time she's actually done anything spontaneous for years, and heaven knows she paid for that with the lecture from her mother about mothering not being something you can take or leave and, worse, missing out on seeing Daisy bouncing on the trampoline in her pyjamas the next morning. ('I didn't abandon her in a layby,'

Kate had grumbled. 'I left her with you, and you've always said you're happy to have her.' 'Yes,' Richenda had replied, holding steady eye contact even though Kate longed to close her eyes, or look at her shoes, or anywhere except her mother's cool, I-see-your-bullshit gaze, 'and that's true, but you didn't give me any notice, or really any choice, and that's not how this should work. I know you think you have to take advantage of seeing Melissa when you can, but if she's really your friend she will understand that you can't jump whenever she tells you to.')

Yes, Daisy seems more tired, but all of the play-ground-parents say the same thing, and Jo has even taken to pretending Amelia is ill on the occasional Friday because it seems that a whole week of school is too much for her. Daisy is eating in the same way that she always does: three meals with supplements to help her to digest the food, and picking and graz-ing throughout the day, always notching up enough calories to satisfy Kate by evening. And if Kate has any doubt, there is always hot chocolate with whipped cream, marshmallows and chocolate sprinkles as an accompaniment to a bedtime story. So Kate has resisted the temptation to panic or to flap.

But, when looked at on the percentile chart, Daisy's weight is certainly below where it should be. When Victoria comes in, she is matter-of-fact, and doesn't seem unduly worried; but, with cystic fibrosis, they both know that nothing must be left to chance.

Daisy has a chest X-ray to make sure there isn't a problem in her lungs, which might have a knock-on effect on weight gain. Her supplements are checked again. There is a finger-prick test to check for diabetes – Daisy wails more than she usually does when she has blood taken, but as Victoria says, fingertips do really hurt if you hurt them. Daisy doesn't answer but she glares. Kate keeps her face as calm as she can, strokes Daisy's hair, and thinks of how this pain for Daisy is pain for her, too, though she doesn't show it. Consenting to hurt in the name of health is an almost-impossible thing for a mother to do. And yet these clinic rooms are full of mothers being forced to do exactly that. Fathers too, Kate supposes. A flash of memory makes her close her eyes: the look on Mike's face when he used to see her walking towards to him, the warmth she imagined was love, the way she thought, then, that love meant secrets, thrills and something to be won.

The results of the extra tests are all fine.

'The guidance,' Victoria says, 'is that we wait for six months before making an intervention. But I suggest you see if you can get more calories into her diet. You know the drill.' Kate nods. There will be extra cheese grated onto pasta, peanut-butter sandwiches while watching TV, nuts and dried fruits sprinkled onto breakfast cereal – all strategies that she uses already when she feels as though Daisy needs them. It's not just a question of what she eats, of course, it's a question of what she absorbs. Kate racks her brains for what else she can do for Daisy. Maybe a snack on the way to school as well as on the way back.

'There's another possibility,' Victoria says, and she gestures to Kate to join her out of Daisy's earshot.

Kate leaves the hospital doing a good job, she thinks, of looking calm, and appearing to have taken the information in her stride. But during the drive back to Throckton, as she tells her mother what's happened, she starts to feel shaky. She thinks about all of the grim things that could happen if Daisy doesn't gain weight, and she can barely breathe. Richenda doesn't say much but when they wait for a traffic light to change, she takes Kate's hand and holds it, tight.

'I know it's easy to say, but try not to worry,' Richenda says, as she pulls up along the road from the school gate. 'You're doing all the right things. If you want to talk just let me know.'

'I suppose it's all the usual things. I feel like a terrible mother. I'm never going to get it right. It's only going to get worse.' A sob claws up and out into the air. Kate tries so hard not to worry about Daisy's future.

Richenda holds Kate's hand. 'Why not give this afternoon a miss? It's a beautiful day.'

'I know.' The sunlight of this bright, breath-brittle December afternoon makes Kate want to make the most of it. It's a day to bundle up, and push Daisy on a swing, and then feed her hot chocolate and watch her face go from cold-pink to warm-pink. By the time school is over, the corners of the sky will be darkening, like the edges of a sheet of paper dropped into a fire. The parents and children will scurry for home, and the Christmas tree and decorations that ought to make the flat look cheerful will instead make the space feel cramped and Kate claustrophobic. Right now she wants nothing more than the sky above her and the sense that, under it, anything is possible in the wide world. If the illusion of freedom is all that she can have in her life, she wants to make the most of it.

Daisy stirs in the back seat, opens her eyes, slowly at first and then they snap wide with excitement. 'Is it time? Have you got my costume? Miss Orr says . . .'

Richenda laughs. 'How could I have forgotten it's dress rehearsal?' She says to Kate, 'Say hello to Wendy for me. I can come over to your place later, when she's in bed, if you like.'

'Could I let you know?' Hospital days wipe Kate out, and she has a lot to think about. Even when clinic goes well, she has been known to go to bed at the same time as Daisy. Kate has always assumed that it's to do with being confronted by the many risks that she spends her days actively not thinking about – ensuring Daisy's wellness while doing all she can to not dwell on the implications of her condition. And the bright airlessness of the hospital, and the sound of other children crying. But what might be hardest of all – Kate hates to admit it – is the overheard snatches of pairs-of-parents' conversations that drift into hearing when her door is open. The call-and-response of worry and comfort, planning and thinking, makes her wish she was not so alone.

'Of course.'

Kate gathers her handbag, Daisy's schoolbag and costume, and Daisy herself, waves her mother good-bye, and presses the buzzer on the school gate before she has time to change her mind and head for the swings after all. She's buzzed in, signed in, and walked down to the classroom.

The door grunts on its hinges. The reception class-room is empty. There are piles of school uniforms heaped on chairs. Kate takes off Daisy's hat, scarf, mittens and coat, starts unbuttoning her cardigan, longs for summer as she wrestles her wriggling girl out of her tights. Everything feels difficult today. As she pulls Daisy's vest straight before putting her into her dress, she looks over the familiar little body: barrel chest and long arms and legs, skin and eyes and hair as pale as her own, although Daisy's smile – sudden, wide and certain – is all her father's. Kate can't see that she's missed anything, and still can't believe that Daisy is anything but well. *Breathe, Kate*, she tells herself, *breathe*. She slides the costume over her daughter's head and fastens it at the back. Daisy smooths the skirt down. The silvery taffeta makes Kate's fingers itch, though Daisy doesn't seem to mind it, or is prepared to suffer for her art.

'Come on, then. Shoes,' Kate says. Daisy's silver sandals were bought by Richenda to go with her birthday party dress, although in the event Daisy had gone barefoot, from lawn to bouncy castle to trampoline, for that whole day. Already they are getting too small. *Surely*, Kate thinks again – she'd said it at least three times to her mother in the car – *it's not that Daisy is gaining weight too slowly, it's that she's growing too quickly. Gaining weight slowly indicates illness; a growth spurt, surely, equals health.* Richenda had nodded, but they both know that percentile charts don't lie.

'Mummy?' Daisy is ready to walk down to the hall and join her class. Kate's mind is still full of the weight of the morning, so she hasn't thought about seeing Spencer. Yesterday, she'd let him know they might be late to rehearsal, practising the glacial politeness she'd seen her mother use on her father for years, and she'd been congratulating herself on how well she'd forgotten about him. How silly she was to even give him a second thought, to think a lonely coffee meant anything at all. It's a good job she remembered that she has no time for men – is a disaster with them, anyway – before things went too far. Went anywhere at all.

And then he's there, at the door of the school hall, smiling a welcome, with all of his tallness and his hair freshly cut, a shaving nick on his upper lip. Those eyes. That smell – soap, not aftershave, honest and clean. 'Hello, Daisy,' he says, nodding to acknowledge Kate, but managing to look at the tops of her cheekbones rather than her eyes.

'Sorry we're so late,' Kate answers. 'We had to stick around for an X-ray.'

'You're just in time.' Spencer flicks his gaze to Kate, meeting her eyes for just a second before looking back to Daisy and smiling. 'Have you been practising your words?'

'Tirelessly,' Kate says. 'Daisy?'

Daisy takes a deep breath, coughs, then, 'Follow me!'

'Perfect!' Spencer says. 'Lovely and loud. The mums and dads at the back will definitely be able to hear that, won't they, Mum?'

'They certainly will.' Kate cringes as she always does when anyone other than Daisy calls her 'Mum' or 'Mummy'. If a paediatric ward at a hospital can manage to use her name – to make her feel like an actual person in her own right, not just the owner of the uterus that grew Daisy – she doesn't see why Daisy's teacher can't. But there it is. God, she's tired.

'Everything OK?' Spencer asks, really looking at Kate this time. 'Does she usually have an X-ray?'

'The X-ray was OK' – Kate tries to keep her voice steady, and almost manages – 'and I'll talk to you or Miss Orr about the rest when you're less busy.'

'I do have camels to wrangle' – Spencer glances over his shoulder to his nativity cast – 'but you're welcome to stay and watch. We could talk afterwards. You need to be back to collect her in an hour anyway, don't you?'

'Thank you.' This small, unexpected kindness is almost enough to make Kate cry. She finds a chair at the back of the hall – a teacher-sized one, mercifully – and lets the sound of the rehearsal roll over her. She's grateful for the general commotion, and she laughs, despite herself, at the sight of the shepherds bickering over which of them should hold the crook and which of them the lamb. The singing is enthusiastic and flat; Miss Orr is fulsome in her praise. But by the time the class starts on the second run-through, although her eyes follow the action and her heart is with Daisy, Kate's mind is back in the hospital. She can't stop thinking about the rest of what Victoria said – the part that Kate thinks she will keep to herself, because saying it out loud will hurt as much as hearing it did, and because saying it out loud might make it true.

Kate takes her time helping Daisy change her clothes, watching as the other children file out of the door to meet parents or grandparents or childminders, to be greeted with varying degrees of fuss and interest. When the last of Daisy's classmates has been collected, Daisy fetches her coat.

'We just have to talk to Mr Swanson for a minute,' Kate says, 'about what Victoria told us.' She wonders where Daisy learned to roll her eyes like that. She hopes not from her. Melissa, maybe? 'We won't be long.'

But Mr Swanson is nowhere to be seen. 'He's had to go to a meeting with the Head,' says Miss Orr.

'Oh, he said at the rehearsal—'

'I know, but something's come up. I don't know what, I'm afraid.' Wendy smiles. 'Will I do?'

'Of course you will,' Kate says. 'I was just – well, never mind—' And she starts going through the information from the day: the extra snacks that Daisy will need, at breaks as well as lunchtime now, and the fact that they will have to be even more careful about infection. Wendy nods and makes notes, and smiles in all the right places, and she is so very calm and capable that suddenly Kate is afraid that she's missing the whole point of this, the importance. She has to make her understand. 'When Daisy was two,' she says, 'I took her to a playgroup and there was a girl there with a cold, and I knew I should have taken her straight home again but I felt so' – she shies away from 'lonely' – 'I just needed a change of scene, even if it was only the church hall' – she hears her voice start to sway but she can't stop trying to explain – 'and anyway, Daisy caught something, and although it was hardly a sniffle in the other little girl, not even a temperature, Daisy ended up in hospital on intravenous antibiotics for a fortnight with a chest infection.' She wants to add a good, adult, responsible-mother sentence, the kind of thing she would suggest in response to a parent query on a CF forum: something along the lines of 'so you see how important it is that we work together to make sure that Daisy isn't vulnerable, because something that would have a negligible impact on a fully healthy child can be disastrous for a child with cystic fibrosis.'

But Wendy Orr, with her crocheted cardigan with dried paint on the sleeve, her smile that's welcomed a thousand children with the same warmth and kindness-in-waiting, puts her hand on Kate's arm and says, 'How difficult this must be for you, Kate.' She hesitates. 'I should really call you Ms Micklethwaite when we're in school.'

And Kate says, 'Kate, please. It's Kate.' Because it's ridiculous to have such formality with a woman who is her mother's old friend and is becoming so important in Daisy's life. Wendy came to Daisy's birthday party, and has given Kate, shyly, an invitation to her and Jilly's Christmas drinks party. Just because they are in a classroom, it doesn't mean that they're not friends. And then Kate's crying, trying to cry quietly so that Daisy doesn't notice, although Daisy is giving the dolls what sounds like a mighty telling-off so isn't really paying attention to whatever the grown-ups are talking about. Kate is wiping her tears away before they've hit her chin, smiling an apology at Wendy without looking at her, because she knows that if she once looks properly at that kind, sympathetic face she will bawl.

After a few moments Kate is steady enough to sort-of-smile and says, her voice shaky, 'I'm sorry. It's been a long day. I'll write it all down for you and Mr Swanson and bring it in tomorrow. Come on, Daisy, let's go home. Shall we watch a film and have tea on the sofa?'

'Yes please!'

'We're here to help,' Wendy calls as they leave. Kate nods and raises a hand in acknowledgement. She's full of thanks, though she can't express them at this moment. She'll find a way – Christmas presents, a letter to the Head to say how wonderful Wendy is. And she will start facing down the gossips who talk about Wendy's engagement to Jilly, which happened during October half term. She knows what it is to be gossiped about. She sees that turning her back on those conversations isn't enough. From now on, she'll intervene. Every time.

Daisy looks at her mother with perplexity, asks, 'Are you poorly, Mummy? Because you should have told them at the hospital, and they could have given you medicine.'

Kate has a rule about digestible honesty, so she takes a breath, and says, 'I'm not poorly, but being in the hospital has made me feel a little bit sad and cross inside, and maybe that shows on the outside.'

'It will be all right, Mummy, it always is, you know.' Kate recognises her own words coming back to her through her daughter, and nods, and realises that Daisy's lungs haven't had a lot of exercise today, so she races her to the corner, and then lets herself be chased all the way home. Kate reminds herself of her own strength. She can do it. And anyway, she has no choice.

Chapter 5

Early December, the same day

ONCE DAISY IS IN BED, Kate takes a shower and changes into her pyjamas, even though it's barely eight, partly because she thinks she might go straight to bed but also because she's not quite sure what to do with herself. She didn't think she would ever miss her dissertation, but this would be a perfect time for losing an hour to repagination, proofreading, or anything else that would distract her sad heart and preoccupied brain without asking too much of her intellect.

Kate pulls out her laptop, thinking about posting on one of the CF forums and asking for advice – but she knows what the advice will be and, anyway, she can't bear the thought of writing the day down, making a fact of it, especially the part she didn't tell Wendy, or her mother.

She puts the TV on, but it feels like nothing but noise. She has no energy for other people's lives right now, and pre-Christmas specials bear no relation to her own life. She hadn't even wanted to put the Christmas-tree lights on tonight, but Daisy had insisted. Now she's inclined to turn them off, but she can't be bothered to crawl under the branches to reach the socket. Kate was so happy when she and Daisy moved into the flat at the beginning of August. She thinks of how gladly she packed away her father's gloomy tartan cushions and replaced them with silver-grey faux-fur ones; what a pleasure it was to take down his abstract paintings and hang framed vintage Greenpeace posters in their place; how she filled the tasteful sparseness of his shelves with photographs of her and Daisy's life. The day the lightbox she had ordered arrived, she had opened the packaging and thought she was happy: she and Daisy had spelled out their names and made space next to the photo of the two of them on a teacup ride at the fair the previous summer. Now she sees how pointless this idea of home is. What does it matter where she lives if she can't keep her daughter safe and well? Maybe she should have stayed with her mother. Maybe she can't be trusted on her own.

Torn between going to bed or breaking her no-drinking-alone-on-weeknights rule, Kate is picking idly at her nails when the doorbell rings. She hopes, uncharitably, that she isn't about to get a visit from carol singers, or a PTA member on a mission, or even someone delivering a Christmas card that she wasn't expecting and will have to reciprocate. She almost doesn't go downstairs – she wants nothing more than to pretend she's not in. But the fairy lights are a bit of a giveaway.

What's waiting on the other side of the door is both better, and worse, than anything Kate has imagined. Because in none of Kate's daydreams about Spencer turning up at her door has she been wearing floral pyjama bottoms, a striped vest top, and a cardigan with a frayed hem. Her hair is damp and the coldness of the air on her scalp makes her feel as vulnerable as if she was naked. She wonders if she's dreaming – not an idle fantasy-daydream, but one of those semi nightmares that comes sometimes, as she's drifting off to sleep, where one minute she is walking through her everyday world and the next, something slips out from beneath her and she is plummeting into water, cold and black.

Kate curls her bare feet against the carpet. The floor is solid. He's here. She's here. She pulls her cardigan tightly around her body, keeps her arms crossed in front of her. He says, 'I'm sorry for turning up unannounced. I know it's not very – usual. I heard you'd had a tough day, and I wanted to see that you were OK.'

And she says, 'I'm in my pyjamas.'

'I'm sorry.' He smiles, and it's an understanding sort of a smile, sad at the corners. He begins to turn away. 'I knew this was a bad idea. I'll see you at school.' Behind him the street is empty; there is noise leaking from the Italian restaurant, the ruckus of an early works-do Christmas-party laughter.

'No, no,' she says, 'I meant—' But it's too difficult to explain what she meant, here on the doorstep, or maybe anywhere at all. Because it's as though her own loneliness had somehow called to him. *Stop it, Kate,* she tells herself, *it's that sort of ridiculous romanticism that got you caught up with Mike.* She touches his arm. 'Please. Come in. Daisy's asleep.'

No one sees. No one is on the pavement, no one has stepped out of the restaurant for a cigarette.

Between Spencer and the Christmas tree that is too wide and too tall but was irresistible to her and Daisy because it's just so perfectly Christmas-tree shaped, it feels as though there's hardly room to breathe. Kate asks him to sit down and then she makes tea, without asking whether he wants it, because that way she can watch her own hands, open drawers and cupboards, be busy while she gets used to just the fact of him being here.

'How was your day?' she asks, glancing up.

'I felt bad that I didn't see you after school,' Spencer says, seriously; but before she can respond he smiles. 'I had to go to see the Head about something.'

Kate laughs. 'That's OK. I might not show it, but I do know that you have more to do than teach Daisy.'

'If it was only teaching, being a teacher would be so much easier.' He sounds both wary and tired. Well, that makes two of them.

Across from the kitchen area, two small sofas face each other, a coffee table in between. Kate puts the mugs on the table and then sits opposite Spencer. The sofa seems even smaller with him on it, too. She sits cross-legged, and takes her own mug – pale-blue glazed, bowl-shaped, a gift from her mother – in her hands.

'Tell me everything,' Spencer says. 'Forget what I've heard from Wendy. I want to hear it all from you.'

Kate repeats the tale of the day. 'It's all manageable, really,' she says when she gets to the end. 'I get so used to dealing with CF on a day-to-day basis that I think I am in charge of it, somehow, and I can forget that it can change, and how quickly it can change. It's good that her lungs don't look too bad.' The result of the X-ray had been comparable to the one that Daisy had at her annual review in August. Her lungs aren't strong, but they aren't diseased. This is much more than a small mercy. People in Throckton pity Daisy, Kate knows, but they really have no idea how lightly cystic fibrosis has touched her, compared to some other children. Kate refuses to see her own life as blessed because others are worse off, though. She hates that some of the parents who put their head on one side when they see her and Daisy are likely to be thinking, *thank goodness we are not them*. If you are what passes for normal round here, though – partnered, solvent, with an apparently healthy child – how little introspection you need. How easy it must be to judge, and find yourself and your life perfect.

Kate drinks some of her tea and notices that Spencer's is untouched. She gets up again, brings the sugar-bowl that Daisy painted at a pottery café when out for the day with her granny. Spencer smiles and adds two spoonfuls of sugar to his mug, stirs. 'Thank you,' he says. 'I know I shouldn't. It's my only vice.'

'We love calories in this house. Feeding Daisy is like stoking a furnace. I keep a diary of what she eats and, honestly, I can't believe it myself, sometimes.' Kate thinks of how easy it is to talk to him, about Daisy. *We're having a meeting*, she tells herself, *it's just that I'm in my pyjamas. Sometimes you have to be flexible.*

He looks up. 'I suppose the check-ups are exactly because you don't always notice how things change, day-to-day. They just creep up. No one sees until it's' – he hesitates and Kate wonders whether he was going to say 'too late' and thought better of it – 'really a thing.'

'My mother says something similar. Like how you don't notice you're too hot until you're sunburned, or that when you feel thirsty you're already dehydrated.'

'If there's one thing I've learned since I started teaching, it's that mothers generally know what they're talking about.'

'Yes.' She doesn't mention that she'd snapped back that if Daisy was hot she would take her indoors, and if she was thirsty she would give her a drink, and surely she is not the only one who can see that this is going to need more than platitudes to fix. She must call her mother tomorrow, apologise for her sharpness. Daisy's lack of weight gain is not Richenda's fault. It's no one's but Kate's.

'It sounds hard for you.' Spencer looks straight at her; she looks down, at her hands, which she thinks are starting to look old. She has worried hands. She holds one of them up, stopping him before he says what she thinks he is going to say.

'Please, there's no need to be sympathetic. There are parents of kids with CF who would give their teeth to be where I am right now.'

'That doesn't make it any less difficult for you, though, does it?'

'No, it doesn't.' Kate looks away from the warmth, the empathy in his face. She can't think of what to say so she opens her mouth and lets honesty out: 'But please don't be sympathetic, because I've cried my heart out once already today, and I don't think I want to do it again.'

Spencer puts down his mug. 'Fair enough. If you're sure.'

But she's not sure.

'Kate? Is there something else?' His eyes are clear and concerned as they look at her.

'It's nothing, really.'

'You can tell me. If you want to.' She would like to. But if she couldn't tell her mother, she shouldn't be telling Spencer Swanson.

'It's getting late.'

'Kate,' he says, and he smiles. 'It's ten to nine. I know it's a school night, but even so—'

She laughs, despite herself. 'Ten to nine? Is that all?'

'It is.' He holds out an arm, and a watch pokes out from under his shirt cuff. 'And I'd really like you to tell me what's bothering you, if you feel you can.' Kate half smiles. He half smiles back. 'Don't make me use my teacher voice.'

Their eye contact holds. Kate's skin prickles. She closes her eyes, takes a breath. This isn't about her and Spencer. It's about her and Daisy.

'OK,' she says, deciding. 'Like I say, it's nothing, probably. It just – it just made me think.' She looks at him, checking that – that what? That he's listening, that he means what he said, that he's there? He nods, waits for her to speak. She takes a deep breath. 'Right at the end, the consultant mentioned that some children learn to use eating or not eating as a way of manipulating or punishing their parents. It makes sense, if you think about it. They know that what you need them to do, more than anything else, is to eat properly. So if they don't eat, they have power over you. Or it can be a way of them telling you – maybe subconsciously – that they're unhappy. Daisy's started school. I've been working on my dissertation. I haven't always been the parent I should have been. I have friends who are finishing uni, travelling, and sometimes I . . .' Kate looks away from her hands to the place on the floor she scrubbed the Cointreau stain from. 'Sometimes I resent Daisy. I know I shouldn't, but I do.' She's amazed that her voice is steady, because she has never said these words aloud. She can't, with her mother, because it would be like admitting she wasn't good enough. And if she said anything to Melissa it would unleash an avalanche of 'poor Kate' that she would never, ever get out from under. The only way she can function in the world is by having a brave face she can pretend is real. But talking to Spencer, to a relative stranger who's also, kind of, a professional – it feels OK. And he looks as though he is listening. Not judging. 'So I think maybe she's punishing me, because she's not happy, and it's my fault.' Kate is amazed that she's not crying, although her voice is thinner at the end of her explanation than it was at the beginning.

'Or maybe,' Spencer says, 'Daisy is growing and using more energy at school. I've seen her attack a cheese and ham bagel, Kate. She'd eat the pig raw if it was close enough.'

'That's what I've always thought,' Kate says. 'But—'

'But nothing,' Spencer says, matter-of-factly. Then, more gently, 'Of course, it's possible that she's watching you, and picking up cues. If you're worried, she'll worry. If you're not eating properly, or not hungry, then even though you're making sure she eats, she might feel less hungry. I know it sounds a bit – fluffy – but the two of you have a very strong bond.'

'I suppose so.' Kate turns this around, looking at the different sides of it. 'But I can't pretend not to worry. That won't work on Daisy. And I am worried, so—'

'So, take better care of yourself, and then you'll feel better, and that will make everything easier,' Spencer says. 'If you don't mind my saying something—'

He actually pauses, waiting for permission. Kate smiles. 'Please.'

'OK.' He looks directly at her, his hands on his knees, his mug on the table. 'Daisy doesn't need the best mother that there's ever been in the history of the world. No child does. Daisy just needs a mother who loves her and looks out for her needs. And that's what she's got. It's more than a lot of kids have, believe me.'

Kate pulls her feet up flat on the sofa, hugs her knees. Perhaps she has lost a little bit of weight. Spencer could be right. If she isn't eating properly, Daisy could be following suit.

'Sorry.' Spencer looks unsure of himself, as though he has suddenly realised what Kate saw when she let him in, that he is a teacher who arrived uninvited at the home of a mother who is in her pyjamas. 'I didn't mean—'

'No,' Kate says, 'you're right. You're so right.' Her counsellor for postnatal depression had spent a lot of time helping Kate to understand what motherhood meant to her: how she felt the pressure to be everything and more to Daisy, how she believed, on some level, that cystic fibrosis was a judgement on Kate and that

76

she must be a perfect mother to make up for that, and to keep her daughter safe and well. Kate had thought she'd worked through all those feelings. But her reaction to Victoria's words, and the way she hid them from her mother, suggest not. The postnatal depression was before she had understood – really understood – how she would always be standing on the sidelines of the lives she should have had. She has watched her friends travel, graduate, get great jobs, have relationships that have crashed and burned and that they have moved on from with reckless abandon and no long-lasting consequences. Soon, she knows, she will be going to engagement parties and house warmings, and clicking 'like' on news about promotions on Facebook. And she'll be here, in a flat, doing calorie maths and listening for the sound of Daisy coughing in the night. But only if she can keep her daughter well. Oh, how it all hurts just to think about. She pulls her cardigan more tightly around her. A burst of laughter comes from the party in the restaurant downstairs, and she and Spencer smile at each other, a little blast of mutual sympathy that they are not laughing, they are not drinking and eating and shouting to be heard over the chatter of their friends.

'I hope I haven't upset you.' Spencer is watching her, serious again, worry on his face.

'No,' Kate says, and she smiles, to show him that he hasn't. It starts as a small, reassuring smile, but when he returns it, she feels it broaden. 'Would you like some more tea?' she asks, looking away, reaching for her mug.

'I should probably be going,' Spencer says. As though the meeting is over. Kate doesn't want it to be.

She looks into his eyes exactly at the moment that he's looking into hers; it's a look that might be happening right now in the restaurant downstairs, at one of the corner tables, between two people who have been working their way up to this moment for weeks.

Spencer leans towards Kate, just a little. They'd have to make an effort to touch. Someone would have to get up, to move round the table; but still, he's moving towards her. And she almost does the same, which she could do, easily; she's being pulled that way, a fish on a hook. But Kate has let her heart rule her head before. This time, her head's in charge, and it remembers: 'Can I ask you something?'

'Of course. Ask away.' He leans back.

'You said it was inappropriate to come to Daisy's party. But you're here. Isn't this more inappropriate?' The line slackens; maybe it has broken, although Kate suspects not.

Spencer sighs. 'I honestly don't know,' he says, 'but I'm sorry. There are guidelines about professional behaviour, and it wouldn't have been appropriate to come, but I didn't have to be such an idiot about it.' He has the look of an airbed snagged on a nail, deflated. He's quiet for a moment, watching her. 'As to whether I should be here now . . .'

Kate says nothing. She thinks about her breath, the way she tries to when she needs to be calm: when Daisy won't take her medication, or is crying with distress at a cannula in her hand and the tube that snakes from it and ties her freedom down. When a consultant tells her that there's no immediate reason to worry, reminding her that there are always worries waiting. Or even when Daisy is doing the things any five-year-old might do – having tantrums over growing out of her favourite T-shirt, refusing to go to bed, asking the same question over and over and over. They both sit quietly for a moment, and then Spencer speaks again, more quietly, his voice a little nervous. 'This is going to sound terrible, I know, and I know we barely know each other and you have much more important things to think about – but even without what happened at the hospital today, I really wanted to see you, and, hopefully, be less of an idiot this time.'

'Yes,' Kate says, finding something safe to stand on for a minute. 'Yes, you've been less of an idiot.'

'Good. "Less idiocy" is one of my performance targets for this academic year.'

She looks at him and before she knows it she's laughing, at the ridiculousness of this whole situation; the man she's been fantasising about is in her flat and talking to her about being a good mother while she wears pyjamas so old she wouldn't even wear them in front of Melissa. And he's laughing, too, shaking his head.

But then they stop.

They look at each other again. Spencer's eyes are dark. There's the smallest spatter of stubble on his face. Kate cannot think of another word to say. He stands.

'Well,' he says, 'perhaps I should quit while I'm ahead.'

'Yes,' Kate says, although she means no, and she stands, too, and he moves towards the door and he is next to her, so close that she can see a dimple in the skin of his earlobe where she guesses he once wore an earring. Her fingers itch to reach for it. She twists her own earring instead. His hand, although not touching her, is exactly where it would be if he was about to put it on her waist.

'Are you going to kiss me?' The words blurt from her. He laughs, and she laughs at the sound of his laughter, deep and as clean as the smell of him.

'Well, I think I was,' he says, 'but you've kind of blown my concentration.'

'Sorry.' Kate is laughing more than she should be. 'Sorry. It's just—' He may not be kissing her, but now his hand is on her waist, and it's warm, and she really, really wishes she was wearing anything except the awful cardigan. But she's bra-less under her vest top; taking the cardigan off would make her feel as good as naked.

'It's OK,' he says. He's stopped laughing. She wonders if he's going to try it again or whether he's thought better of it. She takes a breath and tries to explain: 'Sorry. I'm so used to being on my own, or being the grown-up. I just – I suppose I just say what's in my head.'

'That's OK. Really it is. I wish more people did. It would make life easier.' They are still standing. Everything has become uncertain: the kissing-or-not-kissing, the leaving-or-not-leaving. There's something in his face, too: a distance.

'Why don't you stay?' And then Kate realises what she's said. 'I don't mean stay the night, I mean—' She's laughing again. 'Oh, god, I'm sorry. I mean, don't go just yet. Please. Sit down. If you want to.'

'That sounds like an excellent idea,' Spencer says, and he does. Kate sits next to him, and he takes her hand in both of his and turns it palm-up and kisses it, without looking away from her face, which is one of the sexiest things that Kate can remember happening to her, ever, although her experience is fairly limited. And then he lets go of her hand and Kate feels something inside her start to wake from a hibernation so long that she had thought it may as well have been a death. She leans into him, her head on his chest, his arm round her shoulder, and she closes her eyes.

Kate wakes to the sound of the Christmas party discharging itself from the restaurant, in the puzzling glow of the Christmas-tree lights and the unfamiliar sensation of being held. She sits upright, as if stung.

'Whoa,' Spencer says. 'Hold your horses. You're OK.'

'I fell asleep.'

'You did.' Perching on the edge of the sofa, trying to put the components of the day into order, Kate is looking away from Spencer. That doesn't stop her from hearing the gentleness in his voice. 'But that's not surprising. You had a tough day, and then I turned up and nearly kissed you.'

'Oh, god.' Kate puts her head in her hands, the memory washing up through her, making her cringe. 'Spencer, I'm – I'm sorry. It's been such a day even before – did Daisy—'

'Not a sound,' Spencer says. 'Nothing has happened while you've been sleeping. Except for a couple having an argument underneath the window. I think they made up.'

'Right. Well, that's good, I suppose—' Kate has turned to listen to him, watch him talk; in the fairylight glow everything seems eerie, other-worldly. She stands, stretches.

Spencer stands, too, and then – just like that – they are kissing. Kate hasn't had a chance to think that it might be coming, or to remember that he is Daisy's teacher. Since waking she hasn't considered how she hasn't done this in years and she really needs to think about whether it's a good idea or not, properly think about it, instead of daydreaming like she did when she was eighteen. She can't do a pros-and-cons list, because the reality is here, and it's too late for careful consideration. So she can do nothing except kiss, in exactly the way she would have asked for the kiss to be if kisses were agreed beforehand: gently, slowly, but with purpose. And then his mouth moves – to the tip of her nose, the place between her eyebrows, her forehead, the top of her head – and he pulls her towards him. Both of his arms go around her shoulders; hers are around his waist. Although the kiss worked, the hug is awkward, their arms in the wrong places; it would be platonic if it wasn't for the erection pressing at Kate's waist. Her body lets out a great remembering sigh. Spencer holds her more tightly, for a moment, and then steps away, his hands still on her shoulders. He smiles a soft, warm smile.

'I'm going,' he says, 'before we turn into pumpkins. But Kate, I would very much like for us to go on a date, if you'd like to.'

'I'd love to,' she says, half serious, half laughing; she hasn't spent enough time with him to understand what the look in his eyes means, whether his formality is meant as a joke or if he is trying to show her the contents of his heart. (There had been playground gossip about a heart tattoo, from someone who's seen him swimming in the pool at Marsham. At least, it might have been him. And it might have been a heart. The Mysterious Mr Swanson is continuing to drive Throckton crazy.)

'Good.' He moves to the door, puts his hand on the handle. He's smiling. *This is how it should be*, Kate thinks. *Easy*. 'Your life is more complicated than mine, so—'

She nods, smiles back. 'I'll find a time and I'll let you know.'

When he has gone – a kiss, light, on her lips, another smile, an 'I'll let myself out, it's cold' – Kate looks in on Daisy. She sits at the end of her daughter's bed until she feels herself calm, and then she goes and gets into her own bed, and falls into a sleep so deep that when her alarm goes off in the morning, she is convinced it's still the middle of the night. She wakes to Daisy burrowing into her side, snuffling for love, and is tempted to give them both the day off. But Kate wants to see Spencer; and Daisy is very clear that the time between now and the Christmas concert is precious and cannot be wasted. Meryl Streep would envy the level of commitment that Wendy Orr has instilled into her charges. So they get up and get ready – Kate stirs ground almonds into Daisy's porridge, adds a spoonful of honey – and when they set off, they are barely late at all. On the way out, Kate finds a petrol-station receipt with Spencer's phone number on the back lying on the mat. She imagines him going through his pockets in the cold outside, finding something he could write on, looking for a pen. She puts the number into her phone as 'S', and folds the receipt into squares and tucks it into the back of her purse.

Chapter 6

Early December, a day later

'ARE YOU SURE THIS is OK, Mum?'

It's the Saturday after the clinic visit, and two days since the kiss. Kate isn't sure that she should be measuring time by kisses. It's better than counting from bad health news, she supposes. Now she's standing in her mother's hallway, a sullen Daisy clinging onto her hand.

'Of course it is.' Richenda kneels, looks Daisy in the face. 'I know how important your time with Melissa is. And if Daisy didn't come to stay, who else would I bake Christmas tree biscuits with? Who else would I take to the pantomime?'

Daisy's grip loosens, and Kate works her fingers free, puts her hand on Daisy's shoulder instead. Daisy looks up into her mother's face, and says, in a faintly accusatory tone, 'You didn't say pantomime.'

'I thought it would be a nice surprise.' Sometimes, Kate feels resentful of all of the fun things her mother gets to do with Daisy, while Kate is the one with the nebuliser and the homework. It's been a tiring, tiresome morning. Daisy refused to eat her breakfast, Kate shouted, and then she had to shut herself in the bedroom in case she cried. When she came out Daisy was stiff and silent. Kate put a bowl of chocolate raisins on the table, and Daisy ignored them. Then Daisy said she didn't want to go to Granny's, and Kate only just stopped herself from saying the words that gathered in her mouth: *this is the first time I get to go away by myself all year, and you are not going to spoil it for me.* Instead she packed Daisy's mini wheeled suitcase and wondered whether it was really worth going away at all. If Daisy sulked when she left and sulked when she came back, she may as well not bother. A sneaking thought behind that one: if she cancelled going to see Melissa, maybe her mother would babysit and she could go out with Spencer. But, no. Friends first. And the two nights she had spent in London for Melissa's birthday last December was her first real freedom since Daisy was born. It was the trip that had made her realise that she needed to find a way of moving out of her childhood home, making a space to be an adult in her own life, instead of constantly thinking about the parallel path she didn't take when she decided to keep her baby. She is lucky to have so much support, of course, and she would never un-choose her beloved child. But when Melissa texted and asked if she wanted to come down for the party this year, Kate had jumped at the chance.

'I don't always like surprises.' Daisy is undoing her coat with a martyred air.

'Oh dear.' Richenda flicks her gaze to Kate with a smile, but keeps the laugh out of her voice. 'I expect it will be all right when we get there.'

'Mummy is going to Auntie Lissa's party, but I'm not allowed. And Auntie Lissa came to my party. It's not fair. At school we have quick cocoa for parties. Miss Orr says it's the fairest way.'

Kate glances at her mother. 'Quid pro quo,' she says, and Richenda laughs, straightening her face when Daisy looks at her.

'I don't think it's fair AT ALL.'

'Daisy, we've been through this.' Kate can hear the frustration in her own voice, and stops, shakes her head.

'Grown-up parties are boring for children,' Richenda says. 'And Mummy's allowed to have fun, isn't she?'

'That's what Mummy said' – Daisy glances at her mother – 'but when Mummy said it, she said a bad word as well.'

'Why don't you go and find Beatle and Hope, and see if they would like a biscuit?' Richenda asks, and Daisy goes off, with a sigh.

'Sorry,' Kate says, 'rough morning. Oh, and I said "bloody".'

Richenda laughs. 'She'll be fine. You deserve a break.'

'Are you sure?' Whenever Kate has a quiet moment her mind goes back to the hospital, the weight chart, the plunging feeling of having got it wrong. She tries to remember the things Richenda said, and Spencer said, but it's not always easy to let logic and good sense win out over guilt and panic.

'I'm sure. And so long as I have some notice I love to have her. You know that.'

'Thanks,' Kate says. 'And you know I'm sorry about going off with Melissa after Daisy's party. I just—'

'Hey' – Richenda reaches for her – 'I didn't mean it like that. Darling, are you OK? You know I'm here, don't you?' Kate nods, and Richenda continues, 'I hadn't thought, when you moved, that it would be harder to – to be sure that things are all right with you.'

'Oh, Mum.' There's the laughing sound of Daisy in the garden with the dogs, the tiredness of the morning, the worry in her mother's face, and she could cry. 'Honestly, I'm OK,' and then, quickly, before she can change her mind, 'and actually I might get you to babysit, maybe next weekend? I might be going on a' – she can't bring herself to say the word 'date', somehow – 'I might be going out with someone. If you don't mind.'

'Oh.' Richenda looks surprised, and Kate thinks of how depressing it is that the idea of her seeing someone is so shocking. Still, you reap as you sow. 'Who is he? I mean, yes, of course I'll babysit.'

Daisy appears in the doorway. 'The dogs have eaten their biscuits' – she sounds a little like a TV announcer, solemn and slow – 'and it made me think about biscuits for my own self.'

Kate laughs, and opens her arms. 'Come and give me a hug, little one,' she says, 'and I'll see you after school on Monday.' She swallows back a 'be good'. 'Have fun, sweetheart. I love you.'

'I love you. Will you bring me some of Auntie Lissa's birthday cake?'

'Of course I will, baby.'

'Come on,' Granny says. 'Let's wave goodbye to Mummy, then we'll find the human biscuits.' She smiles at Kate. 'You can tell me more about the babysitting when you get home.'

'OK. Her meds and her food diary are in the bag. I've been doing hot chocolate with her breakfast. And she might not have told you, but she likes avocado, now she's five.' Getting Daisy to eat avocado was a godsend, as it's so full of calories and good fats. 'I'll text you the new doses for her tablets, just so you're sure.'

Richenda nods, hugs Kate briefly, and opens the door. 'Thank you. Don't worry. I'll keep in touch.'

Kate shoulders her rucksack and sets out for the station. She doubts there'll be birthday cake at Melissa's, but she can pick up something suitably sweet from the station before she comes home.

Melissa lives in a shared house in Shoreditch in a tiny room. It's almost filled by a queen bed and a clothes rail; Kate's rucksack has to be hung from the hook on the back of the door. Over oat-milk lattes in a café round the corner from the house, Melissa tells Kate she doesn't mind the lack of space in her room because they all hang out in the kitchen most of the time, and anyway, she likes the vibe of the area. Kate agrees it's cool, and it is, as far as she can tell. ('How would *you* know what's cool?' asks the gremlin on her shoulder.) She always finds it strange to walk down a street where no one knows who she is, and where she doesn't know who they are, and she can't link them back to her own family within six moves. On the way to the station, she'd said hello to Jake, the younger brother of a boy in the year below her at school who used to wash her father's car for pocket money, and when she got on the train it was behind the couple who'd bought the house three doors down from her parents' place and then cut down all of the hornbeam trees in the garden. Here, on a not-especially-busy Saturday afternoon in east London, they must have walked past a hundred people in less than ten minutes. The café is full of people wearing headphones, reading, working on laptops, laughing with their friends, but no one turns around when the door opens to see who's coming in.

'Shall I get us some more coffees?' She always forgets how expensive it is to be sociable: coffee, wine, tickets, taxis. She knows she's lucky, to have a year of no rent, and a trust fund from the money her parents had saved for her university career, as well as the benefits she can claim for Daisy; but it would be so easy to fritter money away.

'The party should get going at about ten,' Melissa says when she returns to the table, 'so we've got loads of time. I thought you might want to go shopping.'

'I do.' Kate's boots really don't stand up to scrutiny, and she feels dowdy in her best-of-two-pairs of jeans and blue striped top. Especially when everyone around her is – well, whatever the opposite of dowdy is. Stylish. Cool.

'Great. Well, I thought we'd go to the market, and the vintage shops. I really want some big hoop earrings, and a bowler hat.' Melissa cocks an eyebrow, tilts her head. 'I've been thinking about it all week.'

'Of course you do.' Kate laughs. She can already see Melissa's hazelnut curls bouncing out from under a black brim.

'I reckon I could zhuzh it up with scarves and flowers and – anything really. What do you want?'

Kate doesn't have a list, but she knows the answer. 'To feel less like a—' She's not sure what the word is.

Melissa nods. 'Less frumpy? I'm on it. Let's go.' She leaves her latte half drunk and heads for the door, Kate following in her wake, trying not to be bothered by the 'frumpy', though it's probably true. Although Melissa would consider ninety-five per cent of the population to be frumpy. And Kate doesn't have the time that Melissa has. At home, she gets up and gets dressed in one of her few carefully chosen outfits, all practical and sufficiently 'her' to make her happy, but nothing special. She'd rather spend her money on clothes for

Daisy, and her mother takes Kate shopping, buying her good clothes that will last. But yes, she does feel frumpy, sometimes. And she doesn't want to. And it has nothing to do with Spencer.

Two hours later, Kate is the owner of a pair of black ankle boots with silver buckles. ('They're not too – cowgirl?' she'd asked Melissa, who'd said no, and anyway, could you be too cowgirl, a question to which Kate suspects the answer is 'yes'.) She's also bought a long, tiered floral dress with shoestring straps, which she dismissed as impractical until Melissa pointed out she could wear a long-sleeved top under it. Melissa persuaded her to try on a denim jacket in the second vintage shop they went to and, surprisingly, Kate loved it. She's never owned a denim jacket before; she always thought they weren't quite her. But maybe they are. Or could be.

She's spent all of her money, plus a bit of the Christmas money she hopes will come her way from her mum. But it's worth it. She feels like herself. A better, sassier, more in-control self. Which is odd, because she's never bought vintage clothing, never owned almost-too-cowgirl boots. Maybe the self she could have been would have done these things. Standing in front of the mirror in the corner of the shop, the washed-out denim jacket somehow made her pale face, hair, eyes look interesting rather than peaky. She had stood there and wondered who wore the jacket before she did. Someone who had fun, she hoped. Someone who went on dates and enjoyed themselves and felt as though they had a future.

'How do you know Melissa?'

The man who's asking is called Felix. He's introduced himself, solemnly, shaking Kate's hand, and then asking if she would mind if he sat with her. 'Kate,' he says, once he's settled on the sofa next to her, 'you look like a woman with hidden depths to me.'

Kate laughs. 'Do I, now?'

'Why are you laughing?'

'I'm not laughing. It's my depths making a noise.'

Felix puts his arm around her, leans close. Kate stays upright. 'I like you, Kate. You're funny.'

'Am I? You've hardly had the chance to find out.' She has no idea what she is, once she gets out of Throckton.

'I can just tell.' He taps his nose, lifts an eyebrow, and Kate laughs.

She doesn't mind talking to him, although she had come to sit quietly in the corner for a while, to take a breath and take off her new boots and cross her legs and drink some water. She didn't know how much she had wanted to drink wine from a Mason jar, to dance, circling her arms and spinning on the makeshift dancefloor.

Felix nods. 'You are. How do you know Melissa?'

'School,' she says. 'Though we didn't really become proper friends until we'd left.'

Felix leans back. His expression says that if she wants to lean against him, he'd be happy. But she crosses her legs under her, stays upright, sways with the music. He rubs his hand up and down her back. It would have been nice, maybe, if she was in the market for it.

Kate turns. 'I'm with someone,' she says, a thrill in her gut at the saying of it. The thought of Spencer sends anticipation through her, a shiver from hair-parting to sole. They've been texting, ever since the kiss; and it's nice to be here in London, to have some things to text about that make her sound as though she has more to think about than Daisy and waiting for her dissertation results.

Felix nods, and takes his hand away, a you-win-some-you-lose-some smile on his face.

Melissa is in the centre of the dancefloor, laughing, a bottle aloft in her hand. She found her bowler hat, and she's wrapped some birthday ribbon round the brim; it glows, iridescent, in the near darkness of the candlelit basement. It must be about 3 a.m. Hollie, one of Melissa's housemates, sits down on the other side of Kate, hands her a joint. Kate has started shaking her head – you don't compromise your lungs when you spend all of your life watching a child who will never take the deep, unheeding breaths that you can – but then she thinks of all she has missed out on, doing her degree in her teenage bedroom with a child at her feet. She takes it between her fingertips. She's never even smoked a cigarette. She concentrates, bringing the stubby, glowing joint to her mouth.

The paper is wet and sticks to her lip, and thinking about how many mouths might have already touched it makes her queasy. But she inhales, not too deeply, manages, at least, not to cough. Nothing much happens; if she's light-headed it's the wine and the lateness and the many, many coffees. But she's done it. She's smoked a joint. She hands it back to Hollie, who takes a deep drag, then says, 'You're the one with the kid, yeah? Melissa is her auntie?'

'Yeah,' Kate says. And though Hollie goes on to ask for photos, to tell her how amazing it is to be a mother, to bring, like, an actual human into existence – the night is not quite the same afterwards. 'The one with the kid' is, at least, a little better than 'The one who got pregnant to the married man when she was nineteen' or, worst of all, 'the one with the kid with cystic fibrosis, poor little mite, such a shame'. But how lovely it would be to be 'the one with the first-class degree', 'the one who is training to be a physiotherapist'. Even 'the one with the bowler hat' would be an improvement, in that it would be about her alone, the choices that she made today, not a six-year-old small-town scandal and a five-year-old who has no idea of how she's whispered about. Kate goes to bed before four, checks her phone to see that all is well with Daisy, and sleeps.

Kate wakes at noon. She lies still for a moment, waiting for a hangover to bounce into her stomach, yell in her ear, but she feels only the disorientation of being somewhere other than home. Perhaps she danced the wine away. Kate climbs over Melissa, who is asleep on her back, on top of the duvet, in her clothes. The rest of the house is silent. She showers, dresses, drinks some water, puts on her beloved-already new boots, and after texting Melissa to tell her where she's going, walks down to the café round the corner. She orders avocado toast – wondering whether Daisy might be eating the same thing – and coffee, and scrolls through her phone. Richenda has sent photos of Daisy at the pantomime, clutching a programme and an ice-cream during the interval, and texted a report of her meals and sleep, too. And there's a message from Spencer, hoping she is having a good time. She sends him a photo of her coffee, another of her boots. He sends her photos of his tea, his own feet, in trainers, because he's about to go for a run. The intimacy of it, the closeness, makes her want to cry for her own loneliness. But then he asks how her diary looks for next weekend, and she texts her mum about babysitting, and just like that she has a date for Saturday. Kate has been on barely any dates in her life. Being with Mike, Daisy's father, had been all secret dog walks and snatched sex. She had thought it was romantic, at the time. The terrible way it ended – her slipping and falling into the January water of a lake, Mike drowning while she lay unconscious on the bank – still makes Kate wake with a jolt and a stifled scream some nights. Over the last couple of years, she has been on a handful of dates, some with a fellow Open University student she had worked with on an online group project, one with a doctor at the CF clinic, who had asked her out when he finished his rotation there. The dates had not been terrible, but Kate had found herself wishing she was back at home. She'd decided that she wasn't ready. She might be now. She replies to Spencer's message, signing off with a kiss.

Back at the house, people are moving into life, and after the basement has been cleared of bottles and cans, the ashtrays emptied and the spills blotted – a surprisingly quick and enjoyable task, between eight of them – someone puts on a film. They lie around, half watching, half chatting, Kate on the end of one of the sagging sofas, Melissa stretched out with her head on Kate's lap; Kate thinks about the museums, the shows, the sights she should be seeing, and then she looks around at the affable group of people who are choosing this, and she can think of nowhere else she would rather be. She lets herself sigh. Melissa tilts her head to look up. 'You see, babe?' she says. 'It's all right.'

There's enough time on Monday morning to go to a museum. Kate leaves the house at the same time as Melissa, walks her to the Tube, and stands on the pavement for a moment, feeling the relief of being a small person in a big place. Though Hollie asked about Daisy, no one here much cares about her life, about who the father of her child was. They didn't really care about anything much, these friends of Melissa's, except what was happening right now, and tomorrow, and whether it felt good.

Kate should be more like that. She should make sure Daisy stays that way, too, not asking her to look forwards too far, or reflect too much. She shouldn't be so hard on her, either. After all, it is unfair, when you think about it from her perspective, that Melissa comes to her party and she doesn't go to Melissa's. It's OK to say you're tired, to not want to eat sometimes, to cry with frustration because it's raining or it isn't Christmas morning and you had dreamed it was Christmas Eve, or because your llama socks are in the wash. Kate is an only child; one of her earliest memories is of being at school, and feeling a boiling rage that she has been put in a class with children. She realises now that she spent so much time in the company of adults that she thought she was one. From now on, she will make sure that Daisy glories in being a child.

Play dates, park time, the soft-play centre in Marsham that makes Kate's head ache.

She gets to the British Library in good time, but her rucksack is too big for her to be allowed in with it. So she walks to St Pancras, buys a book, finds a table in a café, and reads, uninterrupted, for an hour and a half. Then she buys a slice of chocolate cake to take away, and asks the bemused waitress to wrap it in a paper napkin rather than put it in a box. Daisy knows how birthday cake is served.

Chapter 7

Mid-December, the following weekend

SPENCER RINGS THE BELL of the flat exactly on time. Kate is ready. She's wearing the new boots, and the new dress, with a black polo-neck purloined from her mother's wardrobe underneath. She was feeling happy – confident, even – until she started sorting out her handbag, which contained a colouring book and pens, three packets of raisins, wet wipes, a rattling tablet dispenser and a conker. Then she'd been hit by the enormity of having a life any different to the one she has now. A weekend in London once a year feels like the limit of her independence – an adventure, an escape, paid for with three days of feeling tired and unsettled, which of course makes Daisy unsettled in turn. The possibility of her everyday life being a new shape had felt, suddenly, impossible – not worth even trying for. She'd scrolled through the messages she and Spencer have exchanged since the kiss over a week ago, and decided that it would be rude to cancel. But she has no hope, anymore.

She looks at herself in the mirror, checking her mascara, and attempts to give herself a stern look. Life is about more than men. She's going to see a film and have something to eat. She fancies him. These are all normal things. If she had a normal life, then a date would have been much less of a big deal. But – especially without her dissertation – it feels as though all Kate has to think about, in the time she's not absorbed by watching Daisy bounce on the trampoline or coaxing one more spoonful of guacamole into her, is Spencer. She owes herself, and Daisy, a better way of living than this. As she goes down the stairs to open the door, Kate straightens her shoulders. She's not a besotted teenage girl.

Except, when she sees him – when she notices that he looks nervous – she may as well be.

'Hello,' he says. 'I've been looking forward to this.'

'Me too,' she answers, because whether this is a one-off or something more, she's going to go honestly into it. 'Though I had a bit of a wobble about it, just now. Come up.'

He passes her and goes up the stairs. Kate closes the door and follows him, remembering the last time he was here. He has been scrupulously professional at school, but she's caught a flash of warmth in his eye when he's looked at her. In the living room, he turns and faces her. He doesn't touch her but he's close enough to. 'Have you changed your mind? If you have, it's OK. I mean' – he laughs, shrugs his shoulders in a 'how can I be making a mess of this already' gesture – 'I'd love for us to go out, but only if you want to.'

And then, she realises how ridiculous she is being. Don't people with kids date all the time? Isn't Daisy safe and well right now? Isn't she allowed to enjoy herself, for crying out loud? Life is short. Mike's was. Daisy's might be. (The floor convulses at the thought.) Why shouldn't she go to the cinema two Saturdays before Christmas?

'I want to.' She steps forward and kisses him, before she can think about it.

They've texted back-and-forth all week about what they might do: Kate had suggested a walk up to Beau's Heights, thinking that they could take Beatle and Hope, but the weather forecast was for wind and rain. A mid-afternoon meal seemed an odd thing, and going for coffee not substantial enough when they had the afternoon and evening. *I know it's not very original, but how about a film, then dinner?* Spencer had texted yesterday. *So long as it isn't a cartoon*! Kate texted back, trying to remember when she last saw a film with a certificate higher than 'U' at the cinema.

The nearby town of Marsham has two cinemas: the multi-screen that's part of the new retail development on the outskirts, and the small independent cinema, lovingly restored to something that Kate suspects is rather better than its former glory. That's where they go. It feels very grown-up. The snacks are small pots of wasabi peas, jelly beans, rice crackers and chocolate-covered coffee beans. Popcorn is served in red-and-white candy-striped cones. Soft drinks come in glass bottles with the metal caps popped off and a paper straw dropped in. There are wines and beers as well as good coffee. It turns out that Spencer is a regular; the staff recognise him and he talks about the films he's seen as they walk up the stairs to the balcony. They are hand in hand again, although they didn't touch, by unspoken consent, as they walked through Throckton's small town square to the place where Spencer had parked his car.

They are in the front row of the balcony, in one of a row of sofas made for two. Spencer sits down and crosses one leg over the other. He puts an arm across the back of the sofa and smiles up at Kate. 'Come and get comfy,' he says. 'I can't believe you haven't seen this.'

'I feel as though I must have done,' she says, 'because everybody has, haven't they? But I have no recollection of it, at all.' She'd asked her mother, when she dropped Daisy off, if she would have seen *It's a Wonderful Life*, but Richenda could only shrug and say probably, but that was the sort of thing her father would have taken her to. Although Kate's parents stayed together until the year after Daisy was born, Kate had never had any illusions that they were happy. She can't remember the three of them doing anything as everyday as going to the cinema together. Family weddings, school events, yes. Even summer holidays, in a house in France, where her mother would read in the garden and her father would walk in the hills, and the three of them would eat together, each with their own book beside their plate at the table. On the nights when she worries about Daisy having only one parent, she remembers her own upbringing, and consoles herself that what she is doing surely can't be worse than the want-for-nothing low-level unhappiness of her childhood.

'Then you haven't seen it.' Spencer shakes his head. 'I think you'd know if you had. I'm glad I get to introduce you to it.'

Kate starts by sitting at the end of the sofa, leaning against the arm, but it's a piece of furniture that's used to having couples in the middle of it, so it tilts her towards him. She tries sitting forward but it feels as though she's ignoring him.

'Kate' – he is smiling, his gaze on hers – 'it's a long film. I'm not going to jump you in a cinema. Come and get comfortable.' So she fits herself into the space beneath his shoulder, and feels how warm he is against her.

'Don't go to sleep,' he says into the hair above her ear as the lights go down. 'Twice looks like carelessness.'

There's a tapas bar in the basement of the cinema, and after the film they eat and Kate cries when she talks about it and Spencer smiles and teases her a little bit.

The way he talks about food, and insists that he won't drink at all because he's driving, makes Kate think that her parents will like him, too. She tells herself off for getting ahead of things.

'I don't know much about you,' she says, in the lull between plates being cleared and coffee arriving.

Spencer tilts his head, half smiles. 'I bet you do.'

Kate laughs. 'I thought we didn't listen to gossip.'

He smiles, the crooked tooth catching the light. 'Well, of course we don't. But if you had – what would you know?'

'OK,' she says, 'if you're sure.' He nods, smiling still. Kate tries to remember what she's heard and what she's imagined, and separate the two. 'Spencer Swanson. No information on possible middle name. Estimates as to age vary, but the consensus is somewhere between twenty-five and thirty-two—'

'Thirty-two? I want to know who said that so I can make their child's life a misery.'

'Born in Dorset, or maybe Devon, grew up in Scotland, possibly Edinburgh, mentioned a sister in conversation at parents' evening, last job was in a school in west London, may or may not go swimming, may or may not have a tattoo—'

His eyes are watching hers, again. Kate thrills at the feeling of it, tension under her skin, heat in her mouth. She remembers how often people tell her how brave she is, as she fights this and that battle for Daisy. Well, bravery comes in more than one form. '—Cannot be found on social media. No information available as to relationship status.'

Spencer smiles and takes Kate's hand across the table. Afterwards, in the morning, she'll remember that although she might have been tipsy, he was as sober as could be. He could have no excuse; he must have meant to take her hand, to talk the way he did. 'Spencer Alexander Swanson. Nobody thought about my initials when they were naming me so I have the choice between SS and SAS. Born in Swanage, in Dorset, to a Dutch mother and Scottish father, twenty-nine years ago on the seventeenth of May. My mother didn't settle on the south coast so we moved to Edinburgh when I was four, just before my sister Annie was born. I chose her name. She's named after one of the trucks in *Thomas the Tank Engine*.'

Kate laughs. 'Seriously?'

'Seriously. Annie lives in Cardiff now, with a man none of us like, two children of her own and two step-children. My parents still live in the house we grew up in, in Edinburgh. I taught in a school in west London for a few years' – he hesitates, looks away – 'but the density of people there got to be too much for me. And there's no air.'

'I don't like London for long,' Kate says, 'except for the museums.' She remembers school trips to the Natural History Museum, everyone else dying to escape to the shops but Kate in love with the colours of the building, the endless samples of rocks and creatures brought back from all over the world, a miracle of knowledge. One of her favourite memories of mothering is the first time she took Daisy there, told her to look at the walls, and watched her face open with delight as she spotted the monkeys carved into the stone, scurrying up arches and along architraves. The journey is just too far to make it a comfortable day trip, but they do it now and then anyway. Last summer they had house-sat for a friend of Richenda who lived in Clapham, and for three days had done everything they could think of to do in London, but the Natural History Museum had remained Daisy's favourite place. They'd looked at the butterflies, pinned out in ranks and rows, Daisy spelling out the names and Kate laughing at the clumsiness and, sometimes, beauty of the words her daughter was enunciating with such care.

Spencer nods. 'It's OK for the first term. Then it gets so that you're always breathing in something that you don't want to.' There's a pause. Kate wishes she hadn't interrupted. She wants to know more, but she doesn't want to ask too many questions. Then Spencer holds her hand a little tighter, and says, 'Has a certificate for swimming a mile and a junior lifesaving award, almost certainly lapsed. Single at the moment, but is hoping that that will change, very soon. And if you want to know whether there's a tattoo, you're going to have to find out for yourself.'

Kate looks at him, looks away. He's so at ease, so flirtatious, that for a moment she wonders whether she is making a mistake. Maybe seducing mothers is what he does. A sort of game. 'I don't think I'd want to have a tattoo,' she says. 'I'd be scared of the pain.'

Spencer leans back in his chair. 'I think there's a lot that people say about tattoos that they could also say about children,' he says, '"they might really hurt" being one of them. And, "what if you change your mind later?" works for tattoos or children.'

Kate laughs. "How do you know for sure?" she says. 'And "how do you choose who you make it with?"'

Spencer smiles. 'Tenuous, but I'll allow it. "Will you regret it when you get older?"'

'What if you don't like it once it's done?' Kate says. And then she remembers being pregnant with Daisy, the way her father tried to make her change her mind, the palpable disappointment of her teachers: 'It's not the sort of thing I'd expect from you.'

'You'll be stuck with it for life, you know.'

As soon as the words reach her, Kate feels her stomach plummet. Daisy's life expectancy isn't something she wants to think about: she pushes her worries about it away, every day, and focuses on keeping Daisy safe. Any other way is unthinkable.

She tries to smile, but Spencer has read her expression. 'Kate, I'm sorry. I was just being silly. I didn't mean to—'

'Honestly, it's fine. It's just that now Daisy's here it's so hard to think about the way people talked about her. Before she was born.'

His hand holds hers, more tightly. 'The last thing I want to do is upset you.'

'I know.' Kate makes herself look up at him, and can't help but smile at the concern in his face. 'I'm not upset, exactly. Just—'

Spencer takes her other hand. 'Shall we go for a walk? We could get some mulled wine at the Christmas market.'

He doesn't press her for conversation, and they wander between the stalls. Kate buys Daisy a wooden bauble with her name on it; Spencer buys an elf hat with ears for himself, for the last day of term.

'Do you know what's been lovely, about this afternoon?'

'Tell me.' Spencer has tucked her arm into the crook of his elbow.

'I haven't worried once about what my dissertation result is going to be.'

Spencer laughs. 'I will take that as the greatest compliment possible.'

'So you should.' She sighs. 'It's not so much the result, but the fact that once I've got it I really need to do something with my life.'

'Raising an amazing child in a fantastic way aside,' Spencer says.

'That aside.' She squeezes his arm. 'Thank you. I just can't imagine how I'm going to do whatever's next – it's all so complicated. I mean, I know I'm lucky not to have to worry too much about money, but – I just can't imagine I'll ever have the headspace to do anything other than look after Daisy. I talk a good game but I don't know that I'll ever really make it happen.' They've moved away from the market square, and the wintry streets are quiet. It's easy to say these things, in the dark.

'I suppose you've been focused on your degree for a long time.'

'Yes, exactly.' At first she had thought that all she wanted was to do nothing for a while, but already her brain is itching and puzzling for something, then feeling defeated when it comes to making any of her ideas reality.

'And having some financial independence – does that make it easier, or harder?'

What an odd question. Kate hesitates; he seems to sense it.

'Sorry. Just thinking aloud, really. Living away from London has made me realise that I won't always be spending most of what I earn on rent. For the last few years there's been too much month at the end of the money.'

'I know I'm lucky like that,' Kate says, 'because I get some space to make decisions. But if I didn't have money to fall back on I'd have fewer choices.' She hears what she's saying. 'God, what an idiot. Listen to me, with my first-world problems. I'm so sorry.'

'So, what would you like to do next?' Spencer asks Kate in the car on the way home. She laughs, an involuntary nervous hic, because what happens this evening is the very thing she was thinking about: how, when Richenda offered to keep Daisy overnight, it had seemed a pragmatic, can-stay-up-late-and-not-worry-about-it idea, an easy yes. But sometime over coffee, the feeling between her and Spencer – the sense of possibility, the easy, strong connection, the beginning of intimacy, and the realisation of just how lonely she has become – made her feel differently. She has an ache that asks, why not salve me now, why wait to ease me away. She could ask him in, kiss him more. She's an adult. He's an adult.

'I hadn't really thought about it,' she says, although she immediately wishes she hadn't. She should be honest.

'Really?' He flicks a glance at her, puzzled, and she realises that he isn't asking whether, when they get back to her flat, she will be asking him to come in.

'Oh!' She laughs. 'I thought you meant—' And the blush does not so much bloom as erupt across her face and neck. She leans away from him so she can rest her skin against the cool of the window.

His left hand finds her right one, briefly, and then goes back to driving; the uncertainty in his voice makes her like him more. 'No,' he says, 'but don't think I'm not thinking about that, too.' It's his turn to laugh, embarrassed. 'I mean – all I mean is—'

Kate has gathered herself enough to help him out. 'It's going pretty well so far?'

'Exactly so.' She doesn't look at him, but she can hear that he's smiling.

'I'm still thinking about this MSc,' she says, after a moment, 'but I need to see what my final result is. And I feel as though I took my eye off the ball a bit, with Daisy. You know. I need to make sure she's back on track.'

They drive the last few minutes of the journey quietly. Kate, looking out of the window, realises she is counting the Christmas trees, something she used to do as a child, something she and Daisy do now. Before long, she sees the cool white light of her own tree, signalling home. She had forgotten to switch the lights of when they went out.

Spencer pulls in a little further along from the flat and turns off the ignition. The radio, which had been burbling Bach cantatas all the way home, has switched off, too. The silence in the car is sudden and loud. 'I had a really nice time, Kate.'

'Me too.'

He shifts round in his seat, turns to face her. 'Can I say something?'

'Of course,' and then a group of early-evening restaurant goers passes the car, talking and laughing, and she feels, suddenly, exposed. Whatever he has to say, it's not going to be made better for sitting in a cooling car and being interrupted every time someone walks past. 'Do you want to come up to the flat and have a glass of wine?'

'That would be great, actually,' he says, and his smile tells her that he's not about to say that this has been a nice afternoon, but. And neither is she. She would say, this has been wonderful, and.

Kate opens one of the bottles of Malbec from the Christmas-wine case her father sent, and pours two glasses of wine. 'Make mine a small one, please,' Spencer says. 'I still need to drive up the hill.'

'Of course.' Kate sits next to him on the sofa, and offers the glass. 'Cheers. I bet you're glad it's not coffee.'

He laughs. 'Too right. You can definitely have too much of a good thing. When it comes to coffee.'

And all of a sudden, Kate isn't thinking about Spencer, or the film, or the wine, or the tightness in her throat when Spencer looks directly into her face. She's thinking of Daisy, the way she watches the same films over and over, the fact that when they get to the end of a book she's enjoyed the first thing she will say is, 'Read it again, Mummy.' Kate half wishes that the same thing, time and again, would make her as satisfied. Would drinking coffee with Spencer every day stop being thrilling? Well, yes. But it might become something else. Something better.

'Kate? Are you OK?'

She takes a breath, comes back from wondering what Daisy is doing now, whether Richenda will get her to bed at a decent time, if she's run around enough to keep her lungs clear today, eaten enough to give her a chance of gaining weight. Thinks about saying as much, but instead she smiles. 'I'm fine. What did you want to say? In the car?'

'Ah' – Spencer laughs – 'before you so rudely interrupted me with wine and warmth?' But then his face turns serious, and he looks down into his glass, then back up at her. 'I thought I should – explain some things.' Kate nods, puts down her glass, holds her own hands. She will have to do her own explaining, at some point, if this is going to go anywhere.

'That day I saw you in the café,' he says, 'I wanted to ask you out, there and then. You watched me leave, and when I looked back through the window I could see you there. I almost went back in. I stood there and I thought, I'll just say, I've really enjoyed this, and I know it sounds ridiculous, but would you like to do it again sometime.'

He goes quiet. Kate smiles encouragement, and the pit of her stomach shivers. 'But you didn't.'

'I didn't. I thought, you have to be so careful, when you're a male teacher, and when you're in a new place. I thought, I can wait. I'll wait until Daisy isn't in my class, at least. Then it won't be – controversial.'

Kate has wondered about this. 'It's not against the rules though, is it? Seeing someone who's a parent.'

'It's not against the rules. There are guidelines, but they're all a bit woolly, and as far as I'm concerned, we're both adults, and what happens between us doesn't affect the rest of the class, or my ability to do my job. But people can be—'

'I know,' Kate says. 'Judgemental, petty, unkind.'

Spencer touches the back of her hand. 'Yes. So I thought I'd wait. There are people who would have a field day about something like this. Staffrooms can be worse than classrooms for bullying. Sometimes I saw you in the playground and I almost came out to speak to you. I wanted to say, "please wait for this year to be over, and then we can be together." But I knew it would sound strange, because all we'd done was have coffee at the same table; and then I pissed you off when I said no to Daisy's party.'

Hearing Spencer swear, oddly, makes her all the more aware that he's a teacher, and that here, now, they are off duty. 'I just felt stupid, for asking you.' He's waiting for her to say more. 'You changed your mind, though. About waiting.'

He smiles, touches her face, and she puts her hand over his, and their fingers slide and curl together. 'I did, but I wanted to make sure you knew that me being here – us seeing each other – people might be unkind.'

Kate feels a great rush of sympathy for him. She kisses his palm and sees that her mouth on his skin has exactly the same effect as his mouth on hers. 'I've been gossiped about before. I know it's horrible. But the thing is, it doesn't change the facts. And if the facts are – if there's nothing wrong with this—'

116

'There's nothing wrong with this. But people will talk. And it's really important to me that you know that, and that you're OK with that.'

There's an expression in his eyes that seems way out of proportion to the difficulty of being the talk of Throckton for a couple of weeks.

'I'm OK with that if you are,' Kate says. And she is. But the thought of being talked about – the sudden silences when she walks into a shop, the looks that follow, the pretend-innocence of questions designed to needle – Kate remembers all of these things from when she was pregnant with Daisy. She remembers how the hurt of it twisted under her skin. She doesn't relish going through it again. But she and Spencer are both single; no one has died. This won't be as bad as last time.

She gets up for the wine, brings the bottle over to where they are sitting. She goes to top up Spencer's glass, but he holds out a hand to stop her. 'I'd better not. I need to drive home.' He looks as though he is holding his breath. She can feel that she is holding hers.

Kate knows what he's asking. She likes that he isn't taking anything for granted. Even though, after the conversation they've just had, him spending the night here might have been seen as a given. She puts down the bottle, touches his face with her fingertips. He tilts the weight of his head towards them.

'I'd like you to stay.' She holds his gaze, so he knows that she knows what she's asking. He holds up the wine glass, and she pours then sits down next to him. He puts his glass on the table and takes her hand. He's slow, careful, and she realises that he's waiting for her – for permission, perhaps, or just to be sure. Her heart opens a little more. She puts her glass down next to his and turns to kiss him.

'Does this come off?' she asks, a little later, her fingers at his shirt collar, and when he nods she unbuttons his shirt. Then she bends to unbuckle her boots, shucks her feet free, tucks them beneath her. He's waiting to kiss her again.

But then he hesitates, and she pulls back, looking at him: the redness of his mouth, the darkness of his eyes. 'What is it?'

Another hesitation, the smallest shake of his head, and then he says, 'Nothing.'

'Are you sure?' Kate doesn't need him to declare undying love, but if he's having doubts at this point, she should probably cut her losses. 'Spencer? Is there something I should know?'

He shakes his head, puts his hand on her shoulder, runs his palm up her neck and cradles the side of her head. She feels herself lean against the weight of it. It feels perfect. They feel perfect. Kate is the one who asks if they should go to bed. She goes downstairs and locks the door, switches off the hallway light. She leaves the Christmas-tree lights on; and that and the light from the streetlights coming through the thin curtains make their skin glow. This is it. She never thought she would have a relationship again, but here she is on the brink of something more real-feeling than anything else in her world. *I should check my phone*, she thinks, *in case there's a message from my mother*; but nothing could happen to Daisy that Richenda couldn't cope with, and there's always the landline if there is an emergency. So, instead she walks towards Spencer – he's standing, and the profile of his face against the light makes her take a quick, thrilled breath – reaches for his hand, and leads him to the bedroom.

And that's where it almost goes wrong. Because Kate realises – feels her body go from pliant to unyielding in the second it takes to put her hand on the door-knob – that she has never had sex in a bed. Never done this most normal of things. How can she hope to have any sort of a normal life? Between Daisy's needs and her own terrible start, she must have been insane to even imagine she could have this chance. Gossip is the least of her worries. Coldness fills her, the hard earth hurtles up to meet her. She thinks of making an excuse – a missed text from her mother, a forgotten errand, a sudden backache. But after the way Spencer has confided his worries, she knows he deserves better.

When she turns to face him, he's looking braced, a pre-emptive hurt in his eyes. 'It's OK,' he says, 'if it's too soon. Or too complicated. I understand.'

She puts her hand to his face, reaching for him the way he reached for her not an hour before. 'It's not

119

that,' she says. 'It's – this is a big deal. There's been no one since Daisy's father.' She laughs, because it's so ridiculous to say what she's about to say. 'And I've never had sex in a bed.'

Spencer pulls her close, against his chest, and she hears his words through her body. 'This is a big deal for me, too,' he says. Then, a breath later, a little more quietly, 'You can trust me, Kate. I promise, you can trust me.' She links her arms behind his waist, pulls herself even closer, feels his breath in her hair as he drops his mouth to the crown of her head. The spinning of her panic subsides, but she isn't sure herself what she is going to do until she does it. She takes his hand. The tattoo on his upper arm calls out to her to be kissed, and so she kisses it, afterwards letting her finger trace its spiked edges. It's hard to make it out in the half light. 'What is it?' she asks.

'That? I've no idea. I got it for a dare on a night out when I was at uni. I don't even remember choosing the design.' He turns, just a little, as though he's not sure what to do, and she leads him through her bedroom door.

It's a small, neat space, with little room between wardrobe, bookcase, and the single bedside table. Spencer sits on the edge of the bed and undoes his shoelaces, and she's glad this isn't going to be a furtive, half-dressed scramble, but something more considered, more calm. Kate pulls her dress over her head, then her top, and stands in her mismatched bra and knickers. Spencer is down to his boxer shorts. 'Well,' he says, holding out a hand, 'shall we give it a go?'

They keep their eyes closed, mostly, taking the occasional peek at each other; it's the opposite of blinking. Afterwards, Spencer goes to dispose of the condom, and Kate climbs under the duvet, remembering the aftermath of sex with Mike: the bundling back into clothes, looking around, scurrying home. She stretches, fingertips to headboard and toes touching the footboard. Turning her head sideways, she looks at Spencer, standing in the doorway, smiling in the way she imagines she is. She pulls back the duvet and he climbs in beside her.

'You're beautiful,' he says.

'You're handsome,' she replies.

'Seriously,' he says, rolling onto his side to face her, eyes soft with sleep and happiness, 'I thought I was falling for you, before. Now I know I am.'

And suddenly Kate is crying, because it cannot be this simple, can it, surely? To meet someone, to feel a connection, to think about it – to understand the landscape – to decide, to reach, to touch. To fit. Is this what it is, to be part of a couple? Kate cannot believe how good it feels to be seen like this, not just her body but all of her. She's not sure why she's crying, apart from the sheer overwhelm of not being lonely, which brings with it the realisation of all the loneliness she has been engulfed in for the last six years. Longer. Maybe her whole life, one way and another.

Spencer rolls onto his back, and she curls into his chest and cries while he lies quietly, his hand warm at the base of her spine. Already it feels like the most natural thing in the world. He makes a noise, not a shushing exactly, because it's not as though he wants her to be quiet. More of a sibilant hum, to let her know he's hearing her, she's not alone with whatever it is that she is feeling.

'I didn't think it was that bad,' he says, when she's become quiet, and she laughs against the damp hair of his chest, rolls onto her back.

'I quite like the bed thing,' she says.

'You wouldn't have had a place of your own, before you had Daisy,' he says. 'You were – what, nineteen? Once you have your own space, you forget what it was like when you lived with your parents.'

'True. Though this is actually my dad's flat; I only have it for a year. I'll probably be home again this time next year.' One of her hands is against his stomach and her little finger is tapping, gently. She stills it. 'I've had two relationships. The first one wasn't long and it was – well, you know. Sofas, rugs. But the second. Daisy's father. I was still at home with my parents and he was – married, so it was mostly outdoors.'

A pause. Perhaps a full stop. She doesn't know how much to say. Spencer doesn't need to know this, does he? Melissa had jokingly offered her a tutorial on going on a date. Kate wishes she'd taken her up on it.

'Go on,' he says, 'if you want to.'

122

'I don't know,' she says. They lie quietly; she wonders if she will sleep, and then, when she realises that she won't, not yet, she wonders if he is sleeping. She turns on her side to face him.

'I'm not much of an outdoorsman, myself,' he says.

Kate laughs, and finds she has more to say after all: 'I used to get home and find bits of moss and leaf in my underwear. I had scratches from twigs, and—' She stops, remembering the too-hasty fingernails, the fear of being caught. It's hard to imagine that she ever thought it was love. He strokes her back, the small of it. 'I was going to say it was necessity, but of course it wasn't,' she says. 'It just felt as though it was. It was very – passionate. Sort of – sort of furious.'

She sits up in bed, looks down at him. Her hair swings forwards and she tucks it behind her ear. 'I'm so sorry,' she says. 'This isn't very – this isn't what you're supposed to do, is it? Talking about your ex on a first night.' She laughs – there is something about them, together, they will both think, separately, later, that makes laughter happen as easily as touch, as breath.

'We can do what we like, can't we?' he asks.

She nods. 'How about you?'

He counts on his fingers: 'Girlfriend in Edinburgh, when I was sixteen. We were together for three years and then she went to uni in Swansea and got a better offer. Six months of one-night stands to heal my broken heart. Serious girlfriend who was on the same course as me. She took a teaching job in Ireland and we just – it

123

just sort of fizzled out. Then' – he stretches his arms above his head, closes his eyes for a moment – 'well, nothing serious since.'

'Something – not serious?' She's not sure what makes her ask, apart from a sudden sense of disquiet, the sounding of a long-ago bell. But he doesn't answer, and when she looks at his face, she thinks he's sleeping.

Kate wakes earlier than Spencer, but it's still late, by her standards, the church clock chiming nine. She thinks about waking him; knows how it would go, with warm morning kisses and eyes-open sex. (They'd woken at 2 a.m. and, surer then than the first time that they would not easily break or shock each other, reached with more confidence.) But it's almost Christmas and there's everything to do, including promising to be at her mother's by noon at the latest so they can have an early lunch and Richenda can go shopping in the afternoon. So she gets into the shower (warm water, aching thighs, tension in her shoulders from the unaccustomed shapes her body has made when sharing a bed), wraps herself in the pale-blue towelling dressing gown she's been wearing since she was seventeen, brushes her hair, and takes the wine glasses from the table, washing them up and leaving them to dry, side by side, on the drainer. Then Spencer emerges from the bedroom, in his boxer shorts, and smiles a sleepy smile at her.

'Well, I hope that wasn't a one-night stand,' he says.

'Unlikely,' she answers, 'but you'll have to wait for the final votes to be counted and verified.' He laughs. There's something in him that allows her to be silly, funny, bright. With her mother she's serious, and vulnerable, because Richenda is her champion and her support and the place where she takes all of her worries. With Melissa, she ought to be an equal, but their lives are too different for Kate to feel parity. With Spencer she might just be able to be herself. She stretches out her hands and he takes them in his own, pulls her close; she rests her face against his shoulder, then nips at his neck with her teeth, laughing as he jumps away.

Spencer takes a shower, and Kate dresses and goes down to the café, returning with almond croissants and lattes. She feels shy, suddenly, as she walks back up the stairs to the flat. But then she sees that he's found plates and knives and laid them at the small dining table in the corner that isn't occupied by the Christmas tree, and it's the easiest thing in the world to sit down opposite him, to slip off her own shoes and tuck her feet against his calf.

'So,' he says, dusting icing sugar from his fingers, 'what happens next?'

'You don't mean wrapping stocking presents, do you?'

'No, I don't.' He pauses and looks at her, seriously. Then he takes a breath, reaches for her hand, looks into her face. 'I would like us to be together, Kate.

A couple. I think we could be' – he pauses again, for breath, to glance down at the table then up again – 'I think we could be happy.'

She almost says, 'I need to think about it,' or, 'it's a bit too soon,' or, 'what about Daisy?' But instead she remembers his voice, last night, telling her that she could trust him. She's entitled to a life. She's been happier in herself, in the last twenty-four hours, than she can recall being in almost any moment since Daisy was born. Daisy brings her own joy, of course. But why shouldn't Kate have more happiness, in the parts of her life where she isn't a mother?

'I think you're right,' she says.

Chapter 8

Mid-December, the week before Christmas

DAISY HAS BEEN AWAKE since dawn, despite Kate's attempts to cuddle her back to sleep. Her bed has gone from being her quiet, undisturbed, thank-goodness-I-got-through-the-day space to somewhere where she aches for company, even though the time she and Spencer have spent in it has been so short. But Daisy was almost vibrating with excitement, her body wriggling top-to-toe against Kate. Kate tried holding her tightly – it worked when she was a baby, and still calms her when she's unwell, or distressed – but Daisy is unquashable, even at 5 a.m. When she said, in a whisper, 'It's the Day, Mummy, it might be better than Christmas Day!' Kate realised that she wasn't going to get any more sleep, and got up to make hot chocolate and porridge. If she was lucky she might get a second breakfast into Daisy before school.

While Kate is heating the milk, Daisy goes off to get dressed 'all by my own self'. Kate lets her – this tiny, independent streak pleases her and breaks her heart in roughly equal proportion. Ten minutes later, a small star sits at the breakfast table, buttons undone at the back but otherwise everything sparklingly in place. Kate tries not to laugh.

'You did very well, Daisy. But you know you have to wear your uniform to school, don't you, sweetheart? And you'll get changed after lunch, before everyone comes to watch the play?'

Daisy looks at her mother with doubt. 'I don't think that's quite right, Mummy. Today is Christmas Play Day. Mr Swanson said it was.'

'Yes, it is. But the morning is going to be a bit more like a normal day.'

'Then why is it not called Christmas Play Afternoon?'

'I don't know. But I think everyone goes with their uniform on so their costume stays nice and clean. That's what Miss Orr said.' Wendy Orr is a useful form of absent authority in many situations. She's also becoming their friend; she often chats, after school, and once she and Daisy met her and Jilly in the bakery and shared a table, making a plan to go dog walking together before they said goodbye. Kate puts the porridge on the table. She's stirred dried fruit into Daisy's, and drizzles honey on top.

Daisy already looks tired. Kate sighs to herself. Christmas is lovely, especially now that Daisy is old enough to be excited, and young enough to still believe in flying reindeer and Father Christmas. But it would be so nice to not feel quite so on her own with

128

it. This will be her first Christmas in the flat, a Christmas morning of just the two of them, although they'll spend the majority of the day with Richenda and Blake, and she feels the weight of being a lone parent. It would be so good, later, to bring a tired child home and then go out for fish and chips while someone else does bath time. Or, after a fractious bedtime (Kate can see the fractious bedtime already, as inevitable as Daisy's desire to sleep in her star costume tonight), to have someone to open a bottle of wine with. Maybe next year she and Spencer will be spending Christmas together.

'Oops, Mummy.' Daisy has dropped porridge down her front, and her eyes are glistening with tears ready to fall.

Kate swallows her sigh. 'Never mind. Let's take it off and I'll wash it.'

'But the play is today!'

'I know, darling, but it's early, so I'll wash it straightaway and put it on the radiator and then it will be dry in no time.'

Daisy looks suspicious, but she agrees. She balks at her antibiotics – 'I'm sure I did already eat these ones once today, Mummy' – and turns down a second helping of porridge, even when Kate offers to add sprinkles to the top.

Eventually, Kate violates her no-TV-before-school rule and settles Daisy on the sofa in the hope that she'll rest, doze, even, before they need to leave. She tucks a bowl of peanut-butter granola next to her. She might nibble at it if she doesn't sleep.

But by the time they get to the door of the classroom, the pale skin under Daisy's eyes is already grey with tiredness, and Kate goes to speak to Miss Orr, explaining the slightly damp costume that needs a little more drying, and Daisy's everything-is-impossible mindset.

'Everything OK?' Spencer appears at the door, and Kate's stomach does a quick round-and-round; she would like to walk over to him, put her head against his chest, feel his arms go round her, automatically, glad that her absence is over. She realises that all of the other parents have gone, while she and Wendy have been talking about how tiring this time of year is for the children, how much there is to think about, to do. Wendy goes back into the classroom and Kate hears her clapping her hands, saying something about pegs and coats and shoes.

'It's fine,' Kate says, 'but Daisy's been up since five.'

'Oh, that does not sound like fun.' In the four days since she kissed him goodbye at the top of the stairs, their mouths tasting of butter and almonds and the hot bitterness of coffee, they've texted and talked on the phone, but only seen each other, briefly, at school. They've agreed that they need to go carefully with Daisy. And anyway, the week before Christmas is full of busyness of one sort and another, so trying to arrange babysitting or mutual free time would be next to impossible. Spencer is going to see his family at Christmas;

Kate will miss him, half-misses him already. Now, she itches to touch him, all the more when he smiles exactly the way he did when he came out of her bedroom and looked at her on Sunday morning. He reaches for her wrist, the exposed place between coat and glove, wraps his fingers round her flesh, squeezes. Happiness rushes through her, chasing the tiredness away. This is how it must be for people who have a partner, as well as a child. She wonders whether it would really be so impossible to see him, later. They don't have to do anything special. They could sit on the sofa together, Kate's feet on Spencer's lap, and talk about how tired they are. That would be something. In a way, it would be better than a date, because Kate would not be alone for the part of the day that she dreads.

Spencer glances over his shoulder, to the hubbub of classroom. 'I need to get back. I was thinking, though, if you like – only if you think it would be OK, I could come over, later, when Daisy's in bed.'

It feels like a mind-reading trick. 'I was just thinking it would be nice to have some company tonight,' she says.

'I can't wait.' He releases her wrist, and she pulls down her sleeve to cover the place where the skin feels chilled now his hand has gone. 'I can't kiss you here but I'm thinking about it.'

By noon, Kate is on her knees with tiredness. She wraps three gifts, realises she hasn't put labels on them, can't remember what they are, and has to unwrap them and start again. So she lies down on her bed and goes to sleep. She has rarely slept during the day, not since Daisy was small and she snatched what rest she could. She assumes that she'll doze for half an hour, maybe an hour, maximum. That will give her time to tidy the flat, change into something clean – she pulled on yesterday's jeans this morning, and there's a peanut-butter handprint on the thigh – and get a seat near the front. Daisy will want to be able to see her.

But as soon as Kate lies down, a deep and still sleep overwhelms her, and she wakes with a start only fifteen minutes before the concert is to begin. She pulls back her hair to disguise the fact that it needs washing, pulls her smart, navy coat out of the wardrobe – it's long enough to cover the mark on her jeans – buckles up her boots and runs.

She's there in time, technically, but of course everyone else has arrived before her. Pairs of parents fill the rows of chairs. Richenda is coming to the after-school performance at 3.30, so there isn't anyone here who could keep her a seat.

Jo, in the second-to-front row, mouths a 'sorry' when she sees Kate, indicating the chair at the end of the row that she must have tried to save. Kate shrugs and smiles in reply. She'll stand at the back; that way Daisy will know she's there.

Her phone buzzes in her pocket. It's a message from Spencer. *Seat in the front row at the end has a reserved sign on. It's for you.* She looks up, sees him smiling through the window that leads from the hall to the classroom, where he's waiting to lead the class in. Kate finds the seat he means and sits on it. 'That's reserved,' says the woman next to her.

'Mr Swanson says I can sit here,' Kate answers, then keeps her eyes front and ignores the noises of disapproval from her neighbour.

Kate is ready to cry from the moment the class files out, led by Spencer and chaperoned into place by Wendy Orr. The children all look so happy, so serious, as they seek out their parents in the audience, wave and smile, before settling into silence and then singing an enthusiastic, if ragged, version of 'O Little Town of Bethlehem'. Daisy remembers her words, and waves her star-wand exactly the way she's practised, standing on a chair at home for full authenticity 'because I do have to climb onto a block on the stage, Mummy'. There's a tricky moment when she has a coughing fit right over the arrival of the Three Kings; Wendy asks them to repeat their lines, and Kate hears a sigh and a tut from behind her, imagines a whisper about Daisy. If she was Melissa, she'd turn in her seat and give those parents a stare. But she isn't. She's had to learn to choose her battles.

Kate is almost dry-eyed until the final chorus of 'We Wish You a Merry Christmas', which everyone is invited to stand up and join in with. Suddenly she cannot hold in her tears; it's as though the worry and hope of the year that's gone erupt from her. Daisy is lucky, she knows: many children with cystic fibrosis are much more limited in what they can do. Daisy doesn't have it easy, certainly, and Kate hates the way she has to feed her constant antibiotics and watch every child that comes near her for fear of infection. But at least Daisy might lead a halfway normal life, for a normal amount of time, if luck is on her side. As Kate looks around at these other parents, heedlessly happy, parents who do not feel they are constantly trying to beat back a tide, she's overwhelmed with tiredness, with happiness that she has got Daisy this far. And that she might not have to keep doing it alone for much longer. She sits on her chair, puts her head in her hands, and sobs.

'Miss Micklethwaite? Are you all right?' Kate looks up to see the woman who tutted at her when she sat down; she recognises her, now, as one of the other teachers.

'I'm fine,' Kate says, 'just a bit – overwhelmed.'

'I see,' the woman says in the tone of one weary of parents, and pats her shoulder. 'Would you like some water?'

'No.' Kate shakes her head. 'Really. Thank you. I'm fine.'

She manages to wave at Daisy as she leaves the hall, hand in hand with one of the shepherds. Kate hopes he wasn't the one that was sniffing all the way through the performance. Parents are to meet their children in the playground for a few minutes before leaving them to prepare for their next show; Kate will have time to dry her tears, find a smile, and be ready to act like any other happy and proud mother.

'Kate? What's happened?' Spencer, under the guise of straightening the wooden benches at the front of the dais, steps over to her, touches her shoulder.

'Nothing.' She looks up into his face, smiles, then repeats, 'I'm just a bit overwhelmed.'

'I've offered to get Miss Micklethwaite a drink of water.' There's a tone in this woman's voice that Kate really doesn't like at all.

'I know these events can be difficult for some parents. Especially with children like Daisy. Is no one with you?'

'Oh, I didn't see you there, Mrs Piper,' Spencer says, and Kate knows him well enough to know that the polite expression on his face is a mask for dislike.

'Evidently,' Mrs Piper says. 'Do you need to get back to your class, Mr Swanson?'

Spencer nods and turns away, glancing the smallest of smiles at Kate as he does so. Kate looks to see Mrs Piper watching her with a bully's speculation. *Don't worry about it*, she tells herself, as she gets up and walks away. But she remembers when her life was nothing except looks like that one. She won't let history repeat.

When Spencer arrives at 9 p.m., Daisy is snoring, Kate has showered and washed her hair, and the world feels calmer and happier. They kiss at the bottom of the stairs, and again at the top.

'Well done,' Kate says. 'It was lovely.'

'Thanks, but to be honest Wendy's the one who really made it happen.' He rubs his hand across his chin, a gesture she already recognises as meaning he is tired. 'It seems to have gone down well. One of the mothers had a meltdown, which means we got the emotional depth spot on,' he jokes, before looking at her seriously. 'Are you sure you're all right? When I saw you with your head in your hands I didn't know—'

'Honestly, it was just – it was a bit much for me. But I'm fine, now.' She thinks it's true, though when Daisy insisted on going to sleep clutching her star wand, she could have sobbed her heart out all over again. 'The playground chat is all very positive. Five-star reviews all round.'

Spencer laughs. 'Not from the the first camel's dad. He thinks his kid was underused. Should have been third shepherd, at least. There's always someone.'

Kate puts the kettle on. 'I'm having tea, if you'd like some? Or coffee. There's wine. And' – she looks in the fridge – 'Orange juice. Pineapple juice. Milk. All of the best beverages.'

'I'd love some tea,' he says, 'and to not think about school anymore for today.'

'Done,' Kate says, but he must pick up the uncertainty in her tone.

'Are you sure? Did Bridget Piper say anything to you?'

'Why do you ask?'

Spencer sighs. 'Because she's always stirring things. Most teachers are great, but there's the odd one that isn't. Bridget is like that. It's all gossip and meanness, and if they see anything they don't like they blow it out of proportion. She doesn't like me, because I'm a man, and so if she can get a dig in, she will.' He comes over to where she is pouring boiling water onto the teabags, touches her waist. 'I've already had a conversation with the Head about it.'

'About what?'

'She went to the Head with some pretend concerns. That I wasn't "participating in the life of the school" because I kept out of the staffroom at lunchtime. I told Jane it was because they go quiet whenever I go in. Now, if they stop talking when I walk through the door, I ask if they were talking about vibrators.'

Kate laughs, horrified. 'You don't!'

'I don't. I have thought about it, though. And I'm sorry you've got caught up in her nastiness.'

Kate turns to face him. 'I'm used to the pointing and whispering. I don't like it, but I can cope with it if I need to.' She had met her mother at school after the 3.30 show, blurted out what had happened, and Richenda, as always, had spoken calm good sense. Nothing in Kate's life was anyone else's business. Some people look for targets. Don't rise to it. She hadn't said anything Kate didn't already know, but it made her feel as though she could manage it, rather than being certain it would crush her again.

'What did Bridget say to you?'

'She didn't say anything. But I knew what she was thinking.'

And then Kate is back five years, pushing Daisy through the Throckton streets in a pram, smiling at her daughter's tiny face, her days always shadowed by her nightmares of drowning in black water. In those first tentative months of mothering she was wary about anyone who approached her, fearful of a barbed comment or a snub, terrified that she might see someone who cared more for Mike's widow than for his child, and not afraid to tell her what they thought of her. She endured it all: faux-sympathy, observations about how like her father the baby was, curt enquiries about how Kate's mother was coping, the implication being that Kate had brought problems to everyone. Her mother had told her to ignore it all – 'This place has its moral roots in 1950, and if they would rather you had left that baby to die in a ditch than bring her safely into the world, then shame on them.' Her father had nodded agreement, but with less enthusiasm: he'd been an advocate of abortion, and could not quite disguise his disappointment that his bound-for-Oxford daughter had chosen the life that she had. They had been horrible times. Kate had gone through them, day by day; she knows the worst is behind her. But that time cast a long shadow, and Daisy's condition means her life is never going to be free of nasty whispers. That feeling of utter overwhelm returns, and before she knows it, she's crying again. She cannot remember a day when she has cried so much in recent years. Spencer is holding her, steadying and calm. When the tears abate, he leads her to the sofa, puts her tea on the table in front of her.

'Sometimes,' she says, 'it all just seems too tiring. I've been through gossip before. It all gets a bit much.'

'I know,' Spencer says. He's drinking his tea, but he never stops watching her. Then his gaze flicks away. 'People will gossip about us. They already gossip about me.'

Kate picks up her blue mug. 'I'm not like this. I mean, usually. I don't cry like this. You must think—'

'Don't guess what I think,' he says, smiling, but his eyes are serious.

This time last week, Kate's brain reminds her, you hadn't even been on a date with him. But that seems impossible. Already he is closer to her than any boyfriend; she knows she would tell him anything. She smiles back. 'I'm sorry.'

'No need to apologise. But do you want to tell me what happened with Mike? Only if you want to. I know you told me a bit, the other night. But it feels as though I should understand it, properly.'

'Really?'

'Really. If you want to.'

So she tells him the whole tale. How she met Mike at the village fete, and flirting with him made her feel special. How unhappy she was, living with her constantly fighting parents, scared of the great and wonderful future that everyone was convinced she would have, and that she could not remember ever signing up for. How she started to bump into Mike, deliberately; it was easy because he walked his dog, late in the evening. How talking led to touching to kissing to sex and before she knew it – no, she corrects herself, not before she knew it, because it was all that she thought about; she was obsessed with seeing him, with trying to make him love her – they spent more and more time together. She shakes her head. 'It was all so – furtive. I thought it was romantic. I don't know what he was thinking.'

Spencer twitches an eyebrow at this, but says only, 'It doesn't sound like he was thinking much at all.'

'I don't know.' She takes a breath. 'He died, because of me.'

Spencer takes her hand. 'I doubt it's that simple.'

Kate continues. She doesn't want to – her stomach has tightened to nausea at just the thought of talking about it – but he may as well hear the full story from her, without the Throckton embellishments. 'We met up after Christmas. It was nearly six years ago. He told me he couldn't see me anymore, but he had sex with me first.' Stated so simply, she wonders if he was really the hero everyone thought. But it doesn't matter now. 'I – I don't remember it very well, but I slipped and fell into the lake. Butler's Pond. There wasn't a fence. There is now. Mike came in after me. He got me out of the water. But he drowned.'

140

Spencer is silent. Kate looks at his profile, wonders if he will make an excuse, leave now. From what he's said, his own life has been so straightforward. A few heartbreaks, staffroom gossip. Not nice, but nothing like this. And that's before you factor in Daisy. Well, he may as well know everything. 'I didn't find out I was pregnant for months, and I only told my mum when I was five months and had some bleeding. I wouldn't say who the father was, but Mike's mother came to see me and told me that Mike was a cystic fibrosis carrier, and so then everyone knew.'

Kate waits.

Spencer hasn't let go of her hand.

He turns to face her and says, 'That sounds awful, Kate, I can't imagine.'

Something deep un-fists. 'It was.'

'Did you love him?' Spencer shakes his head. 'It doesn't matter. I don't know why I asked.'

'I don't know. I mean, I thought I did. Now – I just think how stupid I was. And him. I had no idea of the risks I was taking. I don't mean pregnancy. I mean – I mean' – she feels tears rising but she cannot cry again today, doesn't want to – 'other people's happiness. I didn't care about anything but him. After he died I used to sneak into his garden and leave flowers there. And now' – she laughs, a great hiccup of sound – 'now I carry hand sanitiser everywhere and I have little bags in my handbag in case Daisy needs to spit and I write down every bite of everything she

141

ever eats and sometimes I don't know where that old me went.'

Spencer puts an arm out, and she leans against his side. It's become a simple fit. 'Have you ever talked to anyone about this?'

'I had counselling for postnatal depression. It helped. And I talked to Mike's widow, before and after Daisy was born. That was really hard. I think it helped us both. She's back in Australia now, and Mike's mother died last year, so there aren't the reminders there used to be. So – so I'm sort of OK. But every now and then something makes it all come back.'

He holds her more tightly. 'I'm sorry about what happened today.'

'It's not your fault,' she says. The warmth of his body, the not-aloneness it brings, means that everything feels more manageable than it did this morning. Or last week. Or this time last year. Melissa has been asking for updates ever since the date, and Kate hasn't wanted to say too much, in case she jinxes it. But maybe it's time.

'When I think about Mike and me,' she says, 'it's unreal. I know people talk about how things seem to have happened to someone else but that's honestly how I feel about this. I can remember the – the idea of how I felt about him, but it doesn't seem real any-more. Not like—' She stops, just in time. They've been on one date, for crying out loud; had sex twice and decided to start seeing each other. She should really try to put the brakes on.

'Like us?' he asks, and she can feel his breath, cooling on the dampness of the hair at her crown.

She nods. 'Like us. We're – I mean, already this feels' – what are the words for it, the words that will be true, and not sound ridiculous? – 'deep. And comfortable.'

Spencer laughs. 'Deep and comfortable. I like that. It makes us sound as though we're lying in a really weird bed. I know what you mean, though.'

'Do you?'

She sits up, picks up her mug although the tea is cold now and she doesn't want to drink it anyway. He looks at her, and says, 'You mean that you're falling in love with me.'

Kate feels precarious, off-balance, as though she's being accused of something. She knew she was going too far, telling him everything. She's got it wrong, again. At least she's done it early on, this time, before anything is truly broken. But then she looks at his face, properly, the curl of smile, the way even such tired eyes have a directness that she – yes – loves. She nods.

He nods back. 'I'm glad. Because I'm falling in love with you.'

'Yes,' she says, and just like that, it's done. Simply, honestly, truly. She puts down the mug, lies back against Spencer, and feels his arms encircle her as she closes her eyes.

Chapter 9

Christmas

CHRISTMAS IS THE BUSIEST it's ever been for Kate. After the Christmas play comes the school fair; Kate keeps Daisy as close to her as she can, and steers her away from the coughing, sneezing, sniffing parents and children as far as she is able, without Daisy noticing. She doesn't want her little one to be at any greater risk than usual of catching something that her immune system won't be able to fight off, and she doesn't want Daisy to grow self-conscious and over-cautious. A child with a health condition, not a health condition with a child attached: that's always been her plan for Daisy. But it's hard when Daisy joyfully plunges her hand into the polystyrene-snow-bran tub that so many children have already rooted about in, and Kate is trying not to wince; she cleans Daisy's hand with sanitiser afterwards, but only minutes later, looks around to see Daisy and Amelia taking it in turns to bite the ends off a candy cane.

Jo apologises, which is more than the other mothers would do; then she says to Amelia, 'You know we have to be extra careful about Daisy,' and Kate sees Daisy's face fall. When she glances up from talking to Daisy to see that Mrs Piper is watching her, a cold, dark smile on her face, Kate turns away. There's no need to walk towards trouble. Daisy starts to cough, and Kate takes her to the toilets for her to spit up the mucus and breathe some cooler air.

As the fair gets noisier, hotter, Kate is always aware of Spencer, wandering around the room, joking with pupils and parents. The elf hat he chose on their first official date is proving a great hit, and Kate gets a sweet thrill from knowing that she was there when he bought it. She can see their lives as a slow building up of tiny threads that will make the fabric of a shared life. If she can be this lucky. Can it be as perfect as it seems?

Kate extracts Daisy after an hour, with the bribe of meeting Granny and Blake at the café for hot chocolate and gingerbread reindeer. Richenda and Daisy are soon involved in a complicated game involving two half-eaten biscuits and a lot of clapping; Blake says, 'You look as though you could do with a whisky in that chocolate.'

Kate smiles, pushes her hair out of the way – too late, there's whipped cream on the ends of it. 'It's hard to enjoy these things, and I feel as though I ought to. But I worry . . .'

Blake nods. 'For what it's worth, no one much enjoys a Christmas fair. You can bet your bottom dollar that everyone's glad it's over.'

'I suppose.'

Blake looks over the table, sees that Richenda and Daisy aren't listening – they've moved on to counting the baubles on the Christmas tree. 'I hear the d-a-t-e went well.'

Kate's mood lifts instantly. 'It did.'

'I'm glad. Are we going to meet him? You know I'll need to do a full background check.'

Kate laughs. 'I'm sure you will.'

'I hope he's worthy of you' – Blake looks across the table – 'and of Daisy, too.'

The day before Christmas Eve, Kate, Daisy and Richenda make their way to Jilly and Wendy's home. It's a solid Georgian house, thick-walled and square-windowed, with a drive decorated with Christmas lights and a green-and-gold wreath on the door. 'I believe Jilly's legal practice is very successful,' Richenda says, in answer to Kate's unspoken question, as Kate lifts Daisy to ring the bell.

Wendy opens the door. She's wearing a snowman jumper and jeans; Daisy laughs with delight as she unzips her coat to reveal her own snowman jumper, three dancing, smiling characters on a navy background. 'This is my favourite,' she tells Wendy, 'but when we bought it at the shop it was in the boy section, and Mummy said it was – a big word that means wrong to girls.'

Jilly, who's gone for a plain red dress and snowflake leggings for the occasion, comes up behind Wendy and says to Kate, 'Is it too early to offer Daisy a job? I can just see her cross-examining the shop owner. Come through.' And before they know it, they are in a kitchen-diner that spreads the length of the back of the house, Wendy and Richenda are talking animatedly about someone they both used to know who is about to sell her company for a rumoured fortune, and Jilly is handing Kate a cup of mulled wine that smells so good that Kate's plans for an alcohol-free afternoon are instantly forgotten. 'Cheers,' Jilly says. 'Happy Christmas Eve eve.'

'Christmas Eve eve?' repeats Daisy in amazement.

'Absolutely,' Jilly begins. 'It's a day when Wendy and I see all of our special people—'

But before she can get any further, Daisy is pulling at Kate's free hand. 'Look, Mummy, Mr Swanson is here!'

'Oh, so he is,' Kate says, seeing his head, tall above the two people he is talking to, across the room. He'd said he should be there by the time she arrived; he was right.

He looks over. There must be thirty-odd people in the kitchen, and at least a dozen more in the living room beyond. The door chimes ring. Kate wonders how many people she would invite to a Christmas party, how many would come. And then Spencer smiles, starts to make his way across the room to her.

Daisy says, 'The invitation said Fancy Christmas Dress, Mr Swanson. You could have worn your elf hat if you didn't have a jumper.'

Spencer puts a hand in his pocket and, a second later, his sweater lights up with flashing fairy lights. Daisy's eyes go big. Kate laughs, and then Daisy says, 'You could have worn your hat too.'

'That's true,' Spencer says.

'How are you?' Kate asks. She wonders if she could risk a touch, but you never know who's watching. Spencer puts his hand, briefly, at the small of her back, under the pretext of moving her out of the path of someone behind her.

'I'm fine. I like your top.'

'Thank you.' It's a baseball-style silky T-shirt, pale blue, with 'TEAM RUDOLPH' in navy letters on the front, and the number 25 on the back. Kate wasn't sure about it, but it was better than the few women's jumpers that were left when they arrived at the hypermarket with Richenda first thing this morning, in an attempt to beat the worst of the Christmas-food shopping busyness. Kate should have read the party invitation properly, and then she'd have been more organised. But actually, the T-shirt looks quite good with her skinny jeans and a pair of silver plimsolls she bought in the sale. And she bets she's cooler than everyone else in the rapidly warming kitchen.

'The shop was wrong,' Daisy supplies. 'It was in the men's section.'

'It was this, or a couple of badly placed Christmas puddings. Or a pink fluffy jumper that said "Naughty or Nice?" that gave me an electric shock when I touched it.'

Richenda appears at Kate's shoulder. 'Well,' she says, 'this must be the Mr Swanson I've been hearing so much about.'

'Indeed it is.' Spencer holds out a hand, which Richenda shakes. 'Spencer. You're Daisy's grandmother, aren't you? I didn't get a chance to say hello after the play.'

'Richenda.' Kate's watching her mother's face for signs of approval, disapproval, anything, but there's nothing to see. 'And Kate's mother, too, of course.'

'And also a person in your own right.' Spencer smiles.

'Which goes without saying.' Richenda looks mildly annoyed, which seems unfair to Kate, as her mother would be the first to point out that she is a separate being from her daughter and granddaughter. And it's clear that Spencer was attempting a joke.

'Mummy! I think there is a buffet! And I can see my picture of a butterfly that I gave Miss Orr on the wall!'

'Excuse us.' Kate doesn't really want to walk away – she wants to be privy to all of the conversation between her mother and Spencer – but any chance to get food into Daisy can't be passed up.

'I hear that . . .' Richenda says, but the rest of the sentence is drowned out by Daisy wondering if there

150

will be macaroni cheese, and Kate saying it isn't really a very buffet thing, but they could see if they can find some in the freezer when they get home.

'How did I do?' Spencer had waited for Kate's text to say that Daisy was asleep before arriving; he's holding a bottle of Prosecco, and Kate knows she shouldn't open it because there is so much to do between now and the morning, but the thought of clinking glasses and saying 'Merry Christmas' is impossible to resist. Spencer is setting off on his drive northwards first thing tomorrow. They have agreed not to exchange gifts, and instead to do something special in the new year. Kate knows that Spencer doesn't have money to spare; and anyway, for all they are falling for each other, and they know it, a Christmas gift so early feels fraught with difficulties. Melissa tells her she's over-thinking, but to Melissa, who seems to have spent the last two weeks messaging Kate from Ubers as she runs errands for the magazine where she's interning, Kate overthinks everything.

'My mother says you're very tall,' Kate says.

Spencer nods, clinks glasses. 'Irrefutably true. I'll take that. Unless—'

'She worries about me,' Kate says, 'so she'll want to meet you properly. That's all.'

His face goes serious for a moment. 'I want her to like me. I want her to understand that I'm – that you can trust me.'

Kate laughs. 'Could I remind you of what you said when we first met?' She attempts his accent: 'I'm all modern. You need to watch out for me.'

He holds her gaze with his for a moment; the reflected Christmas-tree lights make his eyes look glassy, cold. And then he smiles, and says, 'If that was supposed to be an Edinburgh accent, I could have you done for crimes against the Scottish people,' and before Kate knows it they are in bed, trying to be quiet, while Daisy coughs and snores her way to Christmas Eve.

'This is my best present of all,' Daisy declares, when she opens a small child-friendly pogo stick, with a thick foam base instead of a spring, from Richenda and Blake. 'Because it is a mystery.'

'Let me show you.' Blake takes Daisy's new and very large teddy and balances it on the footrests. Richenda and Kate lean back on the sofa and laugh. Kate's fingers go to her earlobe, again, feeling the shape of the earring there.

'Are they new?' Richenda asks. 'They're pretty.'

'Yes. They're from Spencer.' She and Daisy had been opening presents from under their own tree in the early-morning half light; Daisy had said, 'I can see another one!' and wriggled under the branches. Just as Kate was saying that she thought she had opened them all, Daisy had emerged with a small, wrapped box in her hand. 'It says "K" on the label,' she'd said, and Kate had thrilled a little. The earrings inside were tiny daisies, silver with a gold-plated centre.

'I thought you said you weren't buying for each other.'

'We weren't. But he said he saw these and couldn't resist them. He hid it behind the tree when he came round the night before last. I messaged him this morning and he said he was going to tell me where it was when we spoke later.'

Richenda looks away. 'But you had an agreement and he didn't respect it.'

'Oh, come on, Mum.' Since her mother left her father, Richenda's born-again warrior-for-women schtick can be a bit much. 'It was a lovely thing to do.'

'If you say so.' Richenda gathers her face into a smile. 'I think we should meet him properly sometime.'

'Of course,' Kate says. 'When we get to that point. We'd need to tell Daisy first, though.' Being sensible about this is hard; she's so sure of Spencer.

'Tell Daisy what?' Daisy's face is pink with excitement and exertion.

Richenda looks at Kate for a beat before saying, 'That it's time to get out the snowflake biscuits we made,' then getting up and heading into the kitchen.

Because Kate had handed in her dissertation late, she hadn't known when exactly she would get the result. She's not sure why she wakes up wondering about it on Boxing Day; it's not as though the Open University will be posting results over the holidays. But after she makes her tea, lines up Daisy's morning medication, and looks in on her still-snoring girl, Kate opens her laptop and does a search of her email. There, in her junk folder, is a notification of a result; it's been there since the day of the Christmas play. Kate holds her breath, clicks the link, and logs on.

The mark she got for her dissertation is the one she was hoping for. And, overall, that means she got a First. A First. A first-class honours degree. Leaning against the kitchen worktop, looking at the screen, she finds herself crying. At the same time she's filled with – she examines, checks – yes, with pride. She did it. For the last four years she's shut herself away in too-small corners of afternoons, and written essays', fifty words at a time. She's set her alarm for 6 a.m. so she could read chapters of books dense with terms she doesn't know, before Daisy wakes. She's kept going even though it has often seemed that the last thing she will ever need in her life is a degree. And now, here she is. Kate Eris Micklethwaite, Bachelor of Arts, first-class honours.

Kate wipes her eyes, makes her tea and takes a screenshot of her results page. She sends the image to Spencer, then to her mother, then to her father, then to Melissa. She knows congratulations will come by return, so she leaves her phone in the kitchen and goes back to bed, where she sits back against the headboard, mug in her hands, and lets herself breathe deeply and think of nothing for a little while. As soon as she starts talking about her result, it will become a fact; and the questions that will follow, about what she will do next, she isn't ready to answer.

And, there's someone else who needs to know first.

Daisy arrives in Kate's bed half an hour later, clutching her new teddy and wondering if it's too early for the foam pogo stick. Kate says she thinks it might be, tucks the duvet round them both, and says into Daisy's hair, 'Mummy passed all of her exams and she got a number one.'

'Well done, Mummy,' Daisy says. 'I'm very proud of you.' Kate laughs at hearing her own words spoken back to her, and then she gets up and makes more tea. Her life is coming together at last.

The week between Christmas and New Year is one of the happiest Kate can remember. Melissa is home, and she and Kate have a night out in Marsham that ends with the two of them calling Melissa's father at 3 a.m. because both of them thought the other had booked the taxi. Jilly and Wendy invite Richenda, Blake, Kate and Daisy around for an early dinner on New Year's Eve eve ('I did not know that there were so many eves,' Daisy commented as she was lifted to ring the bell) and toast Kate's First with champagne; Daisy is delighted to find that macaroni cheese is on the menu. Daisy doggedly masters the pogo stick, and spends cold afternoons bouncing it around Richenda and Blake's garden, being watched by the two bemused dogs. She and Richenda put on hats, scarves and gloves and make up jumping routines on the trampoline, while Kate watches, texts Spencer, and reads a novel from cover to cover for the sheer unadulterated pleasure of it, something she hasn't done since Daisy was born. The family walks up Beau's Heights and the dogs, grown lazy with Christmas titbits, are docile enough for Daisy to hold their leads. Richenda and Kate leave Blake and Daisy watching *Toy Story* and eating chocolate and marshmallows, and go to the sales: Kate chooses a new dressing gown and some satin pyjamas, and Richenda doesn't comment, but pays for them with a smile when they get to the till. Over coffee afterwards, Kate waits for Richenda to say something about Spencer, but she only asks if he is enjoying his Christmas. Kate says that he is, and adds that they are missing each other. Richenda smiles. Kate doesn't push it. She cannot wait for him to come back.

Chapter 10

Mid-January

ON A FROSTED SATURDAY afternoon, Kate drops Daisy off to be indulged by Richenda, and then walks up the hill to make her first visit to Spencer's place. Spencer was away for nine days of the Christmas holidays, and they filled the time with late-night phone calls, endless messaging and quiet longing. He had come to see her as soon as Daisy was asleep on the day he got back, and the first thing he'd said, when the door had closed behind him, was that he loved her. She'd said it right back. Since then, when they haven't been learning the topography of each other's bodies, they have been talking as though they are about to take an exam in each other and both are determined to get full marks. They have swapped histories, from their school days to every ex-girlfriend of Spencer's and the details of Daisy's birth and diagnosis. They have talked about their futures, the ones that are likely and the ones that they might have missed the chance for, Spencer's record shop and Kate's conservation work.

It's an odd feeling, to ring the bell on the rather grand house that's now a dozen flats, to wait for him to press the buzzer that opens the door, and to walk up the stairs, a guest and a visitor. He's waiting on the landing; they kiss, briefly, then again, more deeply, once the door is closed behind them. Kate has brought newspapers and scones; Spencer has put flowers in a jug on the coffee table, and there's a new-looking throw on the sofa. Kate feels a warmth in her belly.

'It's not much of a place,' Spencer says, apologetically. 'I rented it without seeing it, and I thought it would be bigger. And taller.' It's true that the ceiling is low, the walls sloping inward. It's certainly small. But so is Kate's flat.

'It's great,' she says. 'I love attic rooms. I always thought they were romantic.'

'What's happening in Throckton is definitely more romantic than I thought it would be.' Spencer pulls her close. 'Do you want to see the bedroom?'

Later, they sit on the sofa, drinking tea, absorbed in the weekend newspapers, Kate occasionally reading something aloud, Spencer asking her what she thinks of this story or that. Kate leans over to show him a political cartoon, and he takes her wrist, puts down the paper, and looks her full in the face. 'I know we talked about going slowly, and being cautious,' he says, 'but when I look at you all I can think is that there's nothing I can imagine that would split us up.'

They have said vague things already, joking about holidays, talking about Hogmanay in Scotland and how it will be when Daisy is older and Spencer isn't her teacher anymore. Since Spencer came back from Edinburgh, on the day after New Year's Day, he's come to see Kate after Daisy has been asleep, most nights. 'I shall have your face tattooed on my chest at the end of the summer term,' Spencer had said on one of those nights last week as he'd been leaving her flat, late. 'And I shall walk round Throckton with my shirt off, and people will say, ah, what a lovely couple they make, we have been secretly hoping for this since he arrived.'

'I could get a tattoo to match yours,' Kate had said, touching his upper arm, but he hadn't heard. Just as well, as she isn't really sure about a tattoo. Not because of Spencer. Just because of the pain.

But today, on this snowdrop Saturday afternoon, Spencer's words have a serious tone. 'Yes.' Kate's reply is part speech, part exhalation. Because he has just articulated the thing that she hasn't been able to express, the feeling that is there beneath the love and the longing. She can't imagine anything that would separate them, or keep them apart: there is no scenario in which she wouldn't turn to him, naturally, for help or support or to say, I just did the stupidest thing.

'After all, it's Throckton,' Spencer adds. 'There are only so many times that I can knock on your door or you can knock on mine before two and two start making – well – four.'

'You think we should tell people?' Kate knows she has to be sensible about this, that it's a big decision; but at the same time, it isn't a decision at all. The truth will have to be told. And when it has been, they can walk down the street hand in hand. She will say 'Spencer and me' in conversation. And maybe the gossip she is sure is following her will stop if things are all out in the open. Single man and single woman have relationship. Even Throckton can only make so much of a meal of that. There's another thought, one she chooses not to examine too closely: Kate-who-is-going-out-with-the-new-teacher is so much easier to live with than Kate-whose-little-girl-has-cystic-fibrosis-poor-thing or Kate-who-got-pregnant-to-a-married-man-when-she-had-hardly-left-school.

'Well, I was wondering whether we should tell Daisy,' Spencer says. He smiles at Kate. 'And then I could stay over.'

'You could.' She rubs the inside of his arm, where she knows he's ticklish, and he ruffles her hair, which he knows makes her shake her head and laugh. The thought of their love being out in the open is bliss. She hates it when Spencer leaves in the night, even though she could never have Daisy find him in her bed. But lying next to the space he leaves makes her almost as lonely as she was before she knew him.

Kate can find no reason in her heart or her head not to tell Daisy. Her daughter needs to be protected, yes: but she needs to be protected from gossip, and the best way to do that is to give her the facts. She needs to be sheltered from come-and-go relationships, but this isn't one of those. For all of the fizz and frolic of being with Spencer, at the centre of their relationship is the warm stillness of an August garden. It's – well, it's love. They've said it, and she's sure of it.

'I know this is important. I don't want to bounce you into anything. It's your call.'

'Well,' Kate says, 'like you say, people will notice. And my mum and Blake know, so it makes sense. And' – she touches her palm to his cheek – 'I'd like it.'

'Me, too.' Spencer catches her hand, kisses her thumb tip.

'What about school, though?'

'What about it?' Spencer's voice cools, just a degree or so; his gaze slides sideways, towards the window.

'Well – do you have to tell them?'

'Kate' – he speaks as though he has practised this – 'what we're doing isn't illegal. I can show you the teachers' code of practice if you like. You're not a nun, neither of us are married to other people, Daisy isn't a Crown Princess of Europe who needs to have her security monitored at all times. It's all up to us. It's OK.'

'If you're sure,' Kate says. 'I don't want to get you into any trouble.'

There's a beat of a pause, and then that smile, which Kate thinks will always snatch her breath a little. 'It's way too late for that.'

'That was quick,' Richenda says, as Kate fastens Daisy in her car seat then climbs into the passenger seat the following Thursday. She'd dropped them off for their hospital check-up, and Kate had texted less than an hour later to say they were ready to be collected.

'Yes.' Kate buckles herself in. 'What did Victoria say, Daisy?'

'She said, "Well Done Daisy!"' Daisy says.

'Fantastic.' Richenda reaches round to give Daisy a high five, then adds, to Kate, 'Although watching her putting away Toblerone over the Christmas holidays, I didn't think we had too much to worry about.'

'Well, I put on four pounds.' Kate can feel herself starting to blush as she remembers Spencer, when they were reunited, stroking her body as though he could not believe his luck. Kate had felt then that she knows him better than she has ever known anyone. Except Daisy. She feels it still.

'We've piled it on, too.' Richenda laughs. 'Blake's signed up for the Throckton half-marathon in April. He's determined to run the weight off. Are we going straight to school?'

'Well,' Kate says. 'I wondered if we could stop at the supermarket. If you don't mind. If you have time.'

'I have time.' Richenda pulls left rather than right out of the hospital gates.

Five minutes later, they are in the supermarket car park, and Daisy is fast asleep in the back. 'I'll wait here,' Richenda says, switching on the radio. 'Will you get some bananas for me?'

'Sure.' Kate decides to get it over with. 'Spencer is coming over tonight, and we're going to tell Daisy.'

'Right.' Richenda looks straight ahead, through the windscreen. 'I'm glad you're happy, Kate, I really am, but it hasn't been long, has it?'

'Just over a month.' Though privately they agree that their real first date was the day they had coffee together, when Kate was finishing off her dissertation; and that it began, without a doubt, the moment they met – the meeting at school before term began. 'I promise, Mum, I know what I'm doing.' Kate wishes she didn't sound as though she was pleading.

'I just think you might be making it complicated. For Daisy. How is it going to be for her, when her teacher is having breakfast with her on a Sunday morning, with all of you in pyjamas? Or what happens if you split up?'

'We won't.' Kate sounds stubborn now, she knows it, and she doesn't care. 'And I'm not going to sneak around. It shouldn't have to be a secret.'

Richenda puts her hand over Kate's. 'I know it shouldn't. I'm just concerned about you making things difficult for yourself. And Spencer, too. He seems' – she

163

hesitates, weighing – 'nice enough, but we don't know a lot about him, do we?'

'I do. And Melissa says I should go for it.'

'Well, that tells you something.'

'What do you mean by that?' Kate doesn't want a fight, but she won't walk away from it.

Richenda shakes her head, changes tack. 'Nothing. Has Melissa met him?'

'No. He was away all the time she was home at Christmas.'

'Just – Melissa doesn't have things at stake, does she? Not in the same way.'

'We can't keep hiding.' Kate doesn't tell her mother about Spencer sneaking out at 6 a.m. yesterday, while Kate banged around in the kitchen making a noise to drown out the sound of the front door opening and closing. (In fairness, it had never been the intention that he stay the night, they had just fallen asleep, but Richenda is unlikely to take that into account.)

Richenda shrugs. 'Maybe.'

'Are you OK?' Spencer asks, when she answers the door to him at 5.30 that evening. His eyes are bright and his smile is wide. He's carrying a sports holdall and holding a small balloon attached to a stick and a cyclamen in a bronzed pot.

'Yes,' Kate says, with a smile, then, 'I'm a bit nervous.' She'd messaged Melissa, not long before he arrived, and said they were going to tell Daisy tonight. She got a yellow thumbs-up symbol in reply. Her friend's advice has been unequivocal. *Go for it. You deserve some fun. Daisy isn't going to die of her mother getting laid.* Kate had replied, *It's more complicated than that.* And Melissa had texted back, *No it isn't. Also, not to be shallow or anything, but he's hot.*

'I'm nervous, too.' He steps into the flat, closes the door behind him, and pulls her in for a one-armed hug, kissing the top of her head. 'It'll be OK. But it's a big step. I know that.'

'Yes,' Kate says. It feels as though her stomach is in slightly the wrong place.

'Your hair smells all – peachy.'

Kate laughs. 'It's Daisy's shampoo. I've run out of mine. I need to go into Marsham at the weekend and get some more.'

Spencer holds out the plant. 'I didn't bring you forced roses freighted from – wherever they freight forced roses from. I brought you a cyclamen from – well, from about ten yards down the road, but the florist assures me it's native and it would normally flower this time of year.'

'That's so sweet, Spencer, thank you.' The flowers are dark pink, and shaped like falling, drowsy hearts. She holds her face up to kiss him.

'I want to please you,' he says, simply, then, 'Where's Daisy?'

'She's watching a film. Come on up.'

Daisy is so absorbed that Spencer can put his bag in the bedroom before she even registers he's there.

'Daisy,' Kate says, moving between girl and screen. 'I told you Mr Swanson was coming for tea. He's here.'

'Hello, Daisy,' Spencer says. 'I brought you this.' Daisy's face is a picture as she reaches out a hand to take it.

'What do you say, Daisy?' Kate says.

'A balloon on a stick!' Daisy says. She's running her finger along the edges of the butterfly balloon where the foil makes a ridge. Kate and Spencer laugh and look at each other.

'Yes, but what else?' Kate says.

'Thank you, Mr Swanson.'

'That's my pleasure,' Spencer says. 'And you can call me Spencer when we're not in school. Like all the grown-ups did at Miss Orr's party.'

'Wendy's party,' Daisy says, and adds, 'Mummy says she's an outside-school friend so we can call her Wendy outside school.'

'Exactly,' Spencer says. He glances at Kate, a so-far-so-good sort of a look.

'Shall we have supper, Daisy?' Kate says. 'Do you want to wash your hands?'

Daisy trots off to the bathroom, and then returns to the table, where her supplements and tablets sit next to her plate. She takes them without fuss or comment. This is one of the things that makes Kate saddest.

*

Kate has made sure to not make the meal too much of a special occasion. She's heated up the lasagne she bought earlier; there's a salad to go with it, emptied from bag to bowl. There's the usual jug of water, too. No wine, no candles. Just the everyday, plus Spencer, a way of showing Daisy that Spencer will be everyday, too.

'Mummy,' Daisy says in an almost whisper when they are settled with their food around the table. 'Mr Swanson says I can call him something else, but I can't remember the word.'

'It's Spencer,' Spencer supplies. 'It's a bit of an old-fashioned name. My mum likes going to the cinema and she named me after a film star.'

Daisy ponders this. 'Like Jasmine in my class?' she says.

'Well,' Kate says, 'I don't know where Jasmine's parents got her name from, but it might have been Princess Jasmine. Or it might have been because there's a flower called jasmine, like there's a daisy flower.'

'I've never had a Cinderella in my class,' Spencer says.

Daisy considers, looking at her mother. 'I don't know if the wicked stepmother would have let Cinderella go to school.'

'They don't say anything about that in the book.' Kate shrugs, smiles. 'I don't know.'

Chocolate cake from Adventures in Bread follows the lasagne; there's a jug of cream to go with it. Kate had contemplated raspberries, too, but they were out-of-season, and expensive, so she decided against them. 'I'm going to get fat,' Spencer says.

'You don't see a lot of skinny CF parents, that's for sure,' Kate says. Then she looks at Spencer with a small nod; he smiles, nods in return.

'Daisy,' she says, 'I want to tell you something nice.'

'OK,' Daisy says.

Spencer's hand finds Kate's under the table. 'Well, Spencer is going to be my boyfriend, and I'm going to be his girlfriend.'

'OK,' says Daisy, then, 'Amelia's got a boyfriend, but he's invisible.'

'I've heard that,' Spencer says, then, to Kate, 'there are no secrets in my class.'

Kate smiles, but she doesn't want this conversation to get away from her. Anxiety is winning over excitement, in her throat, her lungs, her belly. 'That means that Spencer is going to do lots of things with us,' she says. 'Like coming to Granny's for lunch or helping us walk Beatle and Hope, and doing lots of the things that we do, along with us.'

'OK,' Daisy says again.

Either she's taking it really well, Kate thinks, *or she hasn't understood. But everyone says how clever she is.*

'And,' Spencer adds, and Daisy's head swivels so that her solemn gaze is on him now. 'We will probably do some new things, the three of us together.'

'What things?' Daisy asks.

'Well,' Spencer says, 'we might go on picnics, in the summer.'

'It's too cold for a picnic now,' Daisy agrees.

'Or we might go on some holidays together, or we might do things with my mum and dad as well as your mummy's mum and dad.'

'Who are your mum and dad?'

'They're called John and Sally and they live in Scotland.'

Daisy nods: this seems to be the right amount of information. She turns to look at Kate again. Kate wants to laugh: it feels as though she and Spencer are up before the Head for truancy. She says, 'And Spencer will be having sleepovers here, too, sometimes.'

At this, Daisy's face darkens. Kate realises what she's thinking and adds, quickly, 'In my bedroom. Not in your bedroom, like when Amelia came for a sleepover.'

'You don't have bunk beds,' Daisy says in what Richenda calls her pointing-out-voice.

'We'll manage,' says Spencer. There's a moment of quiet. Daisy returns to her cake; Spencer, who has finished his, takes a spoonful of Kate's, without asking, but with a grin that means she couldn't object even if she wanted to. *This is what my family is*, she thinks, and she closes her eyes against the brightness of her own happiness.

Chapter 11

Late January

THE FOLLOWING WEDNESDAY, Kate and Daisy are almost in the school playground when Jo and Amelia come out to meet them. Spencer stayed over last night; he left after an early breakfast, kissing Kate and waving to a still-sleepy Daisy. 'See you at school,' he had said, and Kate had laughed because it sounded so odd. But she thinks she will soon get used to it, in the same way that she is getting used to the sight of his toothbrush in the bathroom, and the way he puts mugs in the cupboard, with all of their handles facing in the same direction.

'Kate!' Jo is slightly breathless.

'What's happened?'

'Nothing. Nothing. We thought we would come to see you.'

Amelia and Daisy, hand in hand, run in front of them into the playground. Kate looks at her friend more closely. 'Jo? What is it?'

'Just thought I'd come and meet you. That's all.'

Kate laughs. 'Come on. You've never done that before. What's going on?' She looks into the playground and sees the mothers Jo calls the 'Unholy Trinity', heads together. Sarah is the daughter of the school secretary; Cara, Kate knows from her own schooldays – she was a prefect when Kate started secondary school. She now has a child in Daisy's class, a baby in a pram, and a toddler at her side. And Serena organises the PTA. As she watches, Sarah looks around and sees her, and the conversation of the group intensifies. 'Are they talking about me?' Kate asks Jo.

'Yes. I didn't want you to hear so I thought I'd head you off. I need more practice at this sort of thing.'

'Or people need to stop gossiping,' Kate says, her voice low. She feels a barely healed wound, just beneath her heart, start to open again. It still hurts from the teasing she got when she was offered a place at Oxford, the gleeful malice that greeted her pregnancy, the judgement when the news that Mike was the father became public knowledge. Her first thought is to leave Daisy with Jo and go home, or go to her mother, cry and complain. But that won't solve the problem – not today, not tomorrow. Walking away won't help Daisy. Kate is used to staring people down, when they look at Daisy with pretend sympathy, or ask how she manages on her own. But that approach isn't going to work here. She's going to have to confront them. And the sooner the better.

172

She walks over to the group. She knows she's shaking; hopes it isn't visible. She senses Jo a step behind her. Three faces look around at her. 'Hello. I thought I heard my name.'

A look passes between the three; quick, but not quick enough for Kate to miss.

Serena-of-the-PTA gives Kate a cool look. They've never really spoken before; they've had no reason to. Kate knows, though, that Serena was a police officer before she took a career break to raise her children. She probably knew Mike. 'No,' she says, 'I don't think so. We were just talking about Mr Swanson. Apparently he has a girlfriend.'

'Isn't that his business?'

'I suppose it is. It depends, though, doesn't it?' This from Sarah, following Serena's lead. *Honestly*, Kate thinks, *it's laughable*. Except she isn't laughing. She's shaken and she's scared; she's gone back ten years, and she's fourteen and out of her depth. She takes a deep breath. *Don't give them ammunition. Don't show that this hurts.*

'Depends on what?'

'Well,' Serena says, as though to a three-year-old, 'surely a relationship with a mother of a child in the class would compromise his professional integrity? Especially as that child is so clearly a favourite. If my Oliver was caught spitting in the playground, or if he was allowed to eat chocolate and sweets even though they are banned from lunchboxes, well—'

Kate laughs, she's so angry. 'That's because Daisy has cystic fibrosis, not because she's a favourite. And what Spencer does in his own time is none of your business. But if you're concerned you should report him, not spread nasty gossip.'

Cara looks sideways at Serena. 'That's you told.'

'Seriously?' says Kate. She hates conflict but she won't stand for this. Daisy is going to have to stand up to bullies, like every child who is different. So Kate needs to do it, too. She can feel that tears might come, so she blinks-blinks-blinks and wills them away. 'I'm having a relationship that you know literally nothing about and you're bitching about me like we're still thirteen? Grow up.'

There's a collective intake of breath as she turns away. Daisy has lost a glove next to the hopscotch, so Kate retrieves it, then waves her daughter over and tucks it in her coat pocket. Oh, it will be good when winter has gone and they can leave the flat without ten minutes of bundling into more clothes. Kate knows what will be happening behind her back. Eye-rolling, head-shaking and, doubtless, a full debrief on the walk home. Well, let them talk.

Wendy Orr opens the door, inviting the children in, and Kate feels as though she has never been so relieved to see anyone in her life. She can't wait to get away from the school. She hangs back with Daisy, fussing over her zip, so that she won't have to face Serena, Sarah and Cara again. 'I've got to go to the post office,' Jo says, having left Amelia, 'then we can have a coffee?'

'Great.' Kate gives her a grateful smile.

'See you at the bakery in half an hour, then.'

Kate nods, calmer already. She's dealt with it, she's shown she won't be bullied, it's over. But turning back to the playground after she's said goodbye to Daisy, she realises she's not going to be that lucky. Cara is taking her baby from the pram, comforting him as he squalls, and the others are waiting with her. She makes to walk past. Serena makes steady eye contact, and smiles. 'The trouble is, it's all fun and games until somebody falls in a lake, isn't it?'

It's a moment before the words land, with violence, in Kate's solar plexus. By then Serena, Sarah and Cara have left the school playground, and Kate is alone. She puts her back to the wall, her hands on her hips, and tries to breathe deep, but it's difficult, given the speed of her heartbeat and the fury in every cell.

'Kate? What's wrong?' Spencer calls as he comes out of the door. He is across to her, hand on her shoulder, in three strides, his worried face close to hers. Suddenly Kate is aware of Daisy at the window, the fact Serena is probably still within earshot.

'I'll tell you about it later,' she says. 'I'm fine.' She longs to put her face against his shoulder, for just a moment, but doesn't dare. She tries for a smile and walks away, surprised at the steadiness of her legs.

*

As she says to Melissa in a text, while she's packaging Daisy's meds up for the next day, she may as well have brought a chair, sat Spencer on it and then performed a striptease, because by the time she gets back to school to collect Daisy, it's clear that everyone knows that she and Spencer are together. No one – not even Jo – knows what Serena said to Kate: she clearly hasn't seen fit to share that on the PTA WhatsApp group. Kate doesn't want to tell anyone, can't bear for it all to be dragged up and discussed as gossip. She wants to walk up to Serena and say: a man we both knew died. Have some respect. But of course, she doesn't. She can imagine the disdainful look she'd get in response, and her brain is already composing the likely retort: it's a shame you didn't think about respect when you started sleeping with another woman's husband.

But then Spencer arrives with fish and chips, hot in their wrappers, and everything feels easier. Serena, Sarah and Cara are nothing to her, so she shouldn't care. The people she cares about are here. Daisy tries to eat her chips through a coughing fit, and Kate rubs her back, and feels her little ribs, and looks at Spencer, and thinks, *We are the ones that matter. This is my family now.*

'I bumped into your mother on the way to the fish and chip shop,' Spencer says.

'Granny?' Daisy asks.

'Yes.' Spencer smiles at her.

'Where was she going? Was she coming here, too?'

'I think she was probably going to yoga, Daisy.'

'Oh, yes.' Daisy nods knowingly, and Spencer and Kate laugh at her seriousness. Kate will never get used to the happiness of sharing these tiny moments.

'She had time for a chat, though,' Spencer continues, 'and she asked me to lunch on Sunday.'

'That's good.' Richenda's lack of enthusiasm has been weighing on Kate. This sounds like a breakthrough.

'Are you coming?' Daisy asks. 'Because of the being a family?'

'Yes, I am,' Spencer says, then, his gaze back on Kate. 'And I asked her if she thought you should book a date for your graduation.'

Kate sits back, watching Daisy squeeze extra tomato ketchup onto her chips with more enthusiasm than accuracy, and decides not to intervene. 'I don't know, Spencer. It's the grade that matters. I don't really care about the ceremony.'

He nods. 'I know. But your mum and I were saying that you deserve it. Will you at least have a look at the dates? Think about it? And if you can manage it for school holidays, then we can all be there.'

'I'll think about it,' Kate says. She imagines walking across a stage in a cap and gown, looking out over the watching faces, picking out her mother, Daisy, Spencer. She's always telling Daisy that she's done

well, that she's proud of her; why shouldn't she celebrate her own achievements, and show Daisy what's
possible at the same time? 'You clear up,' she says.
'I'll get my laptop.'

Chapter 12

Early February

WHEN SPENCER SUGGESTS THAT they have a weekend away, Kate agrees immediately. She loves the idea, of course she does. It's a milestone in any normal relationship, a moment that says: we choose each other, we commit our time, we matter. Plus, now that she's a school-gate pariah, with only Jo to stand by her, she cannot wait to get away from Throckton, if only for a night or two. The drowning-in-black-water dreams are back, and Daisy must be picking up on Kate's unease, because she's unsettled, too, rejecting her food, short-tempered when things don't go her way. Kate feels weary to her bones. Spencer asks her if they should plan their first trip together or he should organise it. 'Surprise me,' she says. 'I'd like a surprise. If that's OK.'

'Leave it to me,' he says. Then, a little uncertainly, 'We should talk about money, though. I know it's not romantic, but—'

'Oh, God, of course.' She shakes her head. 'I'm sorry, I should have thought. Can we split the cost?

Is that OK? And it doesn't have to be luxurious. I just want to spend time with you.' She's noticed how carefully he watches the dial go round when he puts fuel in the car, sees him take receipts from his pocket and smooth them, keeping them to go through, while she scrumples hers into the bin.

The following Tuesday, Spencer comes round after Daisy is in bed. He knocks, lets himself in with the key Kate has had cut for him, and comes up the stairs two at a time. Kate is reading the online prospectus for a physiotherapy Master's degree, and looks up to see him smiling more broadly than usual, if that is possible.

'We're all sorted!'

'For what?' Kate can't think of anything they need to get sorted for. They've already agreed that when Valentine's Day comes around they'll limit themselves to cards, and there's no way Kate would want to eat out in public, the way things are at the moment.

'Our weekend away. We'll leave after school on Friday, be home on Sunday evening.'

'This weekend?' she asks.

'Why not? I found a good deal, and we're both ready for a break now, not in three months' time.'

'But Daisy—'

'Is going to stay with your mother and Blake. It's all sorted.'

'Really?'

'Really. I went to see them. They said, of course they'd have Daisy.'

'Oh.' Kate is almost more touched by that than the plan to go away.

Daisy, predictably, is less impressed. 'I thought we were going to make our own family,' she says when Kate tells her that Mummy and Spencer are going away for the weekend.

'Well, yes. But part of being our own family is that we can do different things. I didn't come to the panto-mime with you and Granny and Blake, remember?'

'You were going to a birthday party.'

'Yes, Daisy, but that's not the point—' Kate hears irritation in her voice, slows her breath. 'You go to lots of birthday parties without me. You've got Mat-tie's sports party next weekend and Jo is taking you.'

Daisy looks as though she might cry. Kate takes a breath, tries to do better: 'I know it's all a bit strange, but we'll get used to it. And Mummy needs—' She stops herself before she can say 'a break'. 'Mummy and Spencer need some grown-up days. It's like play dates.'

When the time comes to drop her off at Richenda and Blake's, Kate is worried for a moment that Daisy will refuse to get out of the car. (Complaining to her mother about her daughter's obstinacy, once, Rich-enda had raised an eyebrow and said, 'Well, I don't think we need to wonder where that comes from.' So Kate can't really be surprised.) But Spencer takes Daisy's case out of the boot, puts it on the pavement, then opens the door, bows, and says, 'My lady.' Daisy half laughs and unclicks her seat belt, and they walk up the path, the three of them together. Daisy is as end-of-the-week tired as usual, and the being-left-out grumpiness has abated rather than vanished.

Kate is trying to be patient. Her hair is shiny from the cut she had today. The relief of going into Marsham, where she wasn't at risk from Serena, Sarah and Cara smirking when she passed, had made her realise how on edge she was, and how tiring the whispering of Throckton can be.

But they are not quite home free. Standing in the kitchen, unpacking medication and supplements, Richenda says, 'This seems like quite short notice, Kate. Is Daisy OK about it?'

Kate swallows her impulse to say that the time to mention this would have been when Spencer asked her to have Daisy to stay. 'She thinks she should be allowed to come,' she says.

She hopes her mother will laugh – Richenda finds almost everything her granddaughter says to be funny or clever or both – but no such luck. 'She's had some big changes, Kate. Full-time school and now this.'

'Now what? Her mother going away for two nights?'

Richenda puts a hand on her arm. 'No. Of course not. But you're more – you have someone else in your life, taking your attention. She's bound to find that unsettling.'

'She still gets plenty of attention. More, if anything.' Daisy and Spencer sometimes play Jenga in the evening, and Kate hears the crashes and laughter as she takes a shower. Spencer is teaching Daisy card games, too, and when the three of them play, Kate feels as though she is looking through a window into Spencer's happy childhood. Her own parents could never have been civil for the duration of a round of seven-card brag.

'It's still change. And it's all happening quite quickly.'

Oh, for heaven's sake. Am I never to be allowed to have any fun? Kate thinks. Two nights in a hotel will be her first unencumbered adult holiday, unless you count sharing Melissa's bed one or two nights a year. 'Do you want me to tell Spencer to cancel?'

Richenda sighs. 'No, of course not. I just want to be sure that you're not – that you've got your priorities right. And that you're not rushing into this.'

'I've had six years on my own, Mum. Did anyone question your judgement when Blake moved in?' Richenda, who had spent decades putting up with Rufus's infidelities and neglect, had recovered remarkably quickly after their split and soon begun a relationship with Blake. Throckton had raised its collective eyebrows, but if Richenda had cared she hadn't shown it. She and Blake had married shortly after Daisy's third birthday.

Richenda sighs again, and then smiles at Kate. 'Well, yes, they did. You're right, Kate. Daisy will be fine with us. It's just – I want you to be happy. And I want you to be careful. You could be both. It's dangerous to put someone on a pedestal. Nobody's perfect.'

'I am happy. Or I would be if people would understand that I'm not a child and I know my own mind.'

Spencer puts his head around the kitchen doorway, tilts his head. Kate knows he means 'let's go', and just that second of unspoken communication thrills her. She can do anything, now, with Spencer's support; a career, a different life seem possible. But first – a weekend away.

'I think we'll try to get ahead of the traffic, Mum.'

'Very wise.'

Daisy follows Spencer into the kitchen, throwing Kate a bruised look. Kate holds out her arms. She loves Daisy with her whole heart, of course she does, but Daisy is only five. Kate is allowed to overrule her.

'Don't worry about us,' Richenda says, kindness in her tone now; Kate knows that she wants to part friends. Reaching for Daisy's hand, she smiles back at Kate, then looks down into her granddaughter's face.

'We're going to have a lovely weekend, aren't we, Daisy? We might go to the pottery café, I thought.'

'Maybe.'

Kate and Richenda exchange a look. It's Daisy's favourite place, usually.

Richenda picks her up. 'Right, let's say goodbye to Mummy and Spencer. We'll see them on Sunday.' She pauses, and puts a hand on Daisy's forehead. 'Is she a bit warm?' she asks Kate.

'It was warm in the car. She's fine.'

'If you're sure.'

'I'm sure.'

Spencer's hand is on the small of her back; they can be at the hotel in an hour and a half if they are lucky. And Daisy is growing stronger every day. The winter is almost over, and the antibiotics are doing their work.

Kate kisses her daughter's pink cheek, which is plump and giving. Her first ever romantic weekend away beckons. She's bound to be nervous, bound to overthink. And, like Melissa says, she deserves a bit of fun.

By six o'clock that evening, they have checked into the country house hotel that Spencer found a late deal on. Kate had transferred her half of the money to him the evening before, and felt the gentle relief of not having to be in charge, for once. It had felt like a lot – £150 – but how would she know, really, what dinner, bed and breakfast in a hotel should cost? She'd taken some extra money out of her savings at Christmas, in case she needed it, and she hadn't, so it feels less reckless to spend it on herself like this.

Their bedroom is in a turret. The bed is huge and has twisting oak posts and Liberty-print bedding. The bath has clawed iron feet and candles all around it. And the views from three sides, over the South Downs, are mesmerising in their stillness and muted tweed colours.

They look out of the window for what feels like a long time. A cloud drifts across the sky: it seems first to be a dragon, then breaks apart into a series of little submarines. Kate feels suddenly shy. She has shaved her legs and armpits – she doesn't usually bother – and bought sheer black tights to wear with the pale green dress and black heels she bought for her mother's wedding. When she left the hairdresser, she had bought pretty, matching underwear in a silvered sheen, and a new multi-pack of lace-edged knickers to wear with her good black bra. Maybe it's being out in the world with Spencer that makes her self-conscious. It's hard not to feel that she is being watched. It almost feels like a test – will they love each other, away from the school, their homes and the watching eyes of Throckton?

Spencer, standing behind her, his arms around her waist, exhales. 'This is perfect,' he says. And all of Kate's worries disappear. Because it is. He's talked to her when she's been tired and cross. The first time they kissed she was wearing pyjamas, and a cardigan with a hole in it and dried porridge on the sleeve. She's seen him snappy when he's hungry, quiet when he's preoccupied by the unpredictable malice of a primary-school-staffroom. She's offered him cream for the eczema at the base of his back. There is nothing to fear in the intimacy of this weekend – it can only be a good thing. Sometimes things look good because they are good, Melissa says.

Kate leans back, rests her upper body against his chest. 'Perfect,' she says.

It doesn't stay perfect for long.

When Kate wakes up the next morning, dry-mouthed from wine, and makes her way to the bathroom, she sees her phone, which she had switched to silent when they went to bed, alight with a call. Her mother. There's no way Richenda would ring at 7 a.m. unless something has happened to Daisy. The call ends before Kate has time to answer it, and she sees eleven missed calls from 5 a.m. onwards and remembers – the impact of what she's done makes her hands shake as she picks up her phone – that she had said she would send her mother the details of the hotel when they arrived. She forgot. Or perhaps it hadn't seemed important – she always has her mobile with her, anyway.

Spencer turns in the bed, reaches out for her. They haven't fallen asleep together naked since that first night he stayed over at the flat. With Daisy liable to come in search of her mother before the alarm goes off, pyjamas seem safest. She holds his hand, calls her mother with the other.

'What's happened?' she asks, as soon as the call is picked up.

'Kate, it's Blake. Everything's fine, but we're at the hospital.'

'That doesn't sound fine. Is Mum there?' Kate likes Blake, a lot, but he's not the person she needs right now.

'She's with Daisy. I stayed in the car so I could keep calling you. Daisy's got a temperature so we brought her to the hospital.'

Kate frees a hand from Spencer, puts Blake on the speakerphone, starts to cast around for something to wear. Last night's underwear, yesterday's jeans. Spencer sits up.

'What's her temperature?'

'Thirty-eight and rising when we got her here.'

'Right. We'll meet you there.' She presses the button to cut the call off, and grabs her suitcase from the bottom of the wardrobe.

Spencer hasn't got out of bed, though he's sitting up, rubbing the night from his face with the heels of his hands.

Kate says, 'We need to go to the hospital.'

He swings his legs to the floor. 'Shouldn't we have some breakfast, first? Thirty-eight isn't that high, is it?'

Kate pauses and looks at him. He can't have understood. 'It's a danger for Daisy. You know that.' Tights, dress, shoes go into her case; she goes to the bathroom to collect her make-up and toothbrush. She was going to have a lovely, long bath this morning. That doesn't matter now.

He's waiting when she comes out of the bathroom; he's pulled on his jeans, is still shirtless. He pulls her to him, kisses the top of her head. 'Not the morning we were planning, hey?'

'No' – she sags into him for a minute – 'not at all. I'm sorry.'

'It's OK,' he answers. 'But are you sure we shouldn't have breakfast first? It's a bit of a drive.'

Kate looks at him, she is ragged and taut with worry. 'Seriously?'

It's the first time that she hasn't been the one to notice the signs of an infection that's feisty enough to overcome the antibiotics that Daisy takes every day. Usually, it's flushing cheeks and more frequent coughing ramping up over the course of a few hours, and Kate is always on the lookout for it. As she watches Spencer apologise to the receptionist for their sudden departure, she wonders if she would have spotted the problem more quickly if she had been single, still. *No*, she tells herself. Then, with a nauseous honesty, *yes*. She tells herself that there's no point even thinking that. Then she thinks it again. The important thing is that Daisy is in the hospital and Kate is not there with her.

'You're quiet,' Spencer says, as they pull out of the hotel gates.

'I'm not really up for chit-chat.'

'I meant, do you want to tell me about it?'

Kate is not so much thinking as remembering the last time this happened, last May, when it seemed as though summer was on the way, and she was less worried about coughs at playgroups, hand sanitiser, and whether Daisy might be looking peaky. And then she had gone to wake her daughter one morning and found her wilting; pale-faced apart from the bright spots in the middle of her cheeks. The blue vein across the top of Daisy's nose that only shows when she's ill had stood out like a river on a map. Her breathing had been laboured and too fast, her hairline damp, and her hand, when Kate took it, as hot as a stone in a fire pit. These are the things Kate is thinking about as they leave the green-grey of the moors behind them and approach Marsham. She cannot even begin to explain.

Something in her whispers that if she hadn't had this weekend planned, she'd have been more worried about Daisy's temperature. Now she thinks back to the drop-off at her mother's; she realises she should have taken more notice of her daughter's clinginess, her lack of enthusiasm for the pottery café. She should have listened when her mother mentioned that Daisy felt warm. In retrospect, she can remember that there had been the beginning of a blue pallor at her temples.

She rests her head on the cold, car window. 'It's horrible when Daisy is ill,' she says.

'You're not on your own,' Spencer says.

'No,' Kate answers, and she puts her hand on Spencer's, briefly. She cannot help but think of how he didn't really understand what the urgency was, that he would have eaten a full cooked breakfast before setting off if she hadn't objected. She's silent for the rest of the journey, as she runs through all she always does for Daisy, and wonders what crucial thing she has forgotten. Daisy had her flu jab, as normal, at the onset of winter. She had her pre-school boosters, too. Her weight is going up. Her cough is no worse. Kate has even been thinking that they are getting on top of it at last, or that as Daisy was growing her lungs were strengthening. They have such a slick routine with nebulisers and daily physiotherapy that it is never forgotten. Richenda took Daisy swimming last weekend, but she always asks about the chlorine levels in the pool to make sure that they are high enough, and keeps Daisy away from anyone who so much as sniffs. Kate can't think of anything that they've missed. It seems too unfair that the price she should pay for finding someone who really loves her, is feeling that Daisy will suffer.

Spencer pulls up at the hospital entrance as Kate undoes her seatbelt. Now that she's here, her panic is winning out, and she wants nothing more than to run to Daisy's side, to make sure everything that needs to happen is happening, fast. No one should be handling this, except Kate. She should never have left Daisy. Spencer says, 'I'll go and park. Will you be in A&E?'

Kate spits out a laugh. The thought of Daisy's depressed immune system in a room full of people ill enough to be sitting in a hospital emergency department on a Saturday morning is unthinkable. 'No, we'll be in the CF unit.'

'I'll come and find you,' Spencer says, but Kate has already slammed the door, and is running into the hospital's main entrance.

Richenda and Blake are waiting in one of the isolation rooms. Blake gets up to let Kate sit, and Richenda passes Daisy, who is in her arms, across to her mother. Kate wishes for a wriggle, but feels only still, hot weight. She holds her daughter's hand and imagines that she is drawing the heat and the infection out into her own body, pulling it through Daisy's skin into her own, sucking illness out of her little girl, drawing danger away.

Being in the cystic fibrosis unit is like stepping outside of time. Sitting in a hotel restaurant, eating tiramisu from Spencer's spoon, saying yes to another glass of wine because there is nothing to do tomorrow morning except lie in bed, nursing a gentle hangover, phoning down for room service – that feels as though it was a thousand years ago. There is only here, and now; and it's the only place Kate can be, and the only place she can ever imagine being.

Daisy doesn't flinch when the cannula goes in, and Kate feels something in her break at the sight. The diagnosis of pneumonia is swift, but once the treatment is given there's nothing to do but watch and wait. The antibiotics run from a plastic pouch into Daisy's veins as she sleeps. And Kate watches, by the bed, as people come and go. Richenda steps out and Spencer steps

192

in, puts a cup of tea into her hands, places a bottle of water and a sandwich next to her. He doesn't try to talk, just sits alongside her. He takes the tea away when it's cold. And so the day passes.

Daisy's breath rattles her and her cough shakes her and the nurses come and go. After three hours her temperature has stopped rising, but it doesn't drop, either. 'That's a good sign,' Victoria says when she comes to check in at the end of her shift. 'It shows the antibiotics are working. Let's hope they get a hold overnight.'

'What do we do if they don't?' Kate asks. It sounds like a matter-of-fact question in her head but her voice has tears in it when she speaks. She doesn't like it when a doctor says hope. Hope should be for parents: doctors should be certain, in control.

'We try something else,' Victoria says. 'But let's give this a chance first.' Kate nods. She knows the philosophy with acute infection: treat first, refine the diagnosis later. Don't waste a second in case it turns out later that that was the second you needed.

Spencer steps out of the room when Richenda returns, having been to Kate's flat for toiletries, pyjamas for her and Daisy, books and snacks and the pillow from Daisy's bed: 'I thought she might feel more comfortable.' Kate dare not cry, because how would she stop? Richenda says the usual things: don't worry about anything and Daisy will be fine. Kate nods.

'Have they said how long you might be here for?' Richenda asks.

'No,' Kate says, and then she cannot help but cry, after all, feels tears sliding down her face. All the time that Daisy is in this stupor-sleep she isn't eating and drinking. Although Kate understands intellectually that Daisy's body is shutting down everything that's unnecessary so that it can fight the infection, she feels as though she can see her wasting away.

Richenda stands behind Kate, holds her shoulders hard, kisses the crown of her head. 'She'll be sitting up eating ice cream before you know it.'

Kate doesn't say anything. The idea of this frail little creature eating ice cream is as remote as the thought of the four-poster bed she woke up in.

A nurse comes in with a smiling warning: it's almost nine, visiting hours are over, Kate should settle in and get as comfortable as she can. Kate knows the drill: the uncomfortable UPVC-covered armchair that she's sitting on will stretch out into an equally uncomfortable bed for her to toss and turn in. It doesn't matter, so long as she is close to Daisy. But how quickly she has grown used to Spencer's arms around her in the night.

'Spencer's still here,' Richenda says. 'Why not go and say goodnight to him?'

'I don't know.' When Daisy's sick she and her daughter are twin moons sharing an orbit. It feels as though, if she moves away, they will both fall. But there's something that pulls her to Spencer now, too.

'He's just down the corridor. I'll stay with Daisy. She's sleeping herself better. She won't know you're not here.'

'I don't know,' Kate says again. Yesterday she didn't mind leaving Daisy, and look where it got her. She looks at her mother, wishes she was seven, eleven, fifteen, and had no choice but to do as she was told.

'Go on,' Richenda says. 'You might have a long few days. Go and stand outside and talk to Spencer. Breathe some fresh air and stretch your legs. Someone will come and get you if anything changes.'

Kate and Spencer walk down to the main hospital entrance, past the shellshocked criers making calls, and the smokers with their grey faces and their bright dressing gowns, stamping their feet in the cold. They sit on a low wall, bordering a seen-better-days flowerbed.

'How is she?'

'It's definitely pneumonia. She's on an antibiotic drip and fluids. She's stopped getting hotter but she isn't cooling down.' Her voice is steadier than she thinks it will be.

Kate is looking at her hands. She hears Spencer exhale. 'What do the doctors say?'

'They say it's good that she's stopped getting hotter. We need to wait and hope that her lungs don't get damaged. They might need to drain some fluid. It all depends.'

'God, Kate,' he says. 'I can't believe how quickly it happened. Overnight. Literally.'

'I know.' Kate has noticed, over the years, that whenever there's a crisis or emergency with Daisy, everyone needs to go over their latest memories of her, look for details, for clues. 'We shouldn't have left her.'

'We weren't to know,' Spencer says. Kate's not so sure. But yesterday is another world, now. 'Has this happened before?'

'Well, she's been in hospital with infections before, but she's never had pneumonia.' Kate feels her voice start to shake and tries to steady herself. 'But pneumonia is pretty inevitable, at some point, with Daisy's kinds of CF problems.'

'And how are you doing?' He pulls her close. She rests her head against his shoulder. An ambulance siren wails behind them.

'I have absolutely no idea,' she says, after a moment.

She feels him nod. 'Just remember,' he says, 'you're not on your own.'

Chapter 13

Early February

IT'S TWENTY-FOUR HOURS after admittance before Daisy opens her eyes. She's on a drip to keep her hydrated, but the skin on her lips is still drying to a too-pale pink. Kate has found a lip balm in her bag and rubs a little of it along Daisy's lips. It's as she's doing this that Daisy stirs and opens her eyes halfway.

'Hello, sweetheart,' Kate says. 'I'm here. We're in the hospital. Everything's all right.'

Daisy makes a tiny nodding motion before her eyes close again. 'She opened her eyes,' Kate says to everyone who comes in, as though the words are a protection, a charm.

Spencer visits on Sunday afternoon, Richenda in the evening, and they all watch Daisy sleep. Kate won't be moved from her chair, except to take a shower before her mother leaves. She eats little, says less. Daisy sleeps on.

On Monday, Spencer arrives after school. He brings a card, made and signed by Daisy's class. 'I see the hand of Wendy,' Kate says, as she looks at the butterflies that she can imagine everyone was encouraged to draw. The thoughtfulness of it makes her tearful. Everything makes her tearful, today: now that Daisy's temperature is coming down and her breathing is easier, Kate can start to let go of some of the pressed-down fear that's clogged her since the Saturday-morning phone call.

'Wendy and Jilly send their love,' Spencer says. 'And they said they'd love to come in as soon as you and Daisy feel up to it. Lots of the parents are asking after you both.'

'I feel as though nothing but this room is real.' Kate lets go of Spencer's hand to press her palm to Daisy's forehead. The chart at the foot of her bed tracks her temperature, taken by nurses at twenty-minute intervals; but Kate still needs to check for herself. She trusts the feeling of Daisy's skin on her palm more than she trusts a thermometer. 'Is that weird?'

'That's not weird,' Spencer says, and his voice is soft, partly because no one can help but be quiet around Daisy, even though she's clearly so soundly asleep, and anyway they would really all rather she was awake. 'So long as you don't forget about me when I'm not here.'

'Of course not.' Kate thinks about her flat and Spencer's, about school, about the trampoline in her mother's garden, Beatle and Hope snuffling in hedges on walks. She shakes her head as though dislodging a dream.

'Daisy looks so little.' Spencer holds Kate's hand, tight.

'Yes,' Kate says. 'Well she is, really. We forget.'

He's brought a brie-and-bacon on walnut sandwich, and although Kate doesn't think she's hungry she eats it all.

'I spoke to your mum. She's coming in with clean clothes for you both, and magazines and fruit. She says she wasn't sure if your phone was on, but to text her if you want anything else, or I'll let her know when I leave.'

Kate thinks about saying, *all I want is for her to get better*. Instead she nods. Spencer says, 'All of these things must seem so trivial, when you're sitting here.'

He's next to Kate, on an orange plastic chair. Now that she's finished eating, he's holding her hand. But they are both looking at Daisy, as though she is a film about to start.

Kate says, 'Yes.' Then, 'Are you OK?' It feels as though they should have been able to have some more plain sailing before they hit their first storm.

'Don't worry about me,' Spencer says. 'I'm fine. Or at least I will be, when you two are.' She tucks her head onto his shoulder, swings her legs across his knees. He strokes her hair. Kate breathes deeply for what feels like the first time since she got here. *You two*. 'That feels nice,' she says.

'I don't suppose you got a lot of sleep again last night.'

'No.' It had been another night of listening to Daisy's hot, too-fast, too-shallow breath, and trying not to imagine it was getting faster or shallower.

'Well, why don't you close your eyes now,' Spencer says, 'and I'll wake you if anything changes.'

'I can't,' Kate says.

'You can,' Spencer says. 'You can trust me, remember.'

When Kate wakes, she can tell it's evening even though the light in the hospital room doesn't change much. She sits upright almost before she's woken. 'It's OK,' Spencer says, 'she's fine. There's no change.'

'Oh. OK,' Kate says. But if there's no change, then Daisy isn't fine at all. 'What time is it?'

'Half eight,' Spencer says. 'Your mum's been and gone.'

'You could have woken me,' Kate says.

Spencer is standing, stretching; he fills the space, makes Daisy look even smaller. Kate sits on the edge of the bed and takes Daisy's hand in her own. Clammy and hot, still. Daisy's breath comes and goes like wind crossing water. The doctors want to drain some fluid, tomorrow. Kate, who does her best to be unflinching, cannot imagine how awful that will be.

He smiles. 'We did try,' he says, 'but you looked so shattered that we didn't try very hard. She said' – he holds up four fingers, counts things off as he speaks – 'all of your things are in the bag, she's working tomorrow but she'll come in in the evening, she

200

spoke to your dad and he sends his love, text her if you need anything.'

Kate nods. 'Was she OK?'

'We're all upset.'

Kate nods, mute with tears. Spencer, still standing, opens his arms; she stays, sitting on the edge of the bed, one hand on Daisy's, but she puts her head on his chest, her ear fitting against the small soft triangle where his ribcage moves apart. And none of them move until the nurse comes in at nine and says, softly, that visiting hours are over.

Chapter 14

February

IT TAKES LONGER THAN any of them had hoped to get
Daisy well again, and this is the first time in her short
life that, as Richenda says, she seems to be crawling,
rather than bouncing, back. Kate doesn't look when
they put the chest drain in, but holds Daisy still when
she mewls and stirs in her sleep. That evening her temperature falls off the plateau and starts to drop. Blake
is the one to see her open her eyes this time, while Kate
is in the shower. 'I told her you were washing your
hair,' he says, 'and she nodded and said something
about shampoo. Then she went back to sleep.'

'Really?'

'Really.' Blake looks a little pink-eyed. Kate would
like to think Daisy looks better, but apart from those
cheek-spots fading she's too pale for comfort, and too
still for her mother to think of her as being recovered.

After ten days in hospital, when Daisy can sit up on
her own and talk for more than two minutes and is

asking for food rather than having it coaxed into her, they are moved to a room which opens out onto a small garden. The room is for those who are in hospital for months. Although Kate is glad of the extra space and the not-entirely-successful attempts of the hospital Friends to make the place feel more like a home, she is determined that they won't stay there longer than they have to. Daisy doesn't belong in a hospital. Kate has raised her to be a well child, and a well child she will be again. Kate walks into the garden and looks up at the sky while Daisy sleeps. There's a small trampoline, with a handle, on the corner of the grass; Kate longs for the day she will see Daisy bounce again. The air is February-cold; she texts Richenda, asks her to bring in Daisy's hat and mittens, the bright blue coat with furry hood that she loves. She cannot believe that her daughter was made for the constraints of this kind of life. As for Kate, her brain is withering, her body is tired. And of course it doesn't matter – nothing matters, except Daisy getting better – but at the same time, it does. Kate is human. She wants the life she's glimpsed.

Six rooms open onto the garden and the children in them must take turns to be outside, as the risk of cross-infection is so great. The idea is that Daisy can play out in the struggling sunlight, but more often than not all Daisy can manage is to walk out of the door and then sit on Kate's knee while they look at a book. It's fresh air at least, Melissa says; she's come up for the weekend to see Daisy, and has brought Kate a bottle of wine buried in a bag of colouring books and sweets. 'I'm not in prison.' Kate laughs. 'I'm allowed a drink.'

'Feels like prison, mate.' Melissa is wearing a pair of Dr Martens that she has painted stripes onto, jeans, a striped shirt and a silver sweater, and the bowler hat; Kate feels memory rise like nausea when she thinks of that weekend, and how she resented being recognised as 'the one with the kid'.

'It's not too bad.' Melissa has arrived just before their designated hour in the garden. She sits with Daisy on her lap, and the two of them play I Spy, and yawn, and eat Jelly Babies out of Melissa's upturned hat, which Kate has spritzed with sanitiser and lined with a sterile cloth. 'What a pair we are,' Melissa says.

'What a pair,' Daisy agrees.

'You haven't got a hangover, though, have you?'

Daisy holds up her arm. 'No, I've got a cannula.'

Daisy dozes off a few minutes later, and Kate and Melissa sit in silence in the sun. 'If you don't mind,' Kate says, 'I might go and have a quick shower.'

'Not so fast, cowgirl.' Melissa looks at Kate sideways. 'I think we need to talk.'

'What about?'

'Well. About you. About Spencer. And the two of you.'

Kate shakes her head. 'Well, I don't really know how I am, except tired and a bit less terrified than I was two weeks ago. Spencer's been amazing.'

'I've heard that.' There's a dryness to Melissa's tone that Kate doesn't like.

'Have you been talking to my mother?'

'We're just worried, Kate. I mean, he seems great, but—'

'That's because he *is* great. He's been here every day since Daisy got ill, Melissa. I started my period and when I asked him to get tampons he asked what size. He's been amazing. He loves us.' *Why can't people just be happy for me?* she thinks

'Nobody's doubting his amazingness in the current situation,' Melissa says. 'And I'm happy for you, I really am. But – Daisy aside – isn't it a bit fast?'

Kate really, really doesn't need this. And Melissa should know better. She knows what Kate has been through; knows how lonely she has been. 'First of all, there is no "Daisy aside". Secondly, Spencer and I love each other, and we make each other happy. I don't know why that's such a bad thing. And I don't remember being invited to judge your boyfriends, or my mother asking for my permission before she moved Blake in.' Kate hears stubbornness in her voice, tastes tears at the back of her throat. 'And, I seem to remember that you were the one who was encouraging me to go for it. I don't need this, Melissa.' She slumps in her seat.

Melissa, trapped under Daisy's weight still, leans sideways so that her head is on her friend's shoulder. 'I'm sorry. I suppose I was just thinking – if something seems too good to be true, then maybe it is. It doesn't feel like we know much about him.'

'I do,' Kate says.

She feels Melissa nod against her shoulder. 'Well. That's good. Why don't you go and have your shower?'

Kate, under the nurse's supervision, puts the drugs into Daisy's PICC line via the cannula four times a day, flushing it with saline solution afterwards and imagining that she can see the shiver travel up Daisy's arm when the cool salt water goes in. The results of the X-rays show that Daisy's lungs are clearer but not yet clear: she needs to stay in hospital until the doctors are satisfied that there's no immediate risk of a recurrence, and she'll need intravenous antibiotics for a while even after she goes home.

Because their new room is designed for patients who need long-term hospital care, it is more spacious than the acute one and has a real bed for Kate. She and Daisy sometimes doze in the afternoons, before the next round of visitors come. They watch films in the evenings.

'This is bloody awful, but it's also quite nice,' Kate says to Spencer one evening as Daisy sleeps. 'I feel as though I'm in a little nest away from everything else I should be caring about.' Kate pops out for a walk around the hospital perimeter sometimes, when there are others around to keep Daisy amused; Spencer persuaded her out for lunch, once, while Richenda entertained Daisy with a pom-pom maker. But this room has become her world.

In the end, the decision about going to graduation was taken out of Kate's hands. There's no way she could – would – leave Daisy. She hasn't been worrying about what she should do next, or what's going to happen with her and Spencer. Because he's utterly there, utterly theirs, and indulging in even the smallest doubt about him feels as though she is doing him a disservice.

Spencer laughs. 'I feel as though I can't wait to get you out of here. Partly for obvious reasons' – he gestures to the bed where Daisy is snoring, now, one arm flung above her head – 'but mostly so I can have sex with you five times a night every night until we've made up the deficit.'

'We haven't exactly had a honeymoon period, have we?' Kate says.

'We're having a real life,' Spencer says, 'and that's better than anything.'

'You're perfect,' Kate says, and she kisses him.

There's a tap on the door. 'Ten minutes,' calls the nurse.

Chapter 15

Late February

'OH,' SPENCER SAYS, DROPPING in after school the following week, 'I forgot your shower gel. I'll text your mum and ask her to bring it when she comes in tomorrow.' Spencer and Richenda seem to be getting on well enough, and he's even befriended Kate's father, who called while Kate was brushing her teeth one evening. Melissa has asked after Spencer, too, which Kate has taken as tacit acceptance of him being part of her life. All in all, Kate cannot remember what she ever did without Spencer, is glad that she will never have to manage on her own again. When she looks at Daisy, now, she no longer searches for Mike's smile, or wonders what would have happened if things had been different. Rather, she looks back at her eighteen-year-old self with disbelief, with pity. Sometimes she wonders whether she should get in touch with Mike's widow, and say, properly, that she is sorry.

'And I brought your post.'

'Thanks.' Kate kisses him. Daisy, colouring in a horse with four, different coloured legs, glances up with the slightly puzzled expression she always has when she sees her mother being affectionate with someone else. Kate thinks she will get used to it. Well, she'll have to. She smiles at her daughter, takes the envelopes from Spencer.

'Look, Daisy, there's one for you!' It's from Amelia, 'I miss you' picked out in painstaking letters and a picture of the two of them on a trampoline.

Daisy looks as if she might cry. 'I miss Amelia,' she says. 'Why can't she come?'

'We have to be careful about germs, darling,' Kate says, 'for just a little bit longer. It's best to make it only grown-ups.' They've tried Skype calls, but the reception is too patchy in the enclosed hospital garden.

'If you want to make a card for Amelia, I'll take it for you.' Daisy gives Spencer a bright smile – it's good to see them coming back, although the wan half-watt efforts that marked Daisy's first days of recovery were beacons at the time. Kate folds a sheet of A4 paper in half and gives it to Daisy, who sets to, drawing a cloud of butterflies. She sits on Spencer's lap.

'I was supposed to be going to graduation today,' she says, idly.

'Tomorrow,' Spencer says.

'Oh.' Kate shakes her head. 'I've lost all track of time. Is it Wednesday? I thought it was Thursday.'

'Thursday's definitely tomorrow. Because it's PE day, and we're going to have a go at throwing bean-bags into hoops, heaven help me,' Spencer says. 'But that's no concern of yours, Kate Micklethwaite, BA, first-class honours.'

'Yes. And that is how I expect to be addressed from now on, please.'

'But of course.' Spencer laughs, then his face becomes serious. 'I'm sorry you won't be able to go.'

Once Daisy was out of danger, he and Richenda and Wendy had all tried to persuade Kate to take a day trip to attend her graduation – it was less than an hour away – but she was adamant. There was no way she was leaving Daisy in hospital.

'Me too.' She imagines herself in the dress she would have bought for the occasion, her hired cap and gown, the official photographs. She may not have had her Oxford career, but she's found her way back. She's not sure who she's proving anything to, but ever since she got her result, she feels glad she has proved it.

And then Spencer has to go. When Kate goes to bed, she doesn't fall into the deep, relieved sleep she's been enjoying ever since the first day that Daisy opted to play on the trampoline in the garden rather than sit on the bench next to Kate. She hadn't had anything like her usual bouncing energy, and she hadn't gone for height or thrills the way she usually did; but she had beamed as she did a few wobbly jumps, and that had been enough for her mother. No, tonight Kate finds that her mind has moved to the future, and the decisions that she needs to make. She starts with excitement, but before long the logistics are defeating her tired brain: travel, work, and most of all, Daisy. Look at what happened when she tried to have one weekend away. And her weekends with Melissa always have consequences: Daisy becomes anxious, Kate feels guilty, everything is too much. She's only managed this degree by doing it while Daisy slept, or while she was with her granny. And after this – she glances at Daisy, sleeping; the rattle of her breath breaks Kate's heart with love and the fear of loss – can she really risk taking her eye off her daughter? Haven't these last three weeks shown her that she needs to be a mother before everything? What might happen to her little girl if she doesn't have Kate's full attention? The other things Kate cares about – being a good role model, having a career that will help others, having a life (a love life) of her own – feel riskier now than they did before Daisy was admitted to hospital. She would say she was angry, if she didn't fear some sort of karmic consequence.

Except that now there's Spencer. Before this crisis, he told her that she wasn't on her own; now, he's shown her that he means it. These last weeks, there's been no sex, no fun, no flirting, just sitting in too-small too-hot rooms and whispering their days to each other. But still he's here. He says that she can trust him; she always believed it, but now he's showing her that she can. What if she was to try to plan a future as half of a couple, instead of as a left-behind single parent? But she's too tired and it all feels too big, too frightening. The world has shrunk to Daisy's breath and Spencer's arm around her shoulders and she cannot imagine how she will ever manage more.

It's 3 a.m. before Kate sleeps, and 6 a.m. when hospital life begins again, so when that evening comes around and a surprise party in lieu of graduation arrives Kate almost wants to cry with tiredness. Blake comes first, with a tray of canapes and a bag of cocktail napkins and melamine champagne flutes. Richenda brings the fresh orange juice along with the champagne which Rufus has sent, with his love, and a promise to come back and see them soon. Then Wendy and Jilly arrive with a tray of cupcakes. Spencer, who had brought her long floral dress, the perfume from her bathroom cabinet, and a half-hour's notice of the surprise to come says, 'When we are out of here, I promise you a celebration for the two of us.'

'How did you get all this past the nurses?' Kate asks Richenda. Although the staff are kind, they are strict with visitors and steely about noise: quite often, at weekends, there's what Spencer calls 'Daisy tag' as visitors wait in the café for someone to leave Daisy's room and come to the café to send the next person down there, because the two-visitors-per-bed rule is broken only in the sort of dire circumstances that Kate can't even contemplate.

'Well, Spencer charmed them.' Richenda's voice is dry. 'Wendy gave them cake, and I gave them a bottle of champagne for the next time they have a party.'

'So,' Spencer says when glasses are charged. 'Here's to you, our clever Kate.'

'Kate!' comes the echo. Jilly and Wendy are beaming, and Spencer has a tear in his eye. *How strange,* Kate thinks, *that my life partner and two people well on the way to becoming real friends are people I hadn't met until Daisy started school.* Richenda's face looks a little pinched. *The hospital light does strange things to skin, though,* Kate thinks; she had felt her worry about Daisy diminish by several sets of crows-feet the first time she had taken her outside and looked at her face in the puny February sunlight.

It looks as though Daisy will be able to go home next weekend, if the next chest X-ray continues to show improvement, and so they are celebrating that too. 'What are you going to do next, Kate?' Wendy asks.

'I don't really know, yet,' Kate says. 'Sleeping in my own bed is the extent of my ambition right now.'

Daisy, on the other hand, is eating prawns on sesame toasts as quickly as she can get them into her mouth, telling Jilly, 'I like these pink ones best.'

And Kate sits down on her bed, hands her glass to Spencer, lies down, and closes her eyes. Tomorrow she will be able to manage it all better.

*

214

The Saturday after the party, and Daisy seems brighter still. Kate wishes she had been more gracious; she was just so tired. And it was strange, to celebrate like that, when she should have been amongst her student peers, many of whom would have understood – more, even, than Spencer and her mother could – exactly what it meant to achieve an Open University degree. Drinking champagne in a hospital room, where the extent of her intellectual activity had been helping Daisy with the letter sheets that Wendy had brought her, made the degree she worked so hard for feel close to meaningless.

But she should have made an effort. Her people are good and kind.

As if to prove it, Wendy and Jilly arrive mid-afternoon, and send Kate to take a walk. The hospital grounds are nothing special, but the sky is blue and the air still. Kate gets a takeaway coffee and walks to the far end of the car park and back, slowly, watching the toes of her old brown boots as they make their way across tarmac and pavement. Then she sits on a wall near the ticket machine, drinks her cool-enough-now coffee, and watches the people come and go. She looks at the rows of parked cars and she wonders how many people there are here, today, in the hospital, being given good news or bad, having babies or flexing new knees or counting down the minutes until the next painkillers are due. This building is the place where she first saw Daisy, a heart blinking at her from the screen of an ultrasound monitor. Daisy was born here, calmly and naturally, in the birthing pool. Kate remembers sitting in the warm water with her squalling, squirming daughter in her arms, looking up at her mother, and saying, 'she's perfect.' And she was. She is. Although Kate would give anything to fix Daisy's lungs, her faulty pancreas, to make her life easier – she's as perfect now as she was then. If only Kate were the perfect mother she had silently promised that baby she would be.

Wendy and Jilly said to take half an hour, but twenty minutes is as much as Kate can manage away from Daisy. The air in the hospital feels smothering after the moist February afternoon. Jilly and Wendy are sitting on either side of Daisy in the garden. Daisy runs up to meet her mother – she's a little breathless with the effort, but it's so good to see her run at all. Kate sits on the end of the other bench, at right angles to Jilly and Wendy. Daisy joins her, cuddling in.

'You're not bouncing?' Kate asks.

'I've bounced,' Daisy says, 'and now I'm tired.'

'She has bounced,' Wendy confirms, 'very high. Are you OK?'

Kate shrugs. She has no answer to that one, even though people ask her all the time. Something like 'Yes. No. For now,' would probably be accurate. 'This is lovely,' she says, spreading her hands to indicate them all, 'but Daisy's obs are due at four, so one of us will get thrown out.'

Wendy smiles. 'We've got permission to both be here, because we want to ask you something. Well, we want to ask Daisy, actually.'

'Oh, OK,' Kate says. Jilly and Wendy are smiling at each other, at her, at Daisy. They are holding hands, something that's unusual for them: they don't tend to go for public displays of affection. Kate imagines that if she had grown up gay in the 1980s she wouldn't either.

'Well,' Jilly says, 'you know we're getting married?'

Kate nods, smiles. She can enjoy others' romantic happiness better she finds, now she has some of her own.

'We've just set a date for June,' Wendy adds.

'That's great,' Kate says, though from what she remembers of her mother and Blake's small, understated wedding, it seems an ambitious target for all the things that need to be organised – wrapping chairs in hessian, collecting jam jars for flower arrangements, trying seventeen sorts of cake. 'Have you got everything sorted out?'

Wendy and Jilly share a smile. 'Almost everything,' Jilly says.

'In fact,' Wendy adds, 'the only thing we don't have yet is a flower girl.'

'Oh!' and now Kate understands what this is all about. 'Daisy, are you listening?'

Daisy is half dozing in the sunlight, eyelids drooping. Kate shakes her, gently enough to wake her if she's wake-able but not so that she'll disturb her if she really is asleep. Daisy sits up. Kate says, 'Wendy and Jilly want to ask you something.'

Daisy turns her face to them, waiting. Wendy says, 'Daisy, Jilly and I are going to have a wedding and we wondered if you would like to be our flower girl.'

Daisy looks confused. 'I already am a flower girl. A daisy is a flower, too.'

'Ah yes,' Wendy says. 'Maybe we should say, a bridesmaid. Would you like to be our bridesmaid?'

There's a pause. 'Who's getting married?' Daisy asks.

'I'm getting married to Miss Orr,' Jilly says.

'Mummy says your job is not a teacher.' Daisy sounds mildly accusatory as she looks at Jilly.

'I'm a barrister. I help people when they have a problem,' Jilly says. Kate – who has seen that Jilly is nowhere near as comfortable around children as Wendy is – warms to her for the way she has just explained her job so simply.

'And' – Daisy turns to look at Kate, who has a sense of what's coming next – 'you are both ladies. Mummy, can ladies marry each other?'

'Women. Yes, they can.'

Daisy considers. 'But usually, it's a lady and a man.'

'Well,' Kate says, 'it often is, but if people love each other in a special way, they can get married. So a woman and a man might get married, or a woman and a woman, like Wendy and Jilly; or a man and a man, like—' She founders for a couple Daisy will know. Throckton is not overburdened with gay couples.

'Bert and Ernie?' Daisy asks. 'If they were real people, not *Sesame Street* people.'

'Exactly,' Kate says.

Daisy looks at Wendy and Jilly. 'Do you love each other in a special way?' she asks.

'Yes, we do.' Wendy smiles.

'Will you both wear a wedding dress?'

'Yes, we will,' Jilly says. 'We're going to choose them next Saturday.'

'But not big white dresses.' Wendy laughs. 'We're a bit old for that.'

Daisy's expression becomes solemn. 'But will the bridesmaid have a proper bridesmaid dress?'

'Oh, of course.' Wendy looks so serious in response that Kate could kiss her. 'And flowers in her hair, and she will be in charge of carrying the wedding rings on a special cushion.'

'I would expect that the bridesmaid would want to choose her own dress,' Jilly adds.

Kate laughs. 'In that case I expect that the brides would have to be ready for a lot of sparkle,' she says. 'Daisy, would you like to be bridesmaid for Jilly and Wendy?'

'Yes I would.' Daisy nods vigorously, beaming. Kate looks at her, an eyebrow raised, and she tries again: 'Yes please, I would like to be your bridesmaid, thank you very much.'

'Sorry about all of the questions,' Kate says later, as they leave. 'We have quite a small world, and I tend to explain things as they come up.'

'No problem,' Jilly answers. 'I can think of a few people you could explain it to, for us.'

Wendy nods. 'There won't be a lot of invitations going out in the staffroom.'

'I'm so sorry about that. It's unforgiveable.' Kate thinks of what Spencer has told her about the whispering and unpleasantness. If a male teacher is fair game then she can't begin to imagine what kind of stick this wedding is getting.

The thought of Daisy being a bridesmaid – and the pleasure that Daisy will get from it – is already making Kate smile. Then something occurs to her, and before she's thought it through, she says, 'Do you mind if I ask you something?'

'Not at all,' Jilly says.

Kate takes a breath. 'You asking Daisy to be a bridesmaid. It's not because of' – she gestures round the room – 'this?'

Jilly and Wendy look at each other, then Wendy says, 'You mean because she's been ill?'

'Well, yes,' Kate says. 'Because of the CF.'

Jilly takes Kate by the upper arm, firmly. 'We are not the Make-A-Wish Foundation,' she says. 'We want her to be a bridesmaid because you and Daisy and Spencer are part of our lives.'

'Exactly,' Wendy says.

'Get over yourself.' Jilly flashes her smile and kisses Kate on the cheek. Kate watches them walk down the corridor. There was a time when she would have been envious; now she recognises love when she sees it. She goes back to Daisy, who is already drawing bridesmaid dresses.

Chapter 16

Mid- to Late March

D AISY MISSES FIVE FULL weeks of normal life, in the end: four weeks in hospital, then a week of taking it easy at home. Spencer – in his official capacity – tells Kate not to worry about schooling, and to do as much or as little of the worksheets that Wendy sends with him as Daisy feels up to. But Daisy's mind is active before her body, and so the two of them spend time reading and writing, counting and sorting.

On the day Kate takes Daisy back to school – a Wednesday, so she doesn't get tired by a full week to begin with – she's stopped by Mrs Piper on her way out of the gate.

'It's so good to see that Daisy's back.' She's one of the head-on-one-side brigade.

'Yes,' Kate says. 'Thank you for all of your support.'

'Well' – Mrs Piper smiles a smile-that-isn't – 'that's really down to your Mr Swanson. He's been very conscientious.'

Kate feels the involuntary clench of her jaw. 'Miss Orr has been very good to us, too. Exceptionally so. The support from them both has been excellent.'

'Well, I'm very glad.' Mrs Piper nods. 'And please feel you can speak to me if you and Daisy need help in any way at all. Or if you have any – concerns. I'll always be happy to listen.'

'I will, thank you,' Kate says. Thinks, *I bet you would like to hear my concerns*. She takes deep breaths and puts the whole conversation out of her head.

Wendy and Spencer had been shown how to use the PICC line while Daisy was in hospital, so they can give the lunchtime dose of antibiotics at school, but Kate does the rest. Three hours should be enough time to give the flat a good clean and tidy up all of the piles of papers that are accruing. She has such a lot to think about, right now. Her future won't sort itself out, and now that the crisis has passed, there's more to her than being Daisy's mother and Spencer's partner. The idea of doing a physiotherapy Master's keeps niggling at her, but there are so many things to weigh up: her trust fund won't last forever, even if she gets a place on the course, if the psychology component of her degree is enough, and if she can work out not only the logistics of the travel but the implications of it. The weeks since Daisy was taken ill have made Kate even more anxious about letting her daughter out of her sight. Doctors, nurses, family and friends have all queued up to remind and reassure her, directly or indirectly, that pneumonia in Daisy was not evidence of failure on Kate's part. Phrases like 'it comes with the territory', 'these things are bound to happen', 'however well she is she's always going to be vulnerable' were spoken so often in the little hospital room that Kate felt as though she was breathing them in with the dry, hot air. But she knows that she shouldn't have left Daisy to go away with Spencer. He says it doesn't matter, that her mother got her to the hospital at least as quickly as Kate would have done, maybe faster, because when you're a grandparent in loco parentis you're bound to be more vigilant. When he talks like that, although Kate knows he's right, she finds that she goes quiet, because it feels as though he is wrong. She should have been the one to see that Daisy was ill, to get her to hospital. She was neglectful.

And she knows she is bringing all of these feelings when she thinks about studying. Spencer says that becoming a qualified physiotherapist doesn't count as neglect on any official child-protection guidance he's seen, and she knows he's right about that. But, left to herself, even contemplating study that necessitates time away from Daisy feels perilously close to neglect.

'You don't have to decide anything now,' Spencer had said, one night, when he'd got up to get a glass of water at 2 a.m. and found her putting figures in a spreadsheet and mapping likely university-term dates against likely school-term dates. 'You don't have to apply until January and you wouldn't start until the next, what, October? We have time to work it out without staying up all night.' He'd kissed the top of her head, rubbed her shoulders, then reached for her hand and taken her back to bed. He had been asleep before she was. And she'd lain in the dark, thinking about that 'we', knowing that she could be sure of him. When she'd awoken she hadn't felt quite so anxious.

In the here and now, there's another week of school to go before the Easter holidays begin. Daisy is doing well, and they are finding a semblance of a new routine, spending time with Spencer two evenings a week, visiting Richenda and Blake on another. When Daisy is at school Kate still finds herself a little bit lost, emotionally at least, although her days often fill up with the sort of recklessly deep sleep that is never available in a hospital. When she wakes, she finds herself watching TV programmes she'd normally scoff at. She didn't think she would ever miss the days of online university seminars.

She calls Melissa; there's office noise in the background when she picks up. 'What's wrong? Is it Daisy?'

'No.' Kate tries to steady her breath. 'It's just me.'

'Hey, there's no such thing as just you.'

Kate sobs anew. 'I can't stop crying today,' she says, unnecessarily.

'Of course you can't,' Melissa says, as though it's the most obvious thing in the world. 'Let's get on FaceTime. I'll just find a meeting room. Hold on.'

'I say this with love, but you look like shit,' Melissa says, as soon as they've connected.

'I know. I feel it. I'm just so – I can't seem to get it together for long enough to get things going again.'

'Babe,' Melissa says, 'what is it, exactly, that you think you haven't done? How have you failed?' She leans closer to her phone, so all Kate can see is a nostril, a berry-glossed upper lip. 'I forgot to pass a message on to my boss on Friday, and honestly, you'd think I'd driven a ship into a bloody great iceberg. Give yourself a break.'

'I know but—'

Melissa sighs. 'Listen to me, Kate. You haven't got it all sorted. So what? You've just had a major trauma in your life. We all know what could have happened to Daisy. Of course you feel shit. You're shaken. You're upset. And I saw how you held it together when you were in hospital. Don't you think it's about time you fell apart?'

'But—'

'But nothing. Kate, we're twenty-four. You're raising an amazing kid and I had to buy a toothbrush and toothpaste on the way to work this morning because I went home with some random last night. And I'm wearing yesterday's knickers. Who's winning?'

Kate laughs, despite herself. There would have been a time when she would have envied Melissa last night. 'How was he? The random?'

Melissa scrunches up her face. There's a rap on the door, in the background. 'Look, I need to go. Kate, I promise, you'll feel better. Let that man of yours rub your feet, get plenty of sleep, and if I'm not around to talk then watch half an hour of TikTok cat videos. OK?'

'OK. Thanks, Melissa.'

'Love you.' Melissa hangs up. Kate does as she's told and looks at TikTok. It doesn't solve anything, but neither did staring at the spreadsheet.

The days before the Easter holidays pass, and Kate feels herself start to heal, as Daisy grows stronger. She stops feeling as though Daisy's life is as vulnerable as a sycamore seed flying down to earth, and starts to sense the roots and solidity of it, again. She notices that she isn't walking to school pick-up in a panic; she can go to the loo and leave her phone in the other room. The fact that Spencer has texted her, every lunchtime, just a line to tell her Daisy is OK, has definitely helped. And so she herself begins to relax, to remember that she is allowed to be a separate person, to want to be left alone for five minutes or to have an uninterrupted night's sleep, to laugh with Spencer, to be naked against him. To drink a glass of wine too many.

One evening, as she is putting a tired Daisy to bed, she hears Spencer pacing in the living room. She thinks, to begin with, that he must be clearing the table, but they had pasta with bolognese and a salad, so that would be three trips to the dishwasher at most. She hears the sound of his feet going back, forwards, back, forwards, for ten minutes, fifteen.

Daisy has asked for two stories, but she's asleep before the second book is opened; Kate resists the temptation to curl up beside her – she's so very tired herself, still – and instead goes back to the living room. Spencer has stopped pacing and is standing at the window, looking down over the street. She goes to join him. He puts an arm around her shoulder, pulls her in.

'It's so much darker in Scotland,' he says.

'Is that a literal observation, or are we being metaphorical? Because I think I'm too tired for metaphorical.'

Spencer laughs and kisses her forehead, where her parting is. 'Very possibly both,' he says, 'but I was thinking about the light. From the sun, not the metaphorical light. If I was teaching in some parts of Scotland it would be darkening when you picked Daisy up, even at the end of March.'

Kate considers. She has lost so much time to hospital colours and clinical light. It was the end of winter when Daisy was hospitalised. She's missed the early part of spring – there wasn't much of it visible in the hospital car park, just a few struggling crocuses and a mildness in the air, but the temperature of any air outside the hospital's stifling dryness is hard to judge for anything except being blessedly different. Now, with tulips in the village flowerbeds and the last of the primroses in her mother's garden, with the yellows of impending Easter everywhere, she is almost giddy with it all: the sun and smell of spring in the world outside.

'Yes.' He has tilted his head so it rests against hers. Even though they've been talking about what they'll do in the summer holidays, and whether it's feasible for her to apply to do a Master's that will start in January rather than October, it's still a novelty to breathe each other in.

'I could hear you pacing. Is something wrong?'

'No. Yes,' Spencer says. 'It's a storm in a teacup, really.'

Kate takes his hand and leads him to the sofa. 'I could do with thinking about something other than Daisy.' Part of her wants to cross her fingers against having said such a thing. What if she makes her daughter ill again?

'It's just school.' Spencer sighs. 'There are times when I wonder whether I'm in the right job.'

'But everyone says you're a brilliant teacher. Jo has been bringing me up to date with the latest. Your stock is rising.' She adds a suggestive eyebrow, but he doesn't notice. Just as well. She's tired to her bones.

'Really?'

'Really. The playground word is, the children respond well to you, you're good at quieting the boisterous ones down, and bringing the quiet ones out of their shells.'

'The staffroom talk is different,' Spencer says.

'Really? I thought that had blown over.' Although, when she looks back, she realises it's more that he hasn't mentioned school than that he's said that there's nothing going on. Since she and Daisy returned from hospital she's learned a lot of small things that she's been protected from. Her father broke his wrist when he fell on the steps of an art gallery in Florence – only her father would manage to have such a pretentious accident. Blake has been seconded to another police force, disrupting their lives in a way that neither he nor her mother talked to her about while she was in hospital. One of Richenda's biggest clients has gone bust; as she says, she's the bookkeeper, she should have seen it coming, but it had been a quick decline brought on by their biggest contractor going into receivership. Even her friends have felt they can't bother her with what they consider to be trivia: Jo thought she was pregnant, but it turned out to be a false alarm; Melissa's internship has turned into a job.

Spencer shakes his head. 'Nothing blows over in a school. It just festers. Then comes out again, worse.' Kate looks into his face in the hope that he's joking, but there's no flicker of amusement there.

'What's happened?'

'Well, I came back to the classroom early to do some admin at lunchtime, but Wendy stayed in the staffroom. When she came back after lunch I could see she was upset. She wouldn't tell me what was wrong. I thought she might be getting a bit of stick about the wedding.'

'Oh, for heaven's sake,' Kate says. Even her mother's neighbour, who can be what could kindly be described as 'old-fashioned' when it comes to non-traditional relationships (well, non-traditional anything), had taken the news of Wendy and Jilly's wedding and Daisy's role in it with a smile, when they bumped into her on the way to Sunday lunch. 'Ladies can love each other in a special way, Mrs Drury,' Daisy had said, and Kate had been ready to intervene depending on the reply, but Mrs Drury had said only that it's good that people love each other.

'I know' – Spencer strokes her hair – 'but it's a pretty heterosexual place.'

'That's no excuse.' Kate leans into him.

'I wasn't making excuses.' He sounds rattled; Kate pulls away, a little, looks into his face. He smiles and squeezes her hand, an apology. 'Anyway. After school I asked her if someone had mentioned her wedding. That I was her friend and if anything was wrong I wanted to know.'

'Right—'

'It seems there's a lot of – quite ugly gossip going around, about me.'

'Oh, Spencer—' Kate fits herself under his arm, feels him pull her in. She knows how easy it is to talk a good game when it comes to listening to gossip, and how much harder it is to truly ignore what people say.

'I know,' Spencer says, 'but – they're talking about you, too, Kate.'

'What about me? I was in hospital for a month. I can't have done anything worth gossiping about, unless you count not washing my hair for four days.' Kate is aiming for lightness but knows she doesn't manage it.

'I mean, they're saying that you and me – that you're vulnerable and I'm – taking advantage—'

'Oh, that's ridiculous!' Kate's body has gone from leaning-in to tree-trunk-straight in a heartbeat. Spencer puts his hands on her shoulders, looks into her eyes.

'I know it is,' he says. 'We know the truth, and it doesn't matter what anyone else thinks. And I know that in my head, but—' He sits down again. Kate perches next to him, her body turned to face him.

'It's so unnecessary,' Kate says, her mother's phrase. 'And it's not fair,' which is Daisy's.

'The thing is,' Spencer says, 'you don't teach because it's a brilliant career choice, or it's easy, or it's even well paid.' He half laughs, though it's an ugly sound. 'They're advertising for a box-office manager in the cinema and I'd make as much there, pro rata, and minus a hell of a lot of hassle.'

'You worked it out?' In Kate's head, Spencer is so clearly and absolutely a teacher that the thought of him contemplating another job – however briefly – is astonishing.

'Not really. Well, I was waiting for the film to start.' Spencer shrugs. 'Anyway, teaching, it's a vocation and a profession and it's hard work, but everyone just thinks I stick old yoghurt pots together all day and then swan about for six weeks in the summer.'

'They don't think that,' Kate says, but Spencer isn't listening.

'And because I'm a man teaching primary level they think there's something wrong with me, and I have to put down all these stupid rules so that I protect myself from accusations—' Kate thinks of Daisy when it comes to PE day, insisting on her white knee-socks rather than her navy tights: 'Mr Swanson says have a go at putting your tights on yourself, or get one of the other girls to help you, but I can do socks on my own.'

'Surely no one's saying—'

'No, no.' Spencer waves a hand. 'I'm not saying that. I'm saying it's a lot of effort to do this job and I get no credit and a lot of stick from the people who would welcome me with open arms if I was a woman.'

'You don't know that,' Kate says, but she says it without conviction, because she suspects he's right. She thinks of Mrs Piper, whose superior attitude and snide solicitousness had been unpleasant, even in the fifteen-second interaction they had when Daisy went back to school. She can't imagine how wearing it would be day to day.

'I do,' Spencer says, then, 'Well, the old guard don't like anyone different. Wendy got a lot of stick about her and Jilly to begin with, I think. She was telling me about it today. When she started, Bridget Piper kept bringing in newspaper articles for her. About anything vaguely gay. Elton John's new album or Sandi Toksvig presenting *QI*. Asking her which was her favourite Barry Manilow song. Just – awful. Passive aggressive.'

'Why can't people just leave people alone?' It sounds glib, but Kate means it, from every corner of her soul.

Spencer shakes his head: agreement. 'And then she started asking whether Wendy was worried about what the "more traditional" families were thinking about her being "so public" with Jilly. Of course, Wendy told Jilly, and Jilly came to meet her from school one day and had a chat with Bridget about anti-discrimination laws, and mentioned that she was in the legal profession. It's been better since.'

'I should hope so,' Kate says. 'How awful for Wendy, though. Imagine if Jilly hadn't been able to do that.'

Spencer smiles at her, a little sideways. 'Is it too late for you to retrain as a lawyer?'

Kate takes both of his hands, raises them to her lips, kisses his knuckles one by one. 'You know you're doing a good job. You've nothing to fear from Bridget Piper. And we know what we're about.' That 'we' keeps thrilling her: we're taking Daisy to see a film, we'll see you on Sunday for lunch if Daisy isn't too tired.

'Yes,' Spencer says. 'I suppose I can't help but resent it. And I'm worried that you'll believe what they say about me taking advantage of you.'

They look at each other for a long minute, and then Kate smiles and undoes his top button. 'If only they knew,' she says, 'how much I take advantage of you.'

'You're right.' Spencer exhales, his shoulders broadening as tension leaves him. Kate wishes he would smile; there's a heaviness to him tonight that calls out an answering worry in her. 'We still have some catching up to do.'

And all is well, for a while. But later, when he leaves – he forgot his clean shirt for the morning, and decides not to stay – Kate looks out of the window and sees him standing in the street, not moving, looking down at the pavement, and when she goes back to bed she cannot sleep.

Chapter 17

Late March

JUST WHEN LIFE STARTS to feel something like normal, Spencer announces that his parents are coming to visit for the first weekend of the Easter holidays.

They are staying with him for Friday and Saturday night, en route to a fortnight with Spencer's sister Annie, who needs childcare help over the holidays, followed by a week's stay in a cottage on the south coast. Spencer will sleep on the sofa and give his parents his bed. And he will introduce them to Kate and Daisy.

'I'm not going to be nervous,' Kate says to Jo on the Saturday morning. She has taken Daisy to play with Amelia. 'It's the twenty-first century, I have a first-class honours degree' – she still feels a thrill when she says it – 'I am a woman in my own right, and a role model to my daughter. Spencer can make his own choices, and what his parents think of me is irrelevant. They sound nice, from what he's said. Also, we're going to the Italian restaurant for dinner, so I'm not getting involved in some sort of cooking request-for-approval.'

'If you say so.' Jo raises an eyebrow. 'Though if that's the case I'm not quite sure why I'm having Daisy so you can clean your flat. Or why you told me all that without me asking.'

'I will think of an answer to that,' Kate replies, 'before I come back to pick her up.'

'I'll be waiting.' Jo laughs. 'It's good to have you back.'

Kate hugs Daisy goodbye, and goes home via the florist's, where she buys peonies for the coffee table. She needs to be back in three hours, so that she's in time for the lunchtime round of intravenous antibiotics.

Spencer's parents arrived last night. He's taking them around the area this morning; this afternoon, they'll come to collect Kate and Daisy and take a walk up to Beau's Heights, followed by dinner at the Italian restaurant. There's a café halfway up the hill, where Kate and Daisy can wait if it looks as though Daisy is going to be too tired to make it up to the top and down again. Spencer's mother, apparently, loves dogs, so Kate has invited her mother and Blake to meet them in the car park with Hope and Beatle.

'My mum will love that you like dogs,' Spencer had said. 'She always wanted a dog but Annie's allergic.'

'Well then,' Kate had said, 'it's going to be perfect. Daisy won't realise how far she's walking if the dogs are with us. Good for the lungs.'

'And it will be good for the in-laws to meet.' Spencer had grinned. Kate nodded and grinned back, but she'd had that feeling that she gets sometimes. It's as though she's slipping down a gravel bank and everything is going, suddenly, very fast. Or that she and Spencer are a trapeze act that hasn't practised with the net enough before having it taken away. But when she hears him let himself into the flat, when he and Daisy are laughing over his terrible colouring in, when he reaches for her even when he's asleep, she wonders why she ever worries.

Spencer's parents look pale and tired, but they are full of smiles when they arrive at the flat. After the introductions they all stand and look at each other, no one quite sure what to say. Daisy has gone to put on her wellies, as instructed; they all watch her trot off to her room, and then stand in a smiling circle, waiting for someone to start a conversation.

'I'd be as fat as butter if I lived this close to a bakery,' Sally Swanson says. Kate cannot imagine this. Everything about Spencer's mother is wiry, from her dark curly hair to the spring in her step.

'Well, I'm half a stone heavier than I was when we moved in,' Kate says, 'and Daisy has to eat a lot of high-calorie food, so I'm pretty much doomed.'

Sally looks puzzled for a second, and Kate's about to explain, but then John says, 'Ah, a few good walks is all it needs.' His voice has a sing-song cadence that, Kate imagines, makes him impossible to argue with: no matter what he says, it would always sound like poetry. Daisy listens to him with fascination, and Kate sees her storing 'aye' away for future use. According to Spencer, his father is the mild one, his mother more prone to temper and what she calls 'plain speaking'. Spencer obviously gets his height and length from his father. When the two of them stand side by side they make twin silhouettes. Spencer's parents belong to a rambling club and take walking holidays. Kate notes their well-worn-in walking boots and hopes that she'll be able to keep up.

It all works out quite neatly. Blake and John stride ahead with Hope, the greyhound, at their heels; Spencer walks with Richenda; and Kate, Daisy, Sally and Beatle bring up the rear. Sally talks to Daisy about Beatle. 'He's the same number as me,' Daisy says in response to a question about her age. 'We are both five years old.'

'Well,' Sally says, 'that makes you both quite grown-up.'

'Beatle won't get as old as I do,' Daisy adds, 'because he's a dog, and he's already a grown-up dog, but I'm a child, and I'm not a grown-up yet.'

'I see,' Sally says. 'I've always wanted a dog, but we live in a city and it isn't really fair. I'd like the sort of dog who would want to be in a field.'

'Like a sheepdog?'

'A sheepdog would be just the thing for me. And some sheep too.'

'Yes,' Daisy agrees. And then she's off to catch up with Richenda and Spencer. Kate and Sally watch as they turn, smile, and offer a hand each, swinging her along.

'She's a sweet girl,' Sally says.

'Yes,' Kate says, 'she is.'

'Spencer says she's had a rough time of it lately.'

'She's had pneumonia,' Kate says. 'She's been quite poorly. But she's almost back to her usual self. Then the PICC line can come out.'

'Ah, that's what it's for,' Sally says, then adds. 'And it's the holidays now, so that helps. School's hard for the wee ones, I think.'

'I know what you mean,' Kate says. 'Hard for the parents, too. I can't get used to her not being at home with me.'

Sally smiles, but it's an inward, sad smile. 'Ah, well, not all parents are like you.'

Daisy makes it to the top of Beau's Heights with no problem. She takes a puff of inhaler at the top, and is introduced to Kendal Mint Cake by John. She rides most of the way down on Blake's or Spencer's shoulders. Kate talks physiotherapy with John – 'I'm a slave to my back,' he says, and looks at her, hopefully, as though just by considering physiotherapy training, she is qualified to help him. She asks Sally about Edinburgh. They go back to Blake and Richenda's for coffee, as the fair-weather walkers, as John calls them, have taken over the café. Kate does not admit to being a fair-weather walker herself, although she supposes that her trainers give the game away.

After coffee, Spencer and his parents drop Daisy and Kate home, and they arrange to meet at 6.30 at their booked table in the restaurant. Kate tries, and fails, to get Daisy to take a nap, but gets some peanut butter and crackers into her to tide her over to her later dinner time. She catches herself just before she worries that tiredness, excitement, and too many people might get the better of Daisy, and mess things up for her. Daisy matters more than impressing Spencer's parents. Leaving Daisy watching TV, she takes a quick shower, and puts her long floral dress and denim jacket on. She decides against the cowgirl boots and slips on her silver plimsolls.

Dinner is convivial – there's enough goodwill to make it work, even at the moments where the conversation stutters.

'It must be difficult, managing Daisy on your own,' Sally says, in the space between starters and main courses.

'She's not on her own, Mum,' Spencer says. 'That's why we're here.'

Sally rolls her eyes and smiles at Kate. 'Kate knows what I mean. It must have been difficult, managing Daisy on your own, before Mr Knight here turned up on his white charger to rescue you.'

Kate chooses not to pick up the whole 'being rescued by a man' aspect of this, although she would have done had Daisy been listening. She could get hooked on the idea of her daughter needing 'managing', too, but instead she chooses to answer the spirit of the question, which she imagines every mother would want to ask if her son introduced a girlfriend with a five-year-old daughter: what about the father?

'Daisy's father died before she was born,' Kate says, 'so I've always been a lone parent. I have a lot of support from my family.'

John nods. 'Family's important.' Kate and Spencer look at each other; the same look, that says: that was straightforward.

Daisy looks up from her colouring book and adds, conversationally, 'My daddy's name was Michael and he was a policeman. When he died he was saving my mummy.'

'I see,' Sally says, with a look at Kate that says she doesn't, at all. Kate isn't going to go into any more detail, not with Daisy here. Not ever, if she can help it. The dreams where she's drowning have intensified since she and Daisy left hospital. Spencer has to wake her sometimes, and she clings to him as though he is the one who has pulled her from the freezing water.

Then the main courses arrive, and the conversation moves on to safer topics – eating fish if you live a long way from the sea, how different fresh pasta tastes to dried pasta – and everything feels all right again. Although there's no immediate change in atmosphere, Kate feels Sally's gaze on her, quietly, a lot of the time, and her appetite has gone. She forces herself to breathe deeply, and watches Spencer for signs of discomfort. He seems happy enough, holding forth on the subject of childhood holidays and making everyone laugh with his misrememberings.

Kate takes Daisy to put her to bed, leaving the others to finish the wine. They arrive at the flat after a tactful forty-five minutes, when Daisy is sleeping and Kate is ready for the next round of getting-to-know-you chat. This is something else that, she reminds herself, is normal for a new relationship, although it seems odd to her. It feels as though everything she does will have an amplified existence: Kate likes dogs, and tiramisu, Kate's going to be a physiotherapist, Kate is quiet when there are a lot of people around. Kate's daughter is quite blasé about the fact that her father died rescuing her mother. Soon Annie, Spencer's sister, will have all of these details reported to her. Kate supposes that, if she changes her mind about her studies, she will become 'Kate who was going to be a physiotherapist but decided she couldn't cope with the hours away and works in a café instead'. Every conversational gambit has been noted. Of course, she's doing the same thing. She will always think of Spencer's parents with this weekend as the baseline: dark purple jackets, accents that mesmerise Daisy, John loudly declaring that he'll always opt for an alcoholic pudding if there's one on the menu.

Spencer had said he would pay the bill; Kate wishes she had insisted on leaving the money for her and Daisy's meals. She might be better off than Spencer, but his parents might make assumptions.

Kate thinks about how carefully Sally looks away from her and her son when Spencer touches her, reaching for her hand or slinging an arm around her shoulder. Sally had almost winced when Spencer kissed Kate's cheek and the top of Daisy's head as he held the restaurant door open for them when they left. But then, John and Sally barely touch each other, or Spencer. When introduced to anyone, they shake hands, and when Spencer and Richenda had greeted each other with kisses on each cheek Kate had remembered how Spencer had told her he'd never seen that happen, ever, as a greeting until he moved south after his degree. Cultural differences, then, no more.

When Spencer brings his parents up to the flat from the restaurant, they all seem weary.

'I can make tea or coffee,' Kate says. 'Or there's wine. Or you might be awash, I don't know.'

'Awash,' John says. 'Aye, I think that's the word.'

'I should imagine Daisy didn't take much rocking,' Sally says. 'She did well, today.'

'Yes,' Kate agrees, 'she was tired. Please, sit down.'

They do; Sally sits next to Kate and, once Spencer and John are engrossed in conversation about an old neighbour in Edinburgh, Sally says, 'I hope you don't mind my asking, but—'

Kate braces. Why would you preamble a question like that unless you knew it was going to be badly received? She assumes that she and Mike have been discussed, downstairs, while she slipped Daisy's nightdress over her head – she wishes she couldn't feel her ribs so easily – and promised her sleepy girl that they'd have a big, splashy, bubbly bath in the morning, because it was a bit late for one now.

'Yes?' Best to get it over with, whatever it is.

'Well – is there something wrong with Daisy? I mean' – for the first time since Kate has met her, Sally looks unsure of herself – 'I know pneumonia isn't to be sniffed at, but she takes a lot of tablets. And everyone seems very keen to get her to eat a lot.'

'We need to get as many calories into her as we can, because her pancreas doesn't work properly.'

'Oh—' Sally looks more puzzled than before.

'It's one of the facts of life, with CF.'

'CF?'

Kate looks from Sally to Spencer, who is still talking intently to his father, his back turned slightly away so she cannot catch his eye. It seems impossible that his parents don't know this. 'Cystic fibrosis. Daisy has cystic fibrosis. It's a condition that means—'

'Oh,' Sally says in a rush. 'I know what cystic fibrosis is, Kate. I'm so sorry, I didn't realise that was what Daisy has. Poor wee mite.'

'She's very susceptible to infections. She basically takes antibiotics all winter. And she has medication to help her absorb nutrients from her food.'

'That's worrying.' Sally doesn't look worried. She looks anxious. Scared, even. She turns away from Kate and towards Spencer, but he is still angled away from them. Kate has seen a lot of strange reactions to telling people that Daisy has CF, but never someone look as though they want to run from it, as though it's infectious. Especially a woman as sensible, as kind, as Sally seems to be.

If Sally gives a signal to John, Kate doesn't see it, but a second later he looks at his watch and says, 'Well, I think we should head back. We've an early start tomorrow.'

'Of course.' Kate's not sure whether to feel relieved or rebuffed.

When they all stand and say their goodbyes, Spencer moves to Kate's side, but his body feels too straight. Kate tells herself to stop reading so much into everything. Perhaps they're all just tired. Sally must have forgotten about the CF. Or Spencer didn't make too much of a big deal of it, which is what she would always want: Daisy is bouncing, butterfly-loving child first, a girl with cystic fibrosis second.

And then, in a flurry of goodbyes and nice-to-meet-yous and quick, stiff hugs, Spencer and his parents have gone, although Spencer runs back up the stairs and kisses her again, squeezes her bottom, and says, 'You are wonderful and I love you.' Then the flat is quiet until Daisy coughs, which is not a happy sound, but at least comforting in its familiarity.

Chapter 18

Mid-April

'YOU TWO BEHAVE.' Kate doesn't know why she even bothers saying it. Melissa, wearing pyjamas covered in cartoon cats and dogs, is lying flat on her back while Daisy, laughing wildly, tries to throw popcorn into her mouth.

'We absolutely won't.' Melissa sits up and Daisy plonks herself into the dip made by Melissa's crossed legs. Daisy has the best kind of colour on her cheeks: she is bright with pink excitement. Melissa nudges her. 'What did Auntie Lissa tell you while Mummy was getting ready?'

'What happens on sleepover stays on sleepover!'

Kate laughs. 'OK, OK. I'm off now. I'll see you for lunch tomorrow.' She's going to walk down through the village, across the river, and up the hill to Spencer's flat.

Melissa walks her to the door. 'Just enjoy yourself, OK? Make the most of it.'

'Thanks, Melissa.' Kate squeezes Melissa's arm. 'I appreciate this. Especially after what you've said.'

Melissa hugs her. 'I should have written a questionnaire for you. I'd be happier if we knew more about him.'

'We're ready for a night to ourselves. Though I might just go straight to bed.' Being a good mother is exhausting. When Kate brought Daisy home from the hospital six weeks ago, she promised herself that she would never care about anything but Daisy's welfare, ever again. And she hadn't so much as thought about asking her mother to have Daisy to stay over. Spencer said it didn't matter to him what they did so long as Kate was comfortable. But when Melissa offered – well, then Kate realised how much she wanted to drink a little too much, laugh sufficiently loudly to wake a restless child, have sex without an eye on the firmly closed door and an ear out for a waking cough.

And, she and Spencer need time to relax. The fortnight since his parents visited have been strange. She'd mentioned how odd it was that Sally didn't know about the CF; how weirdly she reacted. Spencer said he thought maybe she had a school friend who suffered from it and died. She was probably thinking of that. And when Kate asked him why he hadn't told his mother that Daisy had cystic fibrosis, he'd said that he was following Kate's lead, that CF was not the defining thing about Daisy. Which in many ways was the perfect answer – at least until the pneumonia, and the weeks she and Daisy had spent in hospital. Spencer said he was sure he did mention it, and anyway, he had quite a lot on his mind, at the time; she wasn't the only one who was worried about Daisy, and he had been worrying about Kate too. Kate hasn't brought the subject up again. She's sure he's right; she's probably being over-sensitive. And she really, really doesn't have the energy for an argument about something that has already happened. Maybe Spencer should have told his parents about Daisy's CF. Maybe he did tell his mum, but she misunderstood or didn't hear properly. It's not the end of the world. And nobody's perfect.

The evening air is almost warm, and Kate pauses outside the building that houses Spencer's flat for a moment, enjoying the quiet, and letting her breath even up before she rings the buzzer and climbs the stairs to the fourth floor. Hospital confinement has made her unfit. She ought to take up running, or something, go to yoga with her mother, but somehow she can't find the motivation. She never used to have to catch her breath after a twenty-minute walk; has always been painfully aware of how effortlessly her lungs work in comparison to her daughter's. Twenty-four seems too young for the best years of her body to be behind her.

Goodness, she is maudlin tonight.

Spencer is waiting on the landing; he's wearing jeans and a grey shirt, he's barefoot, his hair is damp. And Kate is overtaken by a swift, sweet rush of love for him, and the certain knowledge that this relationship is perfect for her. She smiles; he smiles; they kiss. But there's something in his face that isn't quite—

'What's wrong?'

He laughs and pulls her towards him. 'Nothing that wasn't solved by you at the door. I made salad niçoise. Is that OK? Wine first?'

'Lovely.' Tuna isn't Kate's favourite, but she can live with it. The wine he opens and pours is crisp and cold on the ridges of her mouth.

They stand and look out over Throckton: the dip of the river, the church, the square. Spencer says, 'I can see your house from here.'

'Oh, yes.' The gable-end of it, with no window. 'I can't see you.'

'My lease here is only a year.' Spencer kisses the top of her head, and she hears everything he isn't saying: that when the lease is up, they might be finding a place of their own. They might even be able to buy a home, between her savings and his salary. Kate knows what Melissa would have to say about that, but Melissa doesn't know everything. Kate leans on Spencer, expecting the comforting press of return pressure, but after a second he steps away. 'I'll get the food.'

The table, under the window in the sloping ceiling, has a candle waiting to be lit; Spencer strikes two matches that sputter out before the wick catches. It looks as though his hand is shaking.

Kate leans against the kitchen island that divides the living space. She imagines him taking the wine glass out of her hand, sitting her up on the worktop, and her wrapping her legs around his waist while they kiss. But he's intent on the salad, adding dressing from a jam jar, tossing it through. He's barely made eye contact since she arrived.

'What's wrong?'

'Shall we eat?'

His words overlap hers; he's speaking in parallel rather than trying to ignore her question. They sit, eat, quietly; Kate tells him about Melissa and the pyjamas and the popcorn, and it barely raises a smile. Her happiness is leaching away with the last of the daylight. It feels as though everything is out of joint.

'What's wrong?' she asks again.

'I'm fine.' Spencer glances away, out of the window.

'You're not. Please, Spencer, tell me what's going on,' Kate says. She puts the wine glass down and crosses her arms, as though she needs to defend the soft centre of her body. Spencer looks at her directly, properly, for the first time since they sat down to eat, and his expression goes from closed and strange to something closer to what she knows. 'I'm sitting here imagining all sorts of things.' It's not until she says it that all of the possibilities crowd in: that he's going to end their relationship, that he's been sacked, that some unthought-of hitch is about to throw their lives off a cliff. He takes a deep breath. She closes her eyes.

'It's a school thing. Probably nothing but it's rattled me.'

'Tell me,' she says. She doesn't let the relief – he's not leaving, they're not over – show. But next to Daisy getting ill again that's what she dreads most.

'A member of staff has made a complaint about me.'

'No prizes for guessing who.' She doesn't take her eyes off him as he talks, although he looks away, out of the window, at his hands, at the candle.

'Got it in one,' Spencer says. 'Your friend and mine, Bridget Piper.'

'What did she complain about?'

'She says—' Kate sees how Spencer takes a deep breath, looks at his hands, as though he's ashamed to look at her. Her heart finds a little extra love for him. She would like to think that gossips don't know how much pain they cause, though something tells her Bridget Piper knows exactly what she's doing. 'She says that I'm having an inappropriate relationship with the mother of one of my pupils—'

'No—' Kate says. She feels herself sit up a little straighter. Witness-box straight.

'Yes,' Spencer shakes his head, still can't look at Kate. 'And she's saying that the relationship is putting children at risk and brings the reputation of the school into disrepute.'

'Oh, that's ridiculous.' Kate's voice has got a shade sharper; she reaches a hand across the table, puts it on top of Spencer's. She sees that she's shaking.

'I know it is,' Spencer says, 'and you know it is, but—'

'But what?'

He sighs. 'It's not that simple.' The look on his face almost frightens her, it's so serious. It's the face of a consultant about to say that Daisy's drug regime isn't working as well as it should, or a nurse trying to get her out of the room before they drain fluid from Daisy's lung. Well, she knows how to handle those moments.

'Hey.' How she wants to see him smile. 'I've got a First, you know. Talk to me. Tell me what you're worried about.'

He smiles, without happiness, and laughs, without humour. 'There's going to be an informal investigation. On Monday.'

'What does that mean?'

'It means,' Spencer says, 'that Jane Hillier is trying to keep the whole thing in proportion. It means that she doesn't really think there's a problem, but she has to do something so that Bridget Piper feels as though she's been taken seriously. The fact that she's doing it straightaway means she wants to nip it in the bud.'

'That's good, then?' Kate reaches for her wine glass with her free hand. The tang of salad dressing claws at the back of her throat.

'Yes,' Spencer says, 'though she also has to be seen to be doing the right thing. If it was serious, she would want to be seen to have acted quickly.'

'But—' Kate wants to say, *of course it's not serious*. But Spencer hasn't finished his thought. It's as though he hasn't heard her.

'If she finds out something that makes her decide that she has to launch a formal investigation then I will probably be suspended and' – she hears tears in his voice – 'well, realistically, it's the end of my career.'

'But you haven't done anything wrong, Spencer. I could go to school and tell them that. And Daisy's being bridesmaid for Wendy and Jilly. Why isn't that wrong?'

'It's a different relationship. A pre-existing one, I suppose. And Wendy is – well, she does everything right, doesn't she?'

'So do you!'

He sighs, a long exhale. When it seems he's empty, he takes a breath and starts talking. 'I wrote the complaints down, because I knew I'd need to give them to my union rep. Do you want to see the list?'

'Can't you just tell me?'

That strange, sad look again. 'I'm having a relationship with the mother of one of my pupils which, while not technically wrong, would be frowned on in some quarters. I let you stay for the dress rehearsal when I didn't offer the same courtesy to other parents who might not have been able to come to the show—'

'That's ridiculous. Who?'

Spencer shrugs. 'It doesn't matter. It's the principle. According to Bridget Piper, anyway. I gave preferential treatment to a parent at a school function.'

'What? When?'

'When I saved you a seat in the front row. I hadn't actually saved it for you – the photographer from the paper had originally said she was coming to the first performance, then changed her mind and came to the second. So, I knew there was one spare. But it looks as though I was playing favourites.'

'Well, if that's all they've got—'

'And I failed to go through the proper channels in a medical emergency.'

'What?'

'When Daisy was taken to hospital. There's a whole lot of steps you're supposed to follow.'

'But you helped us. You supported us. That's the point, surely. And if we're allowed to have a relationship, then—'

'I know, Kate. Oh, and I'm giving undue attention to one of my pupils to the detriment of others.'

Kate shakes her head; she feels as though she is trying to clear water from her ears, after swimming. 'What?'

'Bridget came into the classroom one day before the holidays at the beginning of break. Daisy was struggling to get her coat on over her PICC line so I was helping her with it. The rest of the children were already outside, with Wendy.'

'So? How is that wrong?' He's looking at her as though he's waiting for her to understand, but she can't see why he wouldn't help a child with her coat. 'She's five years old, for heaven's sake.'

He shakes his head, looks away. 'It's a really bad idea,' he says, 'to let yourself be left alone with a child, because at best it looks like favouritism and at worst – well, if people are malicious they can – insinuate—'

No. Surely not. 'You helped Daisy with her coat and she's accusing you of grooming her?'

Kate's hands are shaking. Spencer's are, too, so their fingertips, loosely held across the table, bump-bump-bump. 'No,' he says, 'she hasn't gone that far. If she had I'd be suspended, and this would be a child safeguarding issue and even though I was only helping Daisy with her coat I might as well start looking for a job sweeping the streets.'

Kate is surprised, for a moment, at the sourness in his voice: he sounds like someone else, someone jaded. She, on the other hand, can feel outrage fermenting in her. It's not fair. She's used to life being unfair for Daisy – though she does all she can to mitigate it. Life has not been fair to her, either, not really, though she had thought, lately, that things were about to start going well.

'God, Spencer,' is all she can think of to say. She looks at her hand in his; his face is hidden from her, his other hand across his forehead. She wonders what he's feeling, and whether when he looks back his face will be a mask of formality and excuses before he ends things between them. After all, she's the problem here. If they have no relationship then there's no issue, and there would only be one more term before they don't ever have to see each other again. And apart from the sick, panicked feeling of impending heartbreak, there's the certain knowledge that the life she will go back to will seem worse than it was before, because for a little while it has looked as though Kate Micklethwaite was actually going to be loved, and love back; she was going to be an equal, a partner, part of a couple who adore each other. She was going to be with a man she could rely on. And because of that, she was also getting what she had worked for: the chance to follow a career, to be out in the world, to no longer be defined and constrained by the consequences of a teenage crush. (Not that she doesn't love Daisy. Not that she regrets her. But it has been so good to see a broader horizon.)

She doesn't dare say anything. She just sits, as the candle flame asserts itself against the coming darkness. She breathes and she holds his hand, because he hasn't taken it away, and she watches and hopes and dreads and knows that this sick, heavy feeling won't leave them until this whole wretched mess is sorted.

He looks up. She braces herself. He says, 'If this is all too much I'll understand. It isn't what you signed up for.'

The heaviness in her belly doesn't shift, but Kate's heart unclenches. 'What do we do?' she asks. Her voice sounds steadier than she feels. 'Because I'm not going anywhere. And, Spencer, I know this is awful, and unfair, but you know there's nothing to worry about, don't you? It's obvious that Bridget Piper is trying to make trouble for you. Don't let it rattle you. You've done nothing wrong. And you never have.'

He squeezes her hand. 'I've called my union, and I'll have someone with me if there are any more – conversations – about this. Jane Hillier will talk to whoever she thinks she needs to, to get a true understanding of the situation. Wendy, obviously.'

'Well, that's good.' Kate's hands have stopped shaking, or it could be that Spencer is holding tighter. But the more she thinks about it, Spencer is overreacting. She can see why – it's horrible to be accused like this – but there's nothing for a good person like him to fear.

'It is good,' Spencer says, 'and then Jane will decide who else to talk to and that's when we see just how much preparation Bridget Piper has done for this.'

'Surely Wendy's the only person she should listen to,' Kate says.

'Well, yes, but Bridget could say that Wendy's been unduly influenced by me, or that she's complicit in some way—'

Kate puts her head in her hands. 'But surely when she talks to me—'

'She doesn't have to talk to you.'

'What do you mean? Surely the best way to sort this out is just to—'

'Well,' Spencer says. He looks away, out of the window. It's dark; he will not be able to see Kate's flat now. He rubs at his neck, as though the skin there is suddenly cold. 'Headteachers can run informal investigations however they want to. And – well, if I was up to – no good – then I'd be hiding it from you. Plus, you're not going to think that I'm biased towards you, are you?'

Kate bunches her hand into a fist and puts it over her mouth, before she has even realised what she is doing. She feels tears in her eyes, at the injustice of it all. Spencer reaches over and touches the place between her eyes – a small, gentle stroke that she leans into. 'I wasn't joking,' he says, 'when I said that a school is a mini kingdom. It's in the lap of the gods. Or rather, the lap of Jane Hillier. If Bridget has wound the rest of the staff up enough and they speak against me, then there'll be a formal investigation, and I'm pretty much done for. They'll go back through my records, and—' He stops, shakes his head.

'They won't find anything, though? Or you wouldn't have got this job. We don't listen to gossip, remember.' She thinks of something else he said at their first meeting: 'I'm all modern. You need to watch out for me.'

'Oh, Kate.' He looks as though he might cry. 'There's always gossip.'

'It just seems so wrong.' Kate takes his hand, kisses the knuckles. 'You haven't done anything. All the rules for the kids, about being kind and listening and fairness, and the staff behave like this.'

'I know,' Spencer says.

'You know I'm with you, don't you?' she says. And now the table is too great a distance and she gets up, stands behind him, wraps her arms around his shoulders, puts the side of her face against his face. His stubble rubs at her ear.

'You always smell of summer,' he says.

'You smell of' – imagination fails her – 'you.' She feels him smile.

*

261

They wake early, and Kate suggests that they go to Adventures in Bread for breakfast. But Spencer says he's tired, so goes back to bed, although she hears him sighing and moving around under the bedclothes while she sits, with tea and a book, on the sofa. Trying to read is pointless, though: her mind cannot focus on anything except what's happening to Spencer, not only that he can be accused like this, but that he can be investigated without Kate even being allowed to share her side of things. She thinks of all the ways he has loved her, cared for her, and that he has never so much as flinched when it comes to Daisy and all the complications that CF brings to day-to-day life. The malice of the staffroom has shocked her, but not surprised her: she knows what it is to be gossiped about, to have no way of either confronting, or running away from, whatever it is that people are saying about you just out of earshot. But at least, for Kate, the worst had happened: Mike was dead, she was pregnant, there was nothing anyone could say that either changed those facts or made the pain in her worse. For Spencer, though, the gossip is happening before the worst thing; is causing the worst thing. The gossip is making the disciplinary happen. Yes, maybe Spencer should have been more careful, but Kate very much doubts that anyone would have been concerned about a child like Daisy getting extra care if there wasn't the added dimension of her relationship with Spencer. Perhaps she should go to the headteacher herself; perhaps she should write; but Spencer is sure that that would only make things worse, that if Bridget Piper hears about it she'll make it seem as though Kate has been coerced or Spencer is being unprofessional in involving her.

After an hour of watching these thoughts chase around her head, tea going cold in the mug in her hands, Kate realises that Spencer has gone quiet. She walks to the bedroom, and sees how solidly, calmly asleep he is; it's tempting to get in next to him, warm and safe. But her own restlessness is too great, so, instead, she dresses and leaves, walking home the long way round. She hesitates at her mother's gate, but finds she doesn't want to have to try to explain the mess of outrage on Spencer's behalf and hurt for herself that she feels. Especially when her mother still thinks she's rushed into all this.

She texts Melissa, and bags a table for three in the café. When Daisy rushes towards her she feels her heart exhale; and Melissa's smile, the rattle of her earrings, the way she kisses Kate's forehead, as though she, too, were a child, makes her want to cry. 'Everything ok?'

'I was about to ask you the same thing. You don't look as' – Melissa puts her hands over Daisy's ears – 'shagged out as I was expecting.'

'I'm fine,' Kate says, and she wishes it were true.

'Come on, Kate. The fee for babysitting is full disclosure. Daisy, do you want to have a go with Auntie Lissa's iPad and her special headphones?'

'Can I watch the monkeys again?'

'The documentary? Sure.' Melissa smiles at Kate. 'See? We do educational things, too.'

Resigned, Kate orders a coffee; and, actually, once she's seen that no one from school is around, it's good to talk. 'It's nothing,' she says, at the end of her tale.

'It's probably nothing,' Melissa says, 'so long as you believe he has nothing to hide.'

'Not this again.' Kate is already tired. She doesn't need this, too.

Melissa shrugs. 'I just wish you were a little less – blind. I know you don't want to hear this but there's something he's not telling you.'

'There isn't.' Kate hears her own stubbornness, and doesn't care. She's right, she knows she is.

'So, why did he leave his last job? Or the one before? Come to think of it, how come he's on his third school already? How did he end up in Throckton of all places? Why was his mother so weird about Daisy having CF?'

'She wasn't weird, exactly—'

'You said she was.' Melissa puts her hand on Kate's wrist. 'I'm not saying there is a problem. I'm saying there's no harm in checking that there isn't a problem.'

'Doesn't that make me as bad as the gossips?'

'No' – Melissa looks at Daisy, who is laughing at baby monkeys chasing each other through treetops, oblivious to everything thanks to Melissa's noise cancelling headphones – 'because you've got skin in the game.'

Chapter 19

Mid-April

IN A FIRST, DAISY asks to go to bed. 'I'm tired after the Big Sleepover,' she says. Kate sits on Daisy's bed, and watches her wriggle into her pyjamas.

'Story?'

'If you like, Mummy, I'm going to close my eyes.'

Kate checks her temperature, but she's fine – just tired. Kate takes a book from her shelf and reads a page or two; and when it seems Daisy is no longer listening, she puts the book back on the shelf. But when she bends to kiss her daughter's forehead, Daisy says, 'I liked it when it was just you and me, Mummy.'

'Ssshhh, sweetheart. Time to sleep.'

Kate sits, for a moment, in the dark. She thinks about Mike, about how he let her down, not by dying, but by letting her love him the way that he did. He must have been able to see that she felt so much more for him than he did for her. He was the adult; she was eighteen, adult-shaped at best, though like all eighteen-year-olds, she thought she had nothing to learn. She should have known better, but he should have seen beyond whatever lust or discontent had made him turn to her. He didn't.

Still. Here she is. She's sitting in the dark, mulling over a past that is dead in more ways than one, when a good man who loves her is part of her life. She understands why Melissa and her mother want to protect her, but she knows her mind and she knows her heart.

The next day, Kate and Daisy meet Spencer at Richenda and Blake's, where they'd been invited for lunch. It feels as though Richenda is watching Kate and Spencer especially closely; Kate's glad when her mum is persuaded to go and bounce on the trampoline by Daisy, while Kate and Spencer wash up in near silence. Later, at Beau's Heights, they get caught in two separate April showers; Daisy is well enough bundled up in warm clothes and waterproofs to stay snug and dry, but even so, Kate feels anxiety start to gnaw at her. Maybe they should have gone to the soft-play centre instead. The quiet of the countryside seems to amplify their silence. Every time Kate thinks of something that she wants to talk about, she discounts it. Either it references a happy future – so she sounds as though she's ignoring the possibility of things going wrong for Spencer in the morning – or it's a 'what we could do in a worst-case scenario', but she doesn't want him to think that she has no faith in him. He's obviously, and understandably, preoccupied, but Kate can't help wishing he would understand that she is worried, too. She has skin in the game: Melissa's words won't leave her. Neither will the niggling thought that she doesn't know, for sure, why Spencer came here. She finds that she is saying, 'Are you OK?' with a regularity that she can see is grating on him. And he isn't asking her how she is doing.

At the top of Beau's Heights, he turns to her and says, 'Kate. What will be will be. Let's try to have a nice day.' He smiles and kisses her forehead, but she moves her head, not realising what he intends, and his mouth catches at the side of her temple, sticks in her hair. He laughs, and so does she, and they make the descent back down to Throckton in something that feels more like a companionable silence than a dead space. Kate links her arm through his; when they pass a family who have a child in Year One, Kate feels him stiffen as they say hello, and sees the mother's eyes widen as she realises what she's seeing. As they continue on their way, the furtive hiss of under-the-breath conversation follows them. Kate squeezes Spencer's arm, and he looks down at her and smiles, but it's not a happy smile. Their conversations about how they aren't doing anything wrong, and it doesn't matter what people think, hang around them in the air. Kate remembers the sour, dark taste of being talked about, and tries not think about what might happen tomorrow, when the double-take of a Year One mother might seem like the least of their worries.

Kate is glad when bath time comes, and she can leave Spencer to his thoughts, while she gets pulled into Daisy's talk of being a bridesmaid and whether she might be able to have a sleepover at Amelia's in the summer, whether Granny and Blake might take her on holiday to a beach. She longs for her daughter's sense of possibility.

Once Daisy is sleeping, Kate walks back into the living room to find Spencer waiting for her with a smile. 'This hasn't been our best day,' he says. 'I'm sorry. Everything will be easier when Jane's done her investigation.'

'I don't mind us not having such a great day. But—' She hesitates. Maybe it makes more sense to curl up together, then be ready for what the next week brings. Today has taken more out of it than it's put in.

'Kate—' He looks as serious and remote as he did when she invited him to Daisy's party, seven months ago. 'If there's something bothering you, please tell me. I need to know you're with me.'

'I was just wondering—' And now she's saying it, looking into those honest eyes, she feels unkind for even bringing it up. 'I was just wondering why you left your last job, and the one before that. You said something, on Friday night. About gossip.'

The feeling of betraying him gets too much. Kate goes to the sink, runs water against her wrist until the cold bites, fills a glass. When she looks up at Spencer, he's watching her with a seriousness, a stillness, that makes her blood start to beat a warning in her temples.

He looks at her for a beat too long. 'It was time for a change. That's all. Forget it, Kate.'

She inhales. She knows him well enough – the thought a splinter in her heart – to know he isn't being truthful. 'I think,' she says, 'you had better tell me what happened.' She ignores the part of her that whispers she would really rather not know. Skin in the game. Spencer looks at her, again, as though she's a puzzle he's trying to solve. He puts his head in his hands.

'If I tell you and you tell anyone about it, I'm done for,' Spencer says, into his palms. 'And you're too honest.'

'Tell me.' Kate can feel her heart shaking in her chest, but her voice is cold and calm. She sits opposite him. His eyes look fevered; his hands clench, stretch, clench. It's hard to believe how often they have sat here, laughing, talking, happy, as though together they were the whole universe.

'You don't want to know.' The look on his face tells her that he's right; she absolutely doesn't want to know. But she knows, too, that she absolutely must. She remembers the terrible things that she has coped with in her life: Mike's death; the possibility that she might be carrying a baby with cystic fibrosis; the confirmation that Daisy was going to lead a constrained, curtailed life and that Kate was going to have to step up and make it the best it could be. And the minor crises, too: her parents' divorce, the death of Daisy's paternal grandmother. The postnatal depression. She can cope when she has to. But she really doesn't see why she has to. Not again. It's her turn to put her head in her hands.

When she looks up, he's looking straight at her. 'It's all in the past,' he says. 'That's the first thing I need you to know. It was – it was a long time ago.'

'So was your childhood,' she says quietly, 'but you told me about that.' She is trying to look neutral, to look patient – it's still possible, isn't it, that whatever it is that he's worried about is insignificant, or is some bit of classroom business that is hugely important to a school but won't matter at all to her. But already, she knows that it isn't. A flash of hurt, from crown to toe.

He's looking at her, with the seriousness that she loves. Except that now – how quickly things are changing – she suspects that he's calculating: what to tell her, what she might conceivably discover, what he can continue to keep secret. 'Tell me the whole story,' she says, 'beginning to end. Don't leave anything out.'

Spencer nods, leans back, although his hands will not be still. 'It was all—' he begins, but he stops. He looks into her face, and it seems so open, so worried and so anxious – he is almost as pale as she is, for once – that she almost reaches out to touch him, to say, let's talk about it tomorrow. She is tired. They are both tired. It can wait. She opens her mouth to speak and sees that he is hoping for her to put an end to this confession. And then she thinks of how she told him every gruesome detail about her and Mike – the way she followed him, texted him, sneaked out of the house to meet him, left flowers in his widow's garden after he died. There have been plenty of times when he could have told her everything about – whatever this is.

'Just start at the beginning.' She tries to sound gentle; her voice comes out afraid.

He sighs, slumps, resigned now to whatever it is. Kate sits back, knots her fingers, listens, although now that it's coming she doesn't want to hear it after all. 'It was my first teaching post,' he says. 'A year's probation, which is fairly standard. It was a school near Maidenhead, bigger than the one here, two-form entry and up to Year Six. I was teaching Year One. There were twenty kids in my class, and one of them was Elise.' He is speaking more and more quietly, and Kate is leaning in to hear him.

'Elise was an only child with Down's syndrome. Her mother was single, and older. Her father lived abroad. Elise was a sweet kid who got frustrated easily. Amanda, her mother, picked her up most days and part of Elise's routine was to walk her through the classroom, tell her what had happened during the day. It seemed harmless enough. The teaching assistant and I would clear up, they would walk around; Elise would talk about what she'd done.

'Amanda used to chat to me, just a little bit, while Elise was putting her coat on. I wasn't very happy. It was a new place and I was lonely, and having worked so bloody hard to get into teaching I wasn't really sure whether I should have done. It seemed to be a lot more nose-wiping and a lot less shaping the future than I'd dreamed, in my heady idealistic student days.' She can see that he's said it that way on purpose, in the hope that Kate will laugh at him, but she keeps her face tight and still. She won't be deflected. 'She was – nice. Funny. Clever. She seemed to really know what she was about.'

'Like me?' Kate asks.

'Yes,' Spencer says, then, 'No.' He shakes his head. 'There's no right answer to that, is there?'

'There might have been, if you'd told me before now.' Now that the tide of panic has dropped in Kate, now that she can see the outline of what Spencer is going to tell her, Kate can feel that she is going to be angry. She isn't yet. But it's coming. And she has no time for Spencer's self-pity.

'One day she asked me how I was getting on. I told her I was struggling. It was a Friday. I had been wondering about going home to Edinburgh that weekend.

I would have more or less had to turn round and come home as soon as I'd arrived. And I was worried that if I did go home, I would never come back. She listened. She didn't say much but invited me to come over and have a drink, when Elise was in bed. I did.'

'And?'

'Do you need to know the details?'

'Yes. I do.' Kate thinks of herself at the hospital, watching all of Daisy's medical procedures as though she is an examiner, only crying and shaking when it is over and she has turned away. 'What was she like?'

'What was she like?' He repeats the question, as though he doesn't understand it, but Kate holds his gaze and he drops his head. 'She was in her early forties. She seemed very confident and sorted. She wore jasmine oil for perfume. She was' – he waves his hand in mid-air – 'not very tall. And a small build. She did martial arts. She had a smile that made her look a bit sarcastic. Blue eyes. Brown hair.' Kate finds herself adding details: linen trousers and silk shirts, high-thread-count cotton bedlinen. Goes to gallery openings and has a cleaner. *Stop it, Kate*, she tells herself. *Amanda is not your enemy.* Something strikes Kate: *it sounds as though Amanda had money. More than me, probably, but money all the same. That's something she and I have in common.*

'Amanda.' Kate's brain is working overtime; she thinks of something else. 'Your tattoo.' Spencer looks surprised, as though this is the last thing he expected her to say. But then he looks away, and Kate knows. If she trusted herself to touch him she would reach for his shirt, pull it loose, and take a close look. But she doesn't need to. She knows, now, what the oddly angular design is. 'It was an "A" and an "S" and you've gone back and had it changed.' Once she's seen that the tattoo is made up of overlapped letters she can't unsee it.

'Yes,' he says. 'The tattooist said half of his work was disguising old tattoos.' Kate remembers how he said that he would have her face tattooed on her chest; it was a joke, of course it was, but it seems a tattoo is the way he tells someone he loves them. Kate wants to write down every loving thing he ever said to her, examine their meanings anew.

'Does Amanda have the same tattoo?' Kate asks. Her brain can't seem to focus on the important things, like Elise, and Down's syndrome, and Spencer telling her that part of the trouble at school was the suspicion that he was exploiting a vulnerable parent of a vulnerable child. She can't ask those questions. Not yet.

'No,' Spencer says, and he laughs, a short, bitter sound that makes Kate look away. 'She said I was an idiot. She's got a scorpion, on her ankle. She's a graphic artist and that's her – well, signature, I suppose you'd call it.'

Kate makes a noise that comes from the back of her mouth: a snort or the beginning of a sob. She doesn't know which it is. She touches her face; her eyes are dry. He looks at her, as though he's checking for permission to continue. She nods.

'Well, we started – seeing each other.'

'Did it start that night?'

'Yes,' Spencer says.

'How?' She doesn't want to know and at the same time she can't not ask. Part of Kate already knows that this will be important, later, that she will have to lay her and Daisy's relationship with Spencer next to that of Amanda and Elise, and see how much they match. And from there, decide how much of this story is going to be coincidence, how much she has been manipulated, used. Does he love her, or is it a vulnerable woman with a child with special educational needs and a bit of money in the bank that he's after?

'Well' – Spencer rubs his hand across his eyes, as though he is trying to remember, but she doesn't buy it, not for a second – 'she was very – sure of herself. Direct. She actually said, "Would you like to come to bed, Spencer, you do know you can't stay the night." I said I did. It had been six months since I'd split up with Billie—'

'Oh yes, you told me about *her*,' Kate says, emphasising the last word.

He continues as though he hasn't heard; maybe he hasn't. It seems that now he's begun he seems determined that she should know everything. 'And the sex was over before it started. I was embarrassed. I thought she would just ask me to leave. But she said we'd do it her way when I'd recovered.'

Kate nods.

'I love you, Kate,' he says. It's a plea.

'Did you love Amanda?' she asks, then, more quietly, 'Did you love Elise?'

'I didn't have a lot to do with Elise, outside school,' he says. 'It wasn't like – this. Elise had a routine and she slept well and though she had issues and sometimes problems they were – predictable. It was a three-storey house and Amanda had a bathroom, a bedroom and a walk-in wardrobe on the top floor. Elise was on the first floor. If she did get up we'd hear her' – Kate sees how he winces at that 'we', maybe because he sees how it makes Kate flinch – 'and I'd just' – but he stops, because Kate is not laughing exactly, but making a laugh-shaped sound, with the humour taken out.

'You hid in the wardrobe?' she says. 'Spencer, that's ridiculous.' But then she thinks back to how, before Daisy knew about the two of them, she would watch to make sure he didn't fall asleep, bundle him out and into the night.

'I know,' he says.

'So, what went wrong?' Kate asks. She's had enough detail, now. She's got the measure of Amanda, her independence, her income. She's full of a dark sadness. Lately she has thought she is able to read Spencer. She imagined she could tell, by looking at him, how his day was; whether he is tired or calm or about to suggest they go and do something. Her subconscious has learned to calculate based on mouth and eyes and set of shoulders and the clothes he's chosen to wear. She thought they were close enough for her to do this; she thought she knew when to ask him what was wrong and when to greet him with a grin and pull his hands round her waist and say, 'Daisy's asleep already, let's play.' But she didn't know him at all. Not really. 'Something must have happened, something bad, or you'd have told me about her. I thought we had told each other everything.' She means it as a statement, but it comes out as something feeble, childish almost. He reaches out to touch her. Although she doesn't move away, her skin stiffens under his touch. He takes his hand back into his lap.

'It was me,' he says. 'I read more into it than there was. Amanda was – she wasn't like anyone I'd ever known before. She was so unapologetic. She had enough money – really enough, so that she didn't have to think about money at all. I'd never known anyone like that before. I mean – there were a few people like that, at uni, but none of them were training to be teachers. She had a full-time nanny and she worked from home. She picked and chose what she wanted to do, so although she always collected Elise from school, she very rarely brought her, because she preferred to work in the morning when the light in her studio was good. She ordered sushi in. I'd never eaten sushi.'

Kate says, 'She sounds awful,' before she can stop herself. *This isn't about Amanda*, she tells herself. *It's about Spencer.* She can't tell which part of what he said made her react: the money, the nanny, the studio, the sushi.

Spencer shrugs. 'It's hard to judge, now. I think what I liked was that she was so different, and because she'd – picked – me, I felt special.' He looks towards the window. The world is dark, now. His voice quiets. 'I think I got a bit obsessed.'

'Obsessed?'

Spencer looks back at her, with an imitation of a smile. 'I don't know what you think of what I've told you, but worse is coming. If you're already done with me, you could save me some humiliation. I'll just go.'

'I think I deserve better than that.'

He raises his hands, lets them drop. 'Of course you do,' he says. 'Of course you do.' His voice is tight, now, as though his throat hurts, and every muscle in his body seems clenched. 'She took me away for the weekend. Elise was with her father. We went to Amsterdam. I'd never been before. We did the usual things.'

'I don't know what the usual things are. I've never been to Amsterdam. I've only ever had one night away with a boyfriend. It was supposed to be a weekend, but my daughter was ill.' Kate can hear how cold she sounds, and she's glad.

Spencer looks at her, pain shining from his eyes. 'We went on a boat on the canals. Walked through the red-light district. Went to the Anne Frank museum. She let me hold her hand. We—'

'I didn't say I wanted to know.' Kate's voice is autumn leaves at first frost. She's thinking of how Daisy whispered that she liked it when it was just the two of them. Well, it's possible that a five-year-old child has better judgement of men than Kate has. When this conversation began, she was waiting for one great hurt. But in fact it's a bouquet of small hurts, each one ready to bloom to a bruise, and leave her with pain everywhere. And she is sure they haven't got to the end of it yet.

He nods. 'I'm sorry, Kate. I know it's too little, too late, but I'm trying to be honest.' She cannot stop herself from snorting, and he nods, accepting. Kate keeps her knees pressed together, her hands in her lap, as though only the tension in her own body can keep her together. 'While we were away, I told her that I loved her, and she said' – she thinks for a horrible moment that he might cry. He doesn't, although his voice gives him away – 'she said, "I know." And then she turned on her other side and pretended she was asleep. Then she went to sleep for real, and I just lay there. All night.'

'What did you think about?'

'What?'

'That night. She slept, you didn't. What did you think about?' Kate is thinking of the times when Spencer has slept and she hasn't; how she's been listening for Daisy, planning their future, regretting her past. How she's watched him and thought of how perfect he was.

'I don't remember,' Spencer says, but he looks at Kate as he says it and it's as though he understands that he must not tell even the smallest lie. 'I thought about leaving, but I couldn't afford to buy a new fare, and anyway we were travelling back the next morning. Then I thought about how she'd led me on, but I knew that wasn't really true. But I think' – he dips his forehead into his hands, and his words are muffled – 'I think I mostly imagined how one day, we'd be on holiday in New York or Rome, in bed, and we would laugh about this. I thought about her saying, "I love you" and me saying "I know" and then we would smile at each other and talk about how far we'd come since we were in Amsterdam.'

'She sounds awful,' Kate says again, but it comes out softly. Spencer should have told her all of this, and she can't even begin to unpick what Amanda and Elise mean for her and Daisy. But she would feel sad for anyone whose lover responded to 'I love you' with 'I know'.

'I was the one who was awful,' Spencer says, taking his head from his hands and looking at her in a way that makes her know she is getting the unfiltered truth now. 'She stopped inviting me over, but I still went. I used to stand on the drive and as soon as Elise's bedroom light went out, I'd knock on the door. She tried to talk to me, the first few times, but I – I didn't want to believe what she was saying. I got the tattoo. A for Amanda, S for Spencer. I showed her and she said she wished I hadn't done it. She started sending her nanny to pick Elise up. The nanny couldn't look me in the eye. I still didn't get the message.' He pauses, but Kate says nothing; watching, waiting. 'She told me to stop going to the house or she would call the police, so I stopped going to the house. But I texted her until she changed her number. So I started to put notes in Elise's book bag.'

'You did what?' This is not the Spencer Kate knows. It's as though the air around her gets colder; her blood has slowed to a crawl. This can't be.

'I know,' Spencer says, shaking his head. 'I feel sick just thinking about it now. And, of course, Amanda did what any right-minded parent would do and she went to the Head. I saw her on the day she came in. She was laughing with the school secretary while she waited. She looked exactly the same. She was wearing a coat I hadn't seen before. It was a sort of' – he looks up, as though the word is above him, in the air – 'brocade, I think it's called. Or embroidered. Heavy-looking, reds and browns. It suited her. I hadn't been sleeping. I'd lost about a stone. I knew then that I needed to give the whole thing up. And the weird thing is, I started to feel better almost as soon as I'd decided.'

'*That's* the weird thing?' Kate says. She has become more and more still as he has talked; first fidgeting through the discomfort, the worry of it; she's quietened, knowing that she needed to hear it. She knows this calm she feels won't last.

He shakes his head, half smiles, though his face drops to seriousness again when she doesn't respond. 'I know. The Head called me in that afternoon. I thought I was a goner, but he said that Amanda had explained what had happened, and that she took some responsibility for the situation and had requested that no formal action be taken, as long as I didn't make any inappropriate contact with her or Elise anymore.'

'That was all?' Kate asks. Considering what Spencer is facing for being with her – for doing literally nothing wrong – this seems absurd. And unfair. Still, Amanda sounds like the sort of woman who could bend the world to her will. Kate closes her eyes, forces herself to take a breath. She imagines Melissa, and her mother, both telling her off for blaming a woman for what a man did wrong. Reminds herself that she was the other woman, once; that Mike was married and what they did was way worse than Amanda, who, objectively, is guilty only of knowing what she wanted. Oh, her head hurts. Not as much as her heart.

Spencer sighs. 'Not really. He tore me off a strip. I can still remember exactly what he said. As though it was yesterday.'

'Tell me.' If she is hurting this badly then he can hurt, too.

He looks at her for a moment, sees that she's serious, closes his eyes, and almost recites: 'He said he was disappointed, that the minimum standard for a teacher, before anything else, was that a child should be safe and protected while in the school's care, and that included being kept safe and protected from any complications in adult relationships. If Ms Lomax—'

'Ms Lomax?' Kate interrupts, even though she knows the answer. She needs to be sure of every detail of this.

'Sorry. Amanda,' Spencer says. Kate hears how his mouth softens those hard 'a's.

'Go on,' she says.

He nods, looking like a man without a coat in a snowstorm. 'He said, if Ms Lomax had chosen to make a formal complaint, then it would have gone very badly for me, and for the school, and I had brought the profession into disrepute. He said I was lucky and that I should consider this episode a warning. I felt like a child, and an idiot.' It looks as though he has run out of breath, of steam. It looks as though he will cry. He rubs his hand across his eyes. Kate is looking at her hands, which are still in her lap. She can hear her own breathing: fast, shallow.

'Is that all?' she asks. She wants them to be at the end of this confession.

'Not quite.' She can see that he's bracing himself to say it, whatever it is, and then it comes out, all in a rush. 'He said that, from the outside, the situation

283

could look as though I was preying on a vulnerable family, and using a child's learning disability to further my own ends.' Kate looks across at him, her hand at her collarbone now, as though it had been pulled on a string. Hearing it said, so coldly, like that – knowing that someone else had articulated the fear that is now making its way through her, from the heart out, from the head down, from the stomach through – she shivers.

'He asked me what I was thinking of doing at the end of my probation year. The message was pretty clear. I said I had been thinking that maybe I should get some experience in a bigger school. He said he thought that was an excellent idea, and as long as I learned from my time here, I could be a good teacher. And that's it.'

'Yes.' She nods. Oh, what she would give for Daisy to wake now, to give her an excuse to move, to be away from this situation. She thinks of all the things she wants to say. They jostle at the base of her throat. *Why didn't you tell me sooner? Did Daisy's condition make me more, or less, attractive to you? How can I trust you? How could you? Don't you know how impossible I thought it was that I would ever meet someone, let alone someone who seemed so perfect for me?* 'This is why you didn't tell your mum about Daisy having cystic fibrosis, isn't it?'

He nods. 'I knew she would be concerned,' he says. 'I thought she would understand, once she'd met you. That this was different.'

Kate nods back, though she's not agreeing, she's not saying it's OK. 'But you still didn't tell me. Until today.'

They sit in silence for a minute, two, three. Then Spencer says, 'I should go.'

Kate looks up from her hands, her ragged, unvarnished fingernails. Amanda doubtless had a fortnightly manicure. She tells herself again that Amanda is not her enemy, closes her hands into fists so she cannot see her nails. 'Yes,' she says. He puts a kiss that she neither accepts nor rejects on the top of her head. Kate finds that she cannot move.

At the top of the stairs, he pauses. 'I always thought Amanda broke my heart,' he says, quietly, 'but I broke my own heart. I didn't listen to her. I didn't read the signs. I thought that wanting her to love me was' – he pauses, swallows – 'was romantic. I broke my own heart, then. But you could break it, now. And if you do, it's everything I deserve.'

'Yes.' Kate doesn't know what she is agreeing with. Maybe she is thinking of Mike, the way she made love out of nothing. Or maybe it's that yes, he deserves every painful word that she could throw his way. She doesn't know, but it is the only word she has, so she says it again, 'Yes.' And perhaps he understands or perhaps he doesn't, but he nods, says he will let her know what happens tomorrow, and then he's gone.

Chapter 20

Mid-April, the next day

KATE SPENT THE REST of Sunday night in a back-and-forth of justifying Spencer then condemning him, of composing texts to him that she deleted before sending, of wondering whether to call Melissa and then realising that if she tried to say any of this out loud she would have to believe it, have to admit that all she thought was true is – well, that's the thing. She just doesn't know. When she wakes, it's with the feeling of a bad dream unremembered.

The Monday-morning school drop-off is a hubbub with only Miss Orr in evidence. Kate texts Spencer to say she hopes that all goes well; because she does, and because she is half-hoping for a reply, for something that will make her feel the misery of last night less acutely. But she isn't surprised when no answer comes. She's not sure there's anything he can say.

She thinks he will let her know the outcome, but all day, Kate's phone refuses to ring. The only texts she gets are from Jo, suggesting that Daisy come for tea one day, and from her mother, offering to babysit one night. She spends a couple of hours looking through photos on her phone, deleting all of the duplicates and the blurred shots of Daisy, moving faster than the camera as she launches herself after the dogs or starts to laugh. Her heart lurches every time Spencer's face appears. When looking at photos gets too much, she heads to Facebook and makes herself cry looking at her friends' lives. Then – she will not be defined by the misery a man visits on her, ever again – she goes and sits in Adventures in Bread, drinking coffee and picking at a ham and cheese croissant, ordering new pyjamas online for her and Daisy, until pick-up time.

There's no sign of Spencer. Kate and Daisy go to the park with Jo, Jack and Amelia: Kate keeps her phone in her pocket rather than in her bag, ringer turned up as high as it will go. On the walk home, she asks Daisy, 'What did you do with Spencer today?'

Daisy looks up. 'It's Mr Swanson at school. You said that.'

Kate laughs, despite herself. 'Sorry. What did you do with Mr Swanson today?'

Daisy ponders. 'We growed some cress, but it won't be ready for a little while. And we talked about vegetables.'

'OK,' Kate says. 'Anything else? Was Mr Swanson there all the time?' *How*, she wonders, *did I become a woman pumping her child for information about her lover?*

Daisy rolls her eyes. 'I was busy,' she says, 'with Amelia.'

When they get home, they do jigsaws and colouring-in until teatime, when Kate suggests that they go to the Italian restaurant and get a takeaway pizza. (As she pays, she realises how much money she's spent today, just because she is sad. She can't let that go on.) She and Daisy eat on the sofa watching TV, tucked under a blanket, and Kate is almost enjoying herself, except that she's desperate to know what's happened to Spencer. It occurs to her, as she sits next to Daisy's bed after putting her light out, that she's acting as though the outcome of the disciplinary interview will tell her what to do next. But in her heart, she already knows what must come next. She cries, quietly, in the silent evening.

Spencer knocks on the door at 9.15, just as Kate was sure that he had left school, packed up the contents of his flat, and was already driving back to Edinburgh, and she would never see him again. It's raining. When she opens the door, he says, 'I didn't feel as though I should use my key.' He steps inside and puts out an arm; Kate walks into the space it makes for her, before she remembers how everything is broken. But the embrace is just right: warm and strong. He kisses the top of her head. 'Well, I still have a job,' he says.

'Come up.' Kate sits where she sat the previous evening, listening to his tale of Amanda and Elise; he sits where he sat, telling her the whole truth, but only because she had called him out on keeping a secret. 'Well? What happened? I was waiting for a message all day. I didn't know what to think.'

Spencer says, 'I know. I'm sorry. But – well, I had to promise to be completely professional in school time and so I thought if I sneaked off to the toilets to text you then that wasn't exactly starting as I meant to go on. But I was thinking of you.' Kate remembers how she loves his face, when it's serious. There's the shadow of a frown on his brow. He moves so he's sitting next to her, touches her face, lays his palm against her neck, below the ear, starts to pull her towards him. She puts her hand on his chest, pushes back. It cannot be this easy. He cannot pretend last night didn't happen.

'Tell me,' she says, 'what happened. Please.'

'Well' – Spencer leans back and looks up, recalling – 'Jane called me in at ten, and she was sitting behind her desk, so I thought it was going to be bad, but she said that she had spoken to several members of staff and although there were some areas of my conduct that I might want to reflect on, she had no real cause for concern and saw no reason to take the matter further.'

He smiles, his face inviting her to smile back, but she doesn't have a smile in her. She waits, tucking her hair out of the way. When the silence has expanded too far she asks, 'So what do you need to reflect on?'

'Well, same old, really. Try to be part of the school community. Although, to be fair, she was good about that – she did say that she can understand why I would stay out of the staffroom. And to make sure I follow the correct channels as far as Daisy is concerned.'

'What does that mean?'

'Oh,' Spencer says, 'nothing that I shouldn't have been doing already. Treating Daisy like any other child. If she's ill I take her to the office, and they call you. That kind of thing. I was a fool not to be doing it in the first place. It just – I know how you worry about her, and it seemed right to keep you updated. I couldn't really go to the office every day and ask them to call you to tell you that everything was OK.' He looks straight at her. 'I'm not saying I was right.'

Kate nods. It's hard to read his face.

'I don't deserve you, Kate,' he says.

'Jane doesn't know about Amanda and Elise?'

'No. If she did it would have been very different.'

'Like it's different for us.' Kate is fighting to keep her voice calm.

She hasn't felt like this since she found out that she was pregnant. Her mind is a Newton's Cradle, thoughts striking thoughts like ball bearings on wires, one extreme reached and then thoughts striking thoughts until they are back to the other extreme. After all, she has been the person that Spencer once was: dazzled by someone older, carried along, rescued from loneliness by something that looked like intimacy but turned out, when viewed from a distance, to be sex. Part of her wants to open her arms to him, tell him that he's been an idiot, and say that she understands. Because, at one end of this spectrum of thought, she does understand.

But. Spencer has lied to her. Spencer has lain in her bed and told her about girlfriends, about internet dating and missed chances. But he has never, once, mentioned Amanda. He has listened to her talk about Mike, about that awful madness and everything that came out of it, and he has never once said, let me tell you of my own disastrous love affair, the one that changed the course of my life.

And he lied about the tattoo. He didn't choose to omit, to brush over, to change the subject; he chose to lie. Kate – or at least the part of her that is looking for a place to hold onto, that will allow her to brush this off, to take a breath and see that it's not as bad as it seems – cannot think of a single lie that she has told Spencer.

He's at the other side of the coffee table, but it feels as though he's a continent away. If Kate reaches out, she feels as though she won't be able to touch him, or if she does, that there will be no answering warmth, nothing that she can feel. Because now she is thinking about why he lied.

A girl with Down's syndrome. Another with cystic fibrosis. It stands to reason that women with children with special needs are more likely to be single. The chances of a relationship withstanding the constant care, the leeching of attention, that a child with special needs requires are, Kate knows, lower than the chance of other relationships surviving. From what she's seen at the hospital and on the CF message boards, a child with CF will either weld a couple together or prise the relationship apart in the places where it isn't strong. *You could argue*, Kate thinks, *that a single teacher is more likely to form a relationship with a single parent of a child with special needs because teacher and parent will spend more time together. There will be meetings, school-door conversations, and if there's the slightest of attractions between the two then there will be opportunity for it to grow.* After all, that's what's happened here, in Throckton. That's what's happened to her.

'Do you mind if I get a glass of water?' Spencer asks.

'Of course not.' He stands, and walks over to the kitchen: Kate looks at his long tall body, the stoop of his shoulders; even though he has his back to her, she can visualise his face, in exact detail, as though she's had to learn him for a test. He turns on the tap, fills the glass, and sits down opposite her again.

'I'm so sorry, Kate. I should have told you, at the start.'

'Why didn't you?' *Say something good*, Kate thinks, *say something that will make this awful taste in my mouth go away. Because right now, all I can think is that you're saying whatever you need to say to put this right. And it's more complicated than that.*

He shakes his head. 'At the start, I thought if I told you, you would put two and two together and make five. I'm not stupid. I know it sounds creepy. And we were in your bed and you talked about Mike and I almost told you about Amanda. But then I thought, if I was you, what would I think of me, if I told you. So I thought if I waited, until you'd got to know me better, then you would understand better.'

'It's not a question of understanding,' Kate says, and she can hear how chill her voice is, but it's not surprising because her heart is growing colder. 'I think you underestimate me if you think I'm not capable of understanding what happened—'

'I didn't mean—' Spencer says, but Kate holds up a hand that would stop traffic.

'I think you underestimate me if you think I'm not capable of understanding what happened,' Kate repeats, 'and I can see why it would be a hard conversation to have, especially at the beginning. But we've spent such a lot of time together. I know it's only been four months, but we've been together such a lot of that time.' There's a pleading in her tone: *go back in time, tell me, fix this*. She thinks of the quiet hospital evenings, Spencer, a fixture from 4 p.m. until 9 p.m., or later if the nurse on duty was a romantic. Weekends where they've barely been parted. Spencer, lying in her bed, stroking her hair, asking questions about her parents, Throckton, the plans she'd had before Daisy: 'tell me more, Kate,' he'd said, and she'd laughed, and said, 'I don't think there's anything else to tell you. You've wrung me dry.'

'I know,' Spencer says. 'I just didn't want to screw this up. I thought I would tell you about it on our weekend away. Then Daisy was ill. When Daisy was in hospital, I didn't want to worry you, and when she was out you looked so tired, and I didn't want to spoil things—'

'What did you think would happen?' Kate can feel herself getting angry now, the numbness that's filled her fading, and the heat setting in. 'Did you think I would never find out?'

'I don't know.' Spencer shakes his head.

'And all this with Bridget Piper,' Kate says, her voice getting louder and then, with a glance at Daisy's bedroom door, deliberately softer. 'Wouldn't that have been a good time to tell me? When you were being accused of an inappropriate relationship with the mother of a pupil with special educational needs? Did that not' – she pauses, takes a breath, measures out the next words – 'jog your memory?'

'I wanted to tell you,' Spencer says.

'Oh, well, that's all right then.' Kate gets up, not because she needs anything, just because she can't stay sitting. She walks to the sink, runs water into a glass, takes a mouthful, pours it away.

'I almost did,' Spencer says. He gets up, walks over to her. 'I'm sorry, Kate.'

'Why didn't you?' Kate asks. 'You're not a child, Spencer. You didn't need permission. I was here. All you had to do was open your bloody mouth.'

'I know' – he says – 'but – well – it's complicated.'

'Really? it seems very simple to me.'

Spencer shakes his head. 'I mean, with school. If I'd told you when – when I told you about what Bridget had said—'

'Which would have been a good time to tell me, all of those other opportunities having been missed—'

'If I'd told you when I told you what Bridget had said—' Spencer repeats. Here's where the argument is bigger than the two of them, unstoppable. Right here. Kate's gaze, which has been fixed on her toes, or maybe her tightly crossed arms, flicks up to his face, down again. 'If I'd told you then, it might have made things worse.'

'Unlike now?' Kate says.

'I mean—' Spencer says, his voice now with a deliberately controlled edge to it, as though he is in the right, and she is being unreasonable. Her heart tightens a little more; something in her sours. 'If I'd told you then, you might have said something to someone – Wendy or Jo – and if you had—'

'If I'd told the truth,' Kate says into the pause, 'because you had put me and Daisy before you and your job, yes?'

'Well, if the Head had got wind of it, she would have had to investigate. It would have looked like – predatory behaviour. Jane probably would have called it as a child safeguarding concern, which would have been how it looked. She would have had no choice.'

Just for a moment, Kate is on his side. She is looking straight into his eyes, and she understands. Her look says that he might be a liar, a terrible boyfriend, that she could retell the tale of their relationship as one in which she was manipulated by someone with a thing for vulnerable women, but that as far as Daisy is concerned, his behaviour is impeccable, unquestionable.

'I wouldn't have said anything, Spencer,' and she hears how his name has two soft S sounds when she says it, 'or thought – what you think I thought.'

'I know.' He stands, takes a step towards her. She takes a half step back. It's almost progress. 'But headteachers can't be too careful. And I would have been suspended, and God knows how long the investigation would have taken. By the time I was cleared, Throckton would be full of people saying that there's no smoke without fire and it would go on my permanent record. That wouldn't have been the end of my career, but it probably would have been the end of my job here – even if I could have come back to work it would have been awful. You can imagine. I couldn't risk telling you in case you said something.'

She can imagine. Kate looks away, down. 'So you risked me – us – instead of risking the career that you've told me you're having doubts about? The career that you think you might give up to work in a cinema.'

'I don't think that's fair.' Spencer looks empty, exhausted.

'Fair?' Kate says, and this time her voice is loud and she's making no attempt to be quiet. 'I don't think that's a word you should be using. Do you think you've been fair? Coming round here and being all—' She wants to cry, but she bites her tears away. 'You've been so – perfect – with all your support and understanding and how lovely you are and how funny and how you've made my life easier, and made me feel as though – as though' – the tears won't stay back, they are running down her face now – 'as though a different life is possible. And now—'

'I'm sorry, Kate. I'm so sorry.' She looks into his face. He is crying too. Well, let him. 'Kate, you have to see. I might be a fool, I might have made a wrong call. But I love you.'

'You could have told me and asked me not to say anything,' she says. She's not accusing him, anymore.

'I know. But I didn't think that was right. I know how honest you are.'

'Then you know how much I value honesty.'

'Yes, I know that.' His voice is quiet and even.

And then they are calm. It's all said: or rather, the appetite for going over it, arguing about it, has gone, from Kate; and Spencer looks as though he has no energy for anything. She looks at him, wiping her eyes; if he can see how hurt, how disappointed she is, so much the better. He has turned out to be too good to be true, right here in front of her eyes.

Cautious, he holds out his arms to her, as though wordlessness might work where words have failed. She walks towards him, puts her head against his chest. His arms go round her, gently, and although she leaves her hands by her sides, not embracing him, the weight of her body cleaves to his.

But only for a moment.

Kate pulls away.

'I'm sorry, Spencer. I can't.' She wishes she could. But there's a hurt here, too deep to be healed by touch, by apology, by the hope that tomorrow will be better. She looks into his face, a sad, tired mirror of her own. 'I want you to go.'

'Go for tonight or go forever?'

'I think – forever.' Kate's voice is quiet. She hears that it has no tone: no disappointment, no malice. There's no point, now. He'll go, and she'll get into bed, switch off the light, lying unmoving with her eyes open, trying to make it feel as though she can bear it. She almost convinces herself that she has borne worse.

Chapter 21

Mid-April, the following Saturday

KATE DRAGS HERSELF THROUGH the rest of the week. It feels long. She lies awake at night and dozes during the day, when Daisy is at school. She finds one of Spencer's ties on the floor by the bed and sleeps with it under her pillow. She tells Melissa about the break up, and Melissa kisses her fingertips, holds them out to her phone screen, and says, 'Babe, I wish I could make this better for you.'

Kate hasn't told anyone about Amanda. She's not sure she ever will. It's too humiliating, to have imagined that she and Spencer had something special when, really, she was no more than his usual – you might say target – woman. SEN child, single, money in the bank. All she says to Melissa is that he isn't as perfect as he seemed.

On Saturday, Wendy, Jilly, Kate and Daisy go bridesmaid-dress shopping. The wedding party arrives in Marsham in time for coffee, Wendy having gamely played I Spy with Daisy all the way in the car and on the short walk to the café that's their first port of call. When they get to 'something beginning with Buh Cuh' (Big Cake) Kate calls a halt. They sit at the table in the window, and while they wait for their coffee and pains au chocolat, Wendy brings an iPad out of her bag and shows Kate and Daisy pictures of the bridal couple's outfits. Wendy will be in a soft, sea-green, silky dress, while Jilly will wear something long, sleek and navy. Kate smiles and does her best to join in with the chatter, to match the excitement, though Wendy's frequent worried glances her way show that she isn't doing a very good job.

Daisy is still looking at the brides' dresses, the smallest of puckers in her smooth little forehead. Time for Kate to intervene.

'Aren't they lovely?' Kate prompts.

'Yes.' Daisy still looks doubtful, though, and Kate can see that she's wondering what the implications of such a non-traditional approach is for her brides-maid's dress. She wonders how her daughter has such clear ideas, already, of what a bride should be. It's depressing. She pins her smile on tighter.

'We think any colour will go with green and blue,' Wendy says, 'so you can choose whatever you like, Daisy. We're going to a very special shop next, and we'll see what they have.'

All of the pink dresses in the bridal shop are taste-ful shades of shell and rose, and perhaps that's what leads Daisy to fix on a bolder turquoise. Whatever her reason, the dress looks beautiful, making her eyes shine and her skin glow. It has what Daisy calls a 'stick-out skirt', her main prerequisite for a bridesmaid's dress, and the neckline, waist and hem have lines of tiny, sequinned flowers. They are halfway through putting it on when Daisy has a coughing fit; Kate rubs her back until it passes, and cannot help but put her hand on her daughter's forehead, just in case. 'I'm not hot, Mummy,' Daisy says, with a slightly panicked expression, 'we don't need to go home early.'

'It's OK, darling,' Kate says. 'I'm just checking.'

'Is there anything you need?' the sales assistant calls through the curtain. She sounds anxious, but to Kate's experienced ear it sounds more like worry for the dress than for the bridesmaid herself.

'We're fine.' Kate pulls back the curtain and Daisy twirls in front of Wendy and Jilly, who make appreciative noises.

'The – equipment – might catch' – the sales assistant looks at Daisy's arm, nervous – 'and would you want something with sleeves to go over it?'

'Oh, the line is coming out next week,' Kate says, and then adds, looking the saleswoman straight in the eye, 'though I don't think it should be a barrier to Daisy wearing what she wants. And anyone who thinks a PICC line has to be hidden in case it spoils a wedding should be ashamed of themselves.'

The PICC-line removal won't come a moment too soon. It's not so much that the line is bothering Daisy:

Kate is more concerned that it isn't, and she's become so used to it that she never gives it a second thought. Kate has noticed that she holds her arm at an angle to stop the line from getting in the way without realising she's doing it, and puts out her arm for Kate to put on the plastic protector as though it's a normal part of anyone's bath time routine.

'Well, that's good,' Wendy says, then adds, 'Not for the wedding, I mean, for Daisy.'

'I know.' Kate smiles. Daisy is standing on a plinth in front of a triple mirror, admiring herself from all sides, while the assistant tries to measure her; the dress is a little too short and pulls under the arms, so it will certainly be too small in seven weeks' time. They will collect a made-to-measure version the week before the wedding. By then, Kate thinks, she might feel better about Spencer. But a part of her – the part that knew, always, that Mike didn't love her, the part that was telling her Daisy was ill even as she and Spencer drove away for their weekend together – doubts it.

Still, she is here with three happy, excited people, and she tries to be carried along with their mood. Off-duty Wendy is funny and playful, trying on veils when the shop assistant's back is turned and making Daisy laugh. Jilly is quieter, and her gaze follows Wendy everywhere she goes. She tells Kate that she and Wendy have been together for almost two decades, and that they have been campaigning for equal marriage for as long as there has been a campaign. But they have waited for their own wedding until Jilly's father died.

'I know we're hypocrites,' she says. Kate shakes her head.

'Things just aren't that easy,' she replies.

All in all, it's a successful day for the bridesmaid-to-be. By the end of it, Daisy has white patent shoes, tights with a sparkle, and the promise of a crown of flowers for her hair on the big day. And she still has energy left for more I Spy in the car on the way home.

'I spy with my little eye, something beginning with Buh,' Wendy says, and Daisy tries Bus and Blue Car before guessing Bridesmaid with a gurgle of laughter. Kate, in the passenger seat, watches the rain on the windscreen and tries not to cry.

Wendy gets out of the car to say goodbye to Kate and Daisy. She hugs Kate, tight, and says, 'If it's any comfort, he's in as much of a state as you are.' Kate doesn't know whether it helps or not. She takes Daisy by the hand and turns away.

Chapter 22

Late April to Early June

IT'S THE THURSDAY OF the following week, and Kate and Daisy are heading to Richenda and Blake's house for dinner. Kate has told her mother, quietly, that everything is over with Spencer. She hasn't said why, and she hasn't said how. She has had no energy left, after getting through the day. And she hasn't said anything to Daisy, telling herself over and over that the time isn't right. The irony of this is not lost on her. But Daisy is a child who deserves protection. Whereas Kate is an adult and she deserved an honesty from Spencer that she did not get.

'Will Spencer be there?' Daisy asks as they round the corner onto her mother's road.

'No,' Kate says, 'Spencer won't be there. He has lots of things to do on school nights.'

'He used to come on school nights, before the Easter holidays,' Daisy says. Kate recognises her own mild tone, used when she needs to help her daughter understand something.

Now is probably as good a time as any. She can get it over with, and then her mother and Blake will be a distraction. 'Daisy, things have changed a little bit. Spencer isn't going to be coming round, anymore.'

'Because he's busy?' Daisy asks.

It's tempting to say yes, but the thought of the untruth spikes at her. 'No. Because he and I have – decided – that he isn't going to be my boyfriend any-more.' *Don't cry*, she tells herself, the way she tells herself most days. Although it's not so much 'don't cry' as 'cry later, when Daisy's in bed'.

Daisy has stopped in the street, and is looking up at Kate. 'But you said we were going to be a family, with Spencer,' she says.

'We were, but—' Kate says. She wishes she had stuck with Spencer being busy, at least for now.

'A family,' Daisy says, stubbornness as well as patience in her voice now, 'is a family. You can't undo a family.'

'No,' Kate says, 'but sometimes things change. And you said you liked it when it was just us, remember?' Kate thinks of the time before she met Spencer, the nights she and Daisy would fall asleep together in her bed.

'Sometimes I did,' Daisy says, darkly, opening the gate to her grandmother's house, 'but you say people are allowed to have a bad mood. I miss Spencer.'

'You see him every day at school.'

Daisy sighs, and looks at Kate as though she is a particularly trying doll. 'That's not what I mean,

Mummy. And anyway, he's Mr Swanson at school. It's not the same.'

Kate can't help herself. 'Why is it different?'

'Because at school he's like a grown-up, and when he's at home he's like one of us. I liked that better.'

'I know, darling,' Kate says. She sees the dogs running down the path to greet them, and she's grateful. 'I'm sorry things are different, but they just are. We need to get used to them.'

'What about the summer holiday things we were going to do with' – she looks puzzled for a moment – 'Mr Spencer?'

'I expect we'll still do some of them. But on our own, or with Auntie Lissa or Granny and Blake.'

She follows Daisy into the garden; Daisy greets Hope, Beatle, and Richenda, in that order, then gets on the trampoline. Her cough is receding as spring starts to edge into summer. Kate hopes that by the time autumn comes again her lungs will be strong enough to withstand the winter.

'Do you want to make a bouncing routine, Granny?'

'I can't think of anything I'd like more, Daisy.'

Kate goes into the kitchen to say hello to Blake and see if there's anything she can do. There isn't, so she sits on the sofa and pretends to read the paper until lunch is ready.

After their meal, Richenda and Kate sit in the garden, drinking wine; Blake and Daisy have taken the dogs for a walk.

'Tell me how you're doing, darling,' Richenda says.

'I don't know.'

Over the last week, Kate has collected up the things Spencer has left at her place over the months. It's a sad little bagful – a toothbrush, a razor, deodorant, shaving balm, the tie she kept under her pillow, socks, a book about cinema classics he'd lent her – and she feels sorry every time she looks at it sitting at the top of the stairs. But, all of that week, even though she'd had times when she could see, very clearly, why he had done the things that he'd done, and that after the first untruth it was more and more difficult to undo the situation he had got himself into, she kept coming back to the hurt of the lies, the roadblock those lies had created for them. She knew she was right when she had said that she couldn't forgive him.

'Do you want to tell me what happened?'

Kate shakes her head. 'It doesn't matter now. All that matters is that it did.'

'Well, if you change your mind, I'll always listen.'

'I know, Mum.' Kate hears how her voice is frayed and shaken. She won't cry. She is so sick of crying. Just for a moment, she wants to tell Richenda all of it, from the beginning, but she cannot imagine saying the words 'Amanda' and 'Elise' out loud to someone else, seeing her mother's face as she understands Spencer's history and what it means for Kate. Instead, she says, 'He told me. The first time I met him. He said, "You should watch out for me." And you warned me, and so did Melissa. If I'm miserable—' she almost says 'heartbroken', but that's such a romantic word, and what she's feeling is a brutal pain, in bone and muscle and blood, '—it's my own fault.'

'Oh, Kate.' Richenda looks as though she is going to hug her, so Kate gets up, quickly. She does not trust herself with comfort, with touch.

'I'll be OK,' she says, but she doesn't believe it.

Richenda sighs. 'Have you given him his things back?'

'That's not going to make me feel any better,' Kate says. The only thing she dislikes more than walking past the bag of Spencer's things at the top of the stairs is the idea of not walking past it.

'It won't make it better, but it might make it easier. Have you and Daisy got plenty of plans? Things to look forward to?'

Kate sighs. 'Melissa did invite me to a party. Not for a month or so.' She's delighted that Melissa's paid internship has turned into a permanent job, but not sure she can celebrate as a friend should. And anything further ahead than tomorrow feels an unimaginable stretch of time away.

'There you go, then. Book your trains now. Daisy can stay here. At least you have half term coming up in a few weeks.'

'Yes,' Kate says, but she means 'no'. Because however awful a possible twice-a-day glimpse of Spencer might be, definitely not seeing him feels worse. She

311

wonders if he'll go to Scotland, if he'll tell his parents that it's over; and she realises with a thud inside that, however much his parents might have liked her, they will be relieved. For them, she will always be an echo, an extension, of Amanda, of their son's ability to find trouble in the shape of women like her.

Later that evening, when Daisy is soundly asleep, her cough rocking her frame, but her eyes firmly closed, Kate texts Spencer and asks him to come and collect his things.

'Is this really it?' he asks when she answers the door.

'I can't trust you,' she says. She tries to make it sound like a fact, not an accusation. She's so tired.

He stands for a moment, arms crossed, looking at his shoes, and then he says, 'Well, I suppose it's what I deserve,' just that, and he takes the bag and goes. After the way they have conducted their relationship – the talking, the touching, the deliberate, committed closeness – it seems the wrong ending, or no kind of ending at all. *But it's the ending I've got*, she thinks as she makes her way back upstairs. *It's time to be an adult about it, and try to feel good about my decision.*

Kate counts down the time to half term. As the next few weeks grumble past, she feels as though she's mastering the art of not-quite seeing Spencer if he's in the school playground. It's easier than pretending to smile. But she can't handle even the glimpses anymore, and

Wendy's sympathetic, school-gate looks make everything feel worse.

As it happens, half term isn't terrible. Daisy goes to two birthday parties, both of which delight her and wear her out; one of them is Serena's daughter's, so Jo offers to collect Daisy and drop her off. Kate imagines she'll have an afternoon of moping – she can't seem to do anything else, no matter how many talking-tos she gives herself – but she falls into a dreamless sleep so deep that the bell doesn't wake her immediately when Jo returns three hours later. When she opens the door, Daisy has her hands on her hips and greets her with, 'I was starting to think you had forgot me.' Kate and Daisy go walking with Blake and the dogs on the days that he's not working; her mother takes a day off and she, Kate and Daisy spend a day in London at the Natural History Museum. There's a morning at the soft-play centre, and a day when Kate and Daisy take the bus to Marsham, go to the cinema, and then go out for lunch, and Kate is almost happy as she and Daisy share a pizza and talk about what they would put on a pizza they made themselves. ('Bananas and avocados and cheese,' Daisy says, 'because then in your mouth there will be a beautiful squish,' and Kate laughs and thinks, *look at that, I can laugh*.) Wendy and Jilly are on what they are calling a pre-honeymoon in Italy, because Wendy can't take time off during the term; but on the weekend before school starts again, Richenda and Blake invite them all for lunch, and Kate looks at her daughter and her family and her friends, and thinks about Melissa and Jo, and decides that if this is her lot she'll be happy. Happiness still seems a long way off, but she'll get there.

When she sees Spencer on the first day back to school, though, she thinks, perhaps, that not-unhappy is a more realistic goal.

The bed is still too big, and the flat is still too quiet, the evenings too long and her body aches for sex and laughter and having someone to match her stride. She supposes she will get used to it, sometime; life, after all, is not so very different to the way it was before she met Spencer. Daisy is thriving in the warming days, all of her test results showing she's as well as she can be. At the hospital, Chantelle asks Kate if she might be anaemic, as she's paler than usual; Kate says she's just tired. But it does feel, a little, as though the colour has gone: from her, from everything.

The next weekend, Daisy pleads for a sleepover at Granny's house, and Kate agrees, even though the last thing she wants is a night in the flat on her own. She'll do some sorting, maybe get together Daisy's too-small clothes and those things of hers that she will never use again, ready to go to the charity shop.

'And tomorrow' – Richenda twinkles at Daisy when she collects her – 'why don't we get the train to Marsham and buy Mummy something beautiful to wear for the wedding?'

'I was going to wear what I wore for your wedding,' Kate says.

'That was December,' Richenda says. 'This wedding's in June. You can't wear velvet. And if Daisy's having a new dress, you should, too. My treat.'

Kate closes her eyes. She thinks of Marsham, Saturday chatter, couples everywhere; the fact that she can't justify a new dress but has to have one bought by her mother. She would much rather spend tomorrow under the duvet, dozing, crying, pretending she isn't checking her phone. But when she opens her eyes, ready to make an excuse, Richenda and Daisy are looking at her, expectantly, and she thinks, *Well, at least Mum will talk to Daisy and I can be quiet.*

By the time they have arrived in Marsham, had coffee, and been to a bookshop, Daisy is hungry and ready for an early lunch; afterwards, they head to the department store that Richenda favours and Kate would never think to go into, where it transpires that Richenda has booked an appointment with a personal shopper. Kate doesn't know whether to run or be grateful; she wishes she'd put on a better pair of knickers, as the ones she's wearing have the elastic coming away around the leg. 'How long have you had this planned?' Kate asks.

'Oh.' Richenda shrugs. 'I made the appointment on the off-chance. I need something to wear for the wedding, too.' Richenda is coming with Kate, as Blake

315

has to work; Spencer will be a guest too, and Kate is almost sure he won't bring a date.

'Hmmm.' Kate is unconvinced, but she does have a mild hangover – she somehow drank a whole bottle of wine herself, last night – and a not improved by the shop's lighting, so she decides on the path of least resistance. Daisy sits on a velvet pouffe and watches as Kate tries on half a dozen dresses. Daisy 'oohs' at them all, and Richenda nods encouragingly, but none of them feel quite right to Kate. One dress is too flouncy, another too low, another too long, another too busy. Then the personal shopper brings in a jumpsuit in dusty purple and a pair of cream mules with gold embroidery and a low wooden heel. Kate puts them on, and looks in the mirror; all three of the adults exhale, in a way that says, mission accomplished, and Daisy claps her hands. The jumpsuit is a perfect fit, tailored and elegant. The personal shopper has brought 'statement earrings', which would look fantastic on Melissa, but Kate will wear plain silver studs, or the daisy earrings Spencer gave her for Christmas, if she can bear to, just to show him that she isn't petty. She has a silk scarf she'll wrap at her throat. But – 'It's awfully expensive, Mum,' Kate says. 'For one day.'

Daisy frowns. 'But it's the most important day of our life, Mummy,' she says. Kate makes a mental note to talk to her about whose important day it is, along with the relative importance of marriage in a woman's life. She knows that princess games are a favourite in the school playground at the moment; maybe she needs to find a way to offset them, somehow. She's been lax of late, letting Daisy watch TV shows she would normally distract her from. *Something else to fix*, she thinks tiredly to herself, *when I have the energy*.

Richenda laughs. 'There are going to be a lot of important days, Daisy. When you become a champion trampolinist, for one.'

'Is that really a job?' Daisy asks, and Kate says of course it is, and goes to change back into her jeans and T-shirt, feeling shabby in more ways than one.

Daisy falls asleep on the train home. She lies with her head on Kate's lap. Richenda, sitting alongside, rests her hand first on Daisy's head and then on Kate's knee. 'You're doing fine,' she says.

Kate shakes her head. 'That's easy for you to say.'

Richenda tips her head towards her daughter, so that their heads touch. 'Well, it isn't. Trust me. I know what it's like to be unhappy.'

Chapter 23

Early June

FRIDAY NIGHTS NOW ARE usually a sort of relief, with the school week over, but not when there's a wedding that Spencer will be attending the next day. Kate goes to bed early, but then lies awake until one, wakes at three in tears, and goes back to sleep an hour later. It feels as though Kate has only just closed her eyes when Daisy is in bed with her: 'Mummy, Mummy, it's Bridesmaid Day!'

Kate looks at the clock. 'It's twenty to six on Bridesmaid Day, Daisy,' she says. 'So we really should stay in bed for a bit longer. Come and cuddle in.' She pulls the warm, wriggly body next to her, and tries to get back to sleep. Kate feels as though her heart ought to be starting to mend by now. It isn't. If anything, she feels worse as time goes on. She puts it down to tiredness. That and the fact that she was a little late collecting Daisy from school yesterday, and it was just her in the playground and Spencer at the classroom door, waiting. He'd looked at her, into her face, for just a second, and she had wanted nothing so much as to put out a hand and say – but that's the thing. Say what? *Why didn't you tell me the truth from the start? I wish things had been different? I miss you?* All of those things would be true but none of them took her anywhere. And by the time she'd thought about it, he'd said, 'See you at the wedding, Daisy,' nodded to Kate, and gone back inside. And she had felt any healing of her heart undone.

There's no way Daisy's going to settle and Kate isn't going to get back to sleep, so they get up and Kate microwaves pancakes and grills bacon and they eat them in front of *Finding Dory*, to fill the time before they need to go to Wendy and Jilly's. Kate will leave Daisy there and go to her mother's, and from there the two of them will go to the hairdresser, then back to her mother's to get ready, and they'll take a taxi to the hotel. Kate would have been just as happy without the fuss, but Richenda insisted, booked and will pay for everything. Kate wonders if it would have been different without her broken heart. But her mum seems to be at least as excited as Daisy about the wedding, rather than taking pity on Kate. Perhaps the elaborate preparations will cheer Kate up. Or at least make her feel sufficiently armoured to get through the day.

As soon as Kate and Daisy leave the flat, look up at the story-book blue sky, and say that it's a lovely day for a wedding, a momentum begins that carries Kate through. She has a glass of Buck's Fizz with the brides, gives Wendy the pack of tablets and snacks and the list of timings, waves to Daisy, who is having her fingernails painted, and then arrives at Richenda's with time for a coffee in the garden before they walk to the hairdresser. Richenda has her hair cut while Kate's is put up, a feat only a hairdresser can manage because it's so soft and slippery. Then it's back to her mother's, for more coffee, and sausage sandwiches provided by Blake, who says, 'You never know how long it's going to be until you get fed at a wedding.' Richenda changes into a fuchsia-coloured dress, and wraps a cream pashmina round her shoulders; Kate puts on the jumpsuit, slips her feet into the mules, and looks in the mirror, where she sees someone who looks – well, like an adult, like a confident, well-put-together woman. That's something. She slides her shoulders back and holds her head high, tries a smile at herself in the mirror. Then she adds her usual slick of mascara and a sheer red lipstick. Her mother's make-up takes a little longer, and Kate sits on Richenda's bed and watches as the foundation, eyeshadow, blusher go on. 'I don't remember ever watching you do this before,' Kate says.

Her mother's reflection pauses, eyebrow pencil in hand, and looks at her. 'I don't think I wore make-up much when you were little,' she says. 'And – well, things are different now.'

Kate nods. 'Did you ever think about being on your own? Instead of with Blake?'

Richenda doesn't hesitate. She's dotting highlighter along the tops of her cheeks, blending it in. 'You say that as though I went from one man to another. But, actually, I went from being lonely and' – she pauses for a moment, takes a breath – 'unseen, to finding real love for the first time in my life. When I split up with your father it was because I had finally worked out who I was and what I needed. I'd have been happy on my own. Though I'm happy that Blake's here. If you see what I mean. Your happiness shouldn't be entirely contingent on someone else loving you, or someone else being there.'

'Yes.' Kate looks at her hands. 'I'm sorry. I didn't mean—'

'There's no need to apologise,' Richenda says. 'But you of all people know that how things look might not be how they are.'

'Me of all people?'

Richenda turns from the mirror; Kate is struck by how bright her eyes are, how the happiness of the last few years has made her mother virtually unrecognisable compared to her childhood-memories mum, who was dull and carping. 'The assumptions that people make about Daisy are a long way from the truth, aren't they?' Richenda asks. 'And the assumptions that people have made about Spencer, too. You know the truth is different. It's not about drawing a line from one thing to another. It's about understanding how complicated life can be.'

'Yes,' and Kate would like to take hold of her mother, hug her; but there's the sound of the taxi's horn and they are on their way. They are driven through Throckton and up, over the hill, along country lanes, towards the country hotel where the wedding will take place. As the car turns up the drive to the hotel, Richenda takes Kate's hand. 'Are you going to be OK? Seeing Spencer?'

'I'm going to have to be,' Kate says, 'and I have to see him at school, most days, anyway.' *It's not about me*, she reminds herself, as she steps from the car, finds her balance and breath. *But it's not school, either.* This is the first time, since he collected his things, that she will have seen Spencer in a setting where they are free to talk to each other if they want to. Kate cannot help but feel herself pulled to him. There is more to her than Spencer. But despite all of her effort, the talking-tos that Kate is giving to herself almost constantly, the yearning for Spencer isn't fading. It's quite the opposite. But the fact remains that – although cystic fibrosis is not Down's syndrome, and Kate is infuriated by people who think medical conditions, physical disadvantages and learning disabilities are all interchangeable – there's something in Spencer's behaviour that she cannot argue away, cannot make peace with.

In the orangery, rows of white chairs, blue organza bows on the backs, are filling up with people. Wendy and Jilly have invited sixty guests to their wedding. It had sounded like a lot to Kate, but she realises, as she surveys the six rows of five chairs on either side of the aisle, that sixty isn't that many people at all, and Spencer is going to be unavoidable. She reminds herself, for what feels like the millionth time, that today is not about her and Spencer, and if she focuses on the wedding, on Daisy, then she will be fine. She and Richenda sit at the aisle-end of the third row, so that it's easy for Daisy to find her mother if she needs to. At the front, the registrar is waiting next to a table bearing a quill pen in a pot, a wedding register, and an arrangement of blue and purple blooms with silver-green foliage.

Then, music swells and the waiting family and friends stand, with a rustle and hum of expectation; the registrar moves to the front and centre of the space at the end of the aisle, holds out her hands in welcome. As rehearsed, Daisy walks down the aisle ahead of Wendy and Jilly, a freesia-and-ivy crown on her head, holding a pillow on which two rings lie. There's a chorus of 'oohs' as she comes. Kate feels Richenda's hand on her arm, but she's not sure who is steadying whom, because all of a sudden she wants to cry, and for the first time in weeks it's nothing to do with Spencer. Daisy looks beautiful, of course she does. But she also looks solemn, and serious, and a lot like Kate and a little bit like Mike. She looks strong and healthy and a million precious minutes from when she was in a hospital bed four months ago, and the next time she will be. Kate is filled with love and pride and the pure, sheer joy of being Daisy's mother, gratitude for her wellness, hope for her future. She stops being brave and lets herself admit that dealing with everything that Daisy faces is hard, a constant stone in the shoe on even the happiest days. Her mother hands her a tissue.

When Daisy has delivered the rings, and been kissed by Jilly and Wendy, she does exactly as rehearsed again, and goes to her designated chair on the front row and sits down. But she can't resist looking round at Kate with a big smile that sets Kate's tears off all over again. Fortunately, she manages not to sob; fortunately, almost everyone in the room is in tears too, as Jilly and Wendy repeat the vows the registrar takes them through, and then make their own. Jilly's sister sings 'It Had to Be You' and then Spencer – who must have been sitting behind Kate and Richenda, because Kate hadn't seen him until now – comes to the front and reads a poem that begins, 'I want to be your friend for ever and ever without break or decay.' Kate grips her own hands, tight, in an attempt to stop her wedding-appropriate tears turning into a heartbroken bawl. Spencer is wearing a navy suit with a pale-blue shirt and a dark pink tie, and is more handsome than ever. He looks from the book in his hand only to Wendy and Jilly as he reads, but as he goes back to his place he grins at Daisy and then catches Kate's eye, gives the gentlest of smiles, and puts his hand to his heart. Kate looks from his face to her hands, gripping each other in her lap, and wishes love was as easy as Wendy and Jilly have just made it seem. She reminds herself that Spencer did the reading because Wendy's family haven't spoken to her since she came out. Nothing is easy. But nothing seems as hard, all of a sudden, as being in the same room as Spencer, but not by his side.

The table plan is kind to Kate. She and Spencer are not in each other's eyelines, so she isn't constantly catching herself sneaking a look at him, or trying not to. Daisy runs between her mother and granny and the brides, and when she is thanked and given a gift she gets a laugh when she looks over and asks, 'Mummy, can I open it now?' When the main celebration is over, people start to wander around; Kate is waved over by Wendy, standing hand in hand with Jilly. Kate leaves Richenda in conversation with one of the other people at their table, a retired school librarian who's worked with Wendy before, and goes to talk to the brides.

'That was beautiful,' she says. 'I trust Daisy behaved? I tried to explain that today was all about the two of you, but I don't think she was convinced—'

Wendy and Jilly smile at each other, and Wendy says, 'She was lovely.'

Jilly adds, 'I've never seen anyone – adult, let alone child – eat so many croissants at one sitting.'

Kate laughs. 'I know.'

Wendy adds, 'She's had all of her meds and she actually fell asleep in the car on the way here, which we thought was probably best.'

'I wondered if she would,' Kate says. 'Thank you for asking her to be your bridesmaid. She'll never forget it.'

'Neither will we.' Jilly touches Kate's arm above the elbow. 'Thank you. It's been a joy to have her as part of our day.'

And then Spencer's there, filling the space in front of them, and Kate can't breathe, for a second. He embraces Jilly and Wendy, then looks at Kate, straight into her eyes, and says, 'Kate.' She realises that she's missed every single thing about him, even the way he says her name.

'Spencer.' Her voice is steadier than she thought it would be. 'Hello.'

She feels Jilly and Wendy start to move away, quells the impulse to take one of them by the hand, to make them stay.

'I'd really like to talk to you,' he says.

'I don't know,' Kate says. She really doesn't. Talking might make things worse, though she can't imagine how. It might make things easier, but she's not sure that she's ready for that, either. She realises that she doesn't want to be over him. Not really.

'Please,' he says.

'Not here.' Kate feels panicky, teary.

Wendy is closer than Kate thought, still within earshot. 'There's a room,' she says, 'out of the double doors, on the left. Where we left our things. You won't be disturbed. If you want some privacy.'

Kate leads the way, aware of Spencer behind her; she looks around and sees that Daisy is sitting on Richenda's lap, talking, laughing. She won't be missed. The room Wendy mentioned is a small sitting room. There are bags – including Daisy's – and jackets, an opened bottle of champagne in an ice bucket on a table. 'This must be where they waited,' Kate says, just for the sake of there being something in the air that isn't the sound of their breathing.

'Looks like it.' Spencer nods. He runs his hands through his hair. He's jacketless now and Kate can see the soft lines from where his shirt has been creased in the packet. 'Now I've got you to talk to I don't know what to say,' he says. 'I have no idea where to start. Except that you look beautiful.'

Kate ignores the compliment, or perhaps stores it away in case she needs it, later. 'Do you think there's anything to say?' She means it as a simple question – she's not sure of the answer herself – but it sounds like accusation. 'You haven't been in touch before now.'

He sighs. 'I know. But I couldn't, could I? Because after everything with Amanda, all I told you, what would you think? If I tried to talk to you when you asked me not to? I would be doing the same thing as I did with her. That's how it would look. You'd think it was a pattern.'

'I—' Kate begins, but she stops. She feels as though she needs a whole new vocabulary, nuanced words for love and fear and disappointment, a way to express herself that will take them back to where it seemed that they belonged.

They are both still standing. 'I've been wishing I'd explained it all better,' Spencer says.

This stings. 'I don't know whether that would have helped. It wasn't the quality of the explanation that was the problem.' Everything she says sounds trivial; whenever she opens her mouth it seems she's starting from the wrong place.

'I mean, the whole thing,' he says. He's walking, two steps one way, two steps another, while Kate stands still, watching him. She can't take her eyes off him. He can't seem to look at her for more than a second or two. 'From the beginning. I should have told you everything. But I knew right from the start that this was it – that you are it, for me – and I didn't want to mess it up.'

Kate tries to speak, but she only succeeds in making a noise, a sort of sigh that seems to mean something to Spencer, because he pauses, looks at her, nods, and stops, facing her, too far away to touch.

'Although I suppose it didn't matter,' he says.

The cat releases Kate's tongue. 'Why didn't it matter?'

Spencer sighs and looks at her, straight at her, and her arm goes out to touch him, an involuntary motion, although she stops it mid-air and brings it back to her side. 'Because,' he says, 'whenever you found out about Amanda that would have been it.

I might as well have told you at the start. It was – insurmountable.'

'Spencer—' He's said what she's thought, over and over, through all of these nights, but there's something not right, when she hears it. Now she can't find another word to come after his name, which she finds that she has spoken softly, a bedroom word.

'And when I thought about it,' he continues, 'not that I've thought about anything else – I thought, well, if I was you, and I had a child with CF, and I found out that the person I'm with had a relationship with someone with a child with Down's syndrome – well, I would have seen a pattern. I think.' He shrugs, and his shoulders seem to land at a lower point than where they began. 'I would have done the same as you. To be safe. Of course I would.'

'But—' Kate says. Spencer looks at her, waiting, but nothing else comes. Her arm, so eager to reach for him a minute ago, won't move. He looks away, down to his shoes, over her head, through the place where the door is ajar as a trolley, rattling with glasses, is pushed past. When it becomes clear to both of them that she has nothing to say, he continues.

'What I'm saying is – I know it's too late. I can see that. I asked to talk to you because I wanted you to know' – Spencer falters, puts a hand to his eyes, takes a breath, and looks straight at her – 'if you can believe it, and I know it seems unlikely, but I want you to know it was just stupid chance. Not a pattern.'

'I—' Kate wants to say 'I know' but she can't, quite.

'I keep thinking that if I were you, I'd feel' – he grimaces, as though the coming word is bitter – 'targeted. I need you to know that it wasn't like that. I loved you. Love you. Amanda had nothing to do with it.'

Now that Spencer has given voice to everything Kate has been thinking she has nothing to say. Her stomach feels empty and her fingertips shake. All she has to do is reach. She sees that he has tears in his eyes.

The door opens and Daisy is there, looking from one of them to the other, and Kate's automatic reactions kick in: 'Hello, sweetheart,' she says, and reaches out a hand.

Daisy says, 'I came to put the box for my bridesmaid present in my bag because it's precious.' She holds out her little arm to show Spencer: Kate's already seen the sweet, charm bracelet with the butterflies and daisies attached. Despite her best efforts to suppress them, Kate feels her tears come.

'That's lovely, Daisy,' Spencer says. Kate can hear the tremor in his voice.

'Wendy says it's really gold,' Daisy says, 'and she says that when I'm bigger and the bracelet part doesn't fit I have to tell her and she'll buy me a bigger bracelet and we can put the butterflies and daisies onto that.' She beams at both of them, then looks at her wrist again.

'I'll put the box away for you, Daisy,' Kate says, trying to avoid what she fears is coming, 'so you can go back to the party.'

It's too late. 'Why are you crying, Mummy?' Daisy asks. 'Why is Spencer crying?'

'We're just a bit sad,' Spencer says. He looks at Kate over Daisy's head, the way they used to when Daisy asked them something, or said something, that they had to coordinate a response to. It makes her tears come faster, rather than slow down; she realises that she gave the pack of tissues from her bag to her mother during the ceremony, and so she dabs at her face with her fingers, then the heels of her hands. Daisy comes and stands next to her, puts a hand on her leg. Spencer holds out a handkerchief, blue like his shirt. Kate takes it. 'That's not a tissue,' Daisy says.

'It's a tissue from the olden days,' Spencer says, 'though we should use them more often, really. I got this out because it's a special occasion.'

'And grown-ups often cry at a wedding,' Kate adds. It's a feeble attempt at distracting Daisy from her line of questioning, but it's worth a try.

'Why are you both a bit sad?' Daisy is nothing if not persistent.

'We were talking,' she says, 'about why we're not a family anymore.' Spencer wipes his eyes with the side of his hand.

Daisy looks at them both. 'I liked it when we were our own family,' she says.

Kate and Spencer look at each other. There's a sad smile between them.

Daisy is on her way to the door when she turns and says, 'Mummy, I thought you said that you and Spencer really loved each other.'

'I did say that,' Kate says.

'If you and Spencer really love each other' – she puts the emphasis on the 'really', rolling it from her mouth – 'why aren't you getting married like Jilly and Wendy?'

'It's—' Kate starts, then realises that saying, 'it's complicated' to a five-year-old won't work. 'Sometimes—'

Spencer looks at Kate: I've got this, his eyes say. She nods. He says, 'Sometimes, Daisy, one of the grown-ups behaves in a way that means the other grown-up can't trust them anymore, and if they do that, they might still love each other, but it makes it too hard for them—'

'Oh, I'm so sorry.' Jilly is standing in the doorway, one foot in the air, mid-stride. 'I thought when I saw Daisy come in here that you must be finished.'

'I think we were,' Spencer says, not looking directly at anyone, then holding out a hand to Daisy. 'Shall we go and find Granny?' And then they're gone.

Kate sits down, puts her head in her hands. It feels as though even her bones are shaking. Everything Spencer said was right, and sounded wrong, like a speech incorrectly translated that starts a war.

'I'm sorry,' Jilly says again. 'I said I'd come and get the other Mrs Orr-DeMellow's handbag for her.' She stands next to Kate, touches her shoulder.

333

'That's OK. I don't think there was anything else to say.'

'From what Wendy says, it's been a hard situation.'

'It's just one of those things.' Kate wonders if she'll feel better if she reapplies her lip gloss. She knows the answer.

'I know it's none of my business, but what Spencer said about trust. Is that fair?'

Kate closes her eyes. Fairness is complicated. Trust is complicated. Parenting is complicated. Love is complicated. And yet it seems that everyone manages these complicated things, except her. 'Probably. He wasn't – honest – about something.'

'That's hard,' Jilly says. She looks as though she is waiting for Kate to say more.

'Yes,' Kates says, then, in a rush, 'but I wasn't always honest. When I was having Daisy, I lied. Her father was married. To someone else. No one knew, until – until afterwards.'

Jilly takes Kate's hands in her own; her wedding ring shines with newness and certain love. 'Nobody's perfect,' she says.

After a moment, Kate says, 'I just – I thought he was.'

Chapter 24

Mid-June

M ELISSA MEETS KATE'S TRAIN, much to her surprise. 'God, you look like shit,' she says.

'Thanks.' Kate can't help but laugh. 'I feel it.'

'Drink?'

'I could do with a coffee,' Kate says.

'I think you could do with an espresso martini.' And before Kate knows it, she's sitting in a booth in a cocktail bar, eating from the various bowls of food that Melissa has ordered – calamari, sweet-potato fries, olives, some sort of pickled salad. It's all delicious – salty and fatty and easy to pick at. Between that and the alcohol and the caffeine, and maybe the fact that Melissa has taken charge so Kate is not the adult, for once, Kate starts to feel something other than numb misery.

'We can talk about him,' Melissa says, 'but as soon as we start speculating, or repeating ourselves, we're done. There's more to life than men, honey. And there's a lot more to you than Spencer.'

'Actually, could we just not? Talk about him?' Kate feels strange saying it, but Melissa didn't ever meet him – they missed each other at Christmas, and on the day Melissa came to the hospital Spencer stayed away so there wouldn't be so many visitors. Whenever they talk about what's happened, Kate finds herself in the strange position of defending Spencer or explaining the assumptions that Melissa makes. As she has thought about little else other than Spencer, her soul and heart are ready for a rest. Even when she gives herself a talking-to and tries to concentrate on thinking about finding a job, or a work placement, or a way to keep studying, she can barely manage ten minutes before her mind wanders away to a memory, or sideways to a what-if. She even googled Amanda Lomax, and found a smart, serious, bright-eyed woman who now chairs a charitable trust that campaigns for disabled children's rights. It made her feel inadequate. What is she doing for Daisy, that's more than the basics? What sort of a role model is she? (*Well*, her sleepless mind countered, *at least you never hid Spencer in a wardrobe. At least you loved him. Love him.*)

Melissa raises an eyebrow. 'If you're sure.'

'I'm just – I'm sick of thinking about it.' Kate shakes her head. She really would have her hair cut short, if it wasn't such a break-up cliche.

'OK,' Melissa says. 'We'll get back to mine, have something to eat, and then there's the party.'

Kate looks at her watch. It's already after seven – she caught the late afternoon train. It's going to be a long night. 'Have we got time for another espresso martini first?' she asks. She's going to need the caffeine.

Kate resisted the full Melissa makeover that was on offer, but agreed to the loan of a pale grey shirt with flowers embroidered across the shoulders; she wears it over the sleeveless black dress she travelled in, rolls up the cuffs, knots it at the waist, and puts her denim jacket over the top. 'Man,' Melissa says as she looks at her, 'you look good.'

'Do I?' Kate looks at herself in the propped-up mirror in the corner, remembers the day she bought the jacket. She stands a little straighter. She can walk through the world alone, if she has to. She knows that now.

The party is taking place on the roof terrace that is shared by all of the flats in the building. It gets going shortly after ten. Groups of people stand and sprawl, laugh and talk, looking out over the north London skyline in the warm summer air. Kate might be enjoying herself. Someone's smoking a joint, but mostly the drug of choice is alcohol – a summery mix of fruit juice, wine and something else (vodka, Kate guesses, or maybe hopes, because she will cope with that better than she would with tequila) passed round in jam jars and replenished from a huge plastic tub. There seem to be friends from university, from work, and from home, as well as neighbours, so no one knows each other very well, and Kate is only as much of an outsider as everyone else. She talks to a trainee tattoo artist, and a French student who lives on the ground floor; when they ask her what she does, she says she's just finished a degree and she's working out what to do next. 'Cool,' says the tattoo artist, 'you could do anything!' And although Kate knows that that's not true, she feels, standing looking over London with the day fading and a drink in her hand, that actually, there are more possibilities for her than she has let herself believe. It's not Spencer or nothing. And so what if she leaves it five years before she trains as a physiotherapist, and in the interim looks for a job in a café? She's only twenty-four, for crying out loud. As Melissa said, on the tube on the way over here, she's missed her dossing-around years. She could have them now. No one would blame her. No one would care.

The alcohol is going to Kate's head and she finds herself laughing at the end of a long story about a lost phone, a taxi, and it-was-in-my-pocket-all-the-time. The sober-ish part of her knows that it's not that funny, really, but there is something about the way the girl is telling it (not a girl, really, a woman, probably older than Kate) that just amuses her. The others around her are laughing, too, the sound of their voices clear in the night sky, and Kate thinks, *this is what my life could have been.* And then, *I could do parts of it, still. Please myself, a bit. Get a tattoo.* And then she is thinking of Spencer; the tangled A and S on his upper arm that he hid the meaning of. The laughter leaves her as suddenly as it came.

Kate moves away from the bulk of the party, and sits on an upturned plant pot, leaning her spine against the parapet that separates her from the sky. She puts her head back, feeling brick against her skull, and closes her eyes. The world is cooling; midnight must be near, ready to tip her into tomorrow, another day done. And her life will feel empty, again. Kate knows, now, that she can do it all on her own. She's proved it to herself, on paper at least. If the sum of her life turns out to be keeping Daisy safe and well, and qualifying as a physiotherapist so that she can help other children like Daisy, that is surely enough? And if she ekes out her Netflix viewing so she has something to look forward to at weekends, so what? If Mike and Spencer are the beginning and end of her love life, does it really matter? At least she won't be one of those women who spends fifty years picking up after a man who stopped noticing her after the first decade. Melissa can say what she likes about more fish, and about not needing a man, not apparently aware that she is contradicting herself. But Melissa isn't Kate, and Kate isn't Melissa. Kate doesn't have whatever it is that Melissa has – resilience, hard-heartedness, time – that lets her hurl herself into one adventure or another without a worry, and pick herself up again as easily. Plus, Melissa can have a one-night stand without arranging a babysitter, can take a job without drowning in logistics.

She wonders if another drink will help. This is the trouble with being sad: it's so easy to blame it all on Daisy, when actually, before Spencer, Kate was happy enough. She could text him, right now. Ask him if he is happy. No. No.

'It's Kate, isn't it?' She opens her eyes, is looking into the face of Felix. She remembers his attentive eyes, the hair pushed behind his ears. 'Mind if I join you? But tell me to piss off if you want to be on your own.'

'Hello,' she says. 'No, it's OK. I might not be very good company. How do you know if you're just drunk or whether the drinking has showed you the terrible truth about your own existence?'

He smiles. 'That's a bold opener. Which answer means you're more likely to talk to me?'

Kate laughs, despite herself. 'Do you think a bowler hat would suit me?'

'It would. But it might slide off your hair. It's very smooth.' He holds out a hand, as though to touch her head, then pauses. Kate angles her head so that he can put his palm on her hair.

Kate laughs. 'Fair point. Sit down. I'm going to hurt my neck looking up at you.'

He has two goes at balancing on a plant pot, but Kate is on the only one that's feasibly big enough to act as a stool, so he lies on the ground, looking up at her.

The flirtatiousness of his smile is almost cartoonish; she's embarrassed, looks away. And there's Melissa, at the edge of a group a few feet away, looking at her and smiling. 'Why not?' she mouths. 'I would.'

So when Kate looks back down at him, she smiles. Her face hurts, a little with it, her heart some more. But she can do it. He reaches up a hand – blunt fingers, clean nails, soft palm – and she slides her own into it.

Later, in his room, Kate is down to her underwear before she changes her mind. It's not him, exactly. He's nice to kiss, hot-mouthed and enthusiastic, and his lips on her neck have made her shiver. But it's just not what she wants. It's Spencer or nothing. So, it looks like nothing. Maybe one day it will be different.

She pulls away. 'I think I've changed my mind,' she says.

Felix lies back with a sigh, puts his head onto the pillow. 'I thought my luck would run out at some point. Got further than I thought I would, if I'm honest.' He swings his legs off the bed, reaches for his jeans. 'I'm going to get you a pint of water, and I'm going to sleep on the sofa. Unless you want to go back to Melissa's now? I could try and sort an Uber.'

Kate almost pulls him back towards her. So many decent men. Why can't she fall for one of those? Perhaps she could, if she tried. But she knows it won't work as long as she has Spencer in her thoughts and heart, under her skin. 'Thanks,' she says.

'No worries.' Felix shambles towards the door. 'I like people who know their own minds.'

Is that me, Kate wonders as she drifts off to sleep, *do I know my own mind?* Given how wretched she feels, she wishes she didn't.

'I brought you sunglasses,' Melissa says, when they meet for brunch the next day.

'I have some,' Kate says. 'I don't feel too bad.' It's sort of true. Having had an emotional hangover since she said goodbye to Spencer, a physical one feels manageable. Balancing, even.

'Well you're a better woman than me,' Melissa says.

'I drank quite a lot of water. Before bed.'

'That's the bit I'm waiting for.'

'I don't know what got into me—' When Melissa raises an eyebrow, Kate laughs. 'That's not what I mean. Going back to someone's place like that. It's not like me. But nothing happened. Well – nothing much. I changed my mind.'

Melissa laughs. 'I was quite surprised that you went for it. But then again, things with Spencer were pretty quick, weren't they?'

'I suppose they were.' It didn't feel like a rush at the time. It just felt natural. But Kate doesn't bother to say so. Melissa's opinion won't alter.

But then Melissa adds, 'Though it sounds like you could have had all the time in the world, and it wouldn't have mattered. You know I'm not saying it was your fault? Just if it had been slower you might not have got so badly hurt.'

Kate nods – not agreement, but acknowledgement, and an inability to say anything more. Melissa will understand. She looks at the menu.

'I think it's going to have to be a full English breakfast and a side of fries,' Melissa says, a few minutes later. 'What do you reckon?'

'Yup.' Suddenly Kate is starving. 'And tea. Much tea.'

'Sorted,' Melissa says, waving at the waiter.

'Sorted,' Kate agrees, but it feels as though nothing is. She has to make an effort, though. 'Let's talk about something else. There's more to life than men, you know.'

Melissa looks offended for a second, and then she laughs. Kate laughs back.

'If you're sure,' Melissa says.

'I'm sure.' She is.

After brunch Melissa goes with Kate to the train station, and they have a goodbye coffee in the place where they had their hello cocktail. 'You look better,' Melissa says.

'I feel it.' And it's true: it's as though, this weekend, Kate has remembered that she is a person, herself, apart from Daisy, apart from Spencer, apart from Mike. She's herself. She's enough.

Chapter 25

Mid-June

BLAKE CALLS WHEN KATE is on the train, and in the three seconds between seeing his name and answering the call, she is already shaking with fright and making lists in her head of things she will ask her mother to bring to the hospital for Daisy.

But Blake's first words are, 'Daisy's fine.'

'Oh.' Kate feels as though she exhales her heart, she's so relieved.

'It's your mother. Don't worry – she fell off the trampoline, and we're waiting for an X-ray. Daisy's with us at the hospital. I just wanted to let you know that we can't pick you up from the station.'

'Right. Is Mum OK? Do you want me to come and get Daisy? I could see if Jo could give me a lift.'

'Her ankle's the size of a turnip, but apart from that she's OK. She and Daisy played I Spy in the car on the way to A&E. I'll let you know when we know how long it's going to take. Could you go and let the dogs out?'

Kate texts her mother a heart emoji, takes a taxi from the station to the flat, drops her bag, and walks to her mother's house. She's standing in the garden watching the dogs wander around when Blake texts to stay they are on their way back; it's a bad sprain, but there's no break. Kate loads the dishwasher, boils the kettle, takes two paracetamol and eats a couple of mini chocolate rolls against her lurking hangover, and thinks about how she has never, ever imagined life without her mother.

'Honestly, I'm fine,' Richenda says when they return half an hour later; but her face is grey and the mascara smudged across her face tells Kate there have been tears.

Blake settles his wife into a chair and puts her strapped-up foot on a stool. 'Do not,' Daisy admonishes the dogs, 'bump Granny's foot. Be very careful. Or you will have to live in the garden.'

Kate makes tea for them all, and listens to the tale – the fall, the sickness that swept through Richenda that made her sure she'd broken something, the relatively quiet waiting room. She has painkillers, instructions to keep weight off her leg as much as possible, and instructions to see her GP in a week. Blake thinks it's going to be worth having some physio, too, just to be on the safe side. When Kate watches Blake taking care of her mother like this, she is lonely to her bones. She pulls Daisy onto her lap. She bought her a notebook and some pens at the station, and Daisy immediately sets about illustrating the accident. 'Because you missed it, Mummy.'

Richenda lies back and closes her eyes. Blake says, 'I'm going to call the station,' adding, to Kate, 'I was supposed to be away on a residential course next week.'

'I'll be fine,' Richenda says.

'No, you won't.' Blake and Kate react in unison, and Daisy laughs delightedly. Kate adds, 'We can come and help, Blake. Can't we, Daisy?'

'You could walk the dogs,' Richenda says, as though she's making a great concession. Kate can see that all she wants to do is sleep.

'Or we could move in while Blake's away,' Kate says, 'couldn't we, Daisy? We could come and look after Granny and take Hope and Beatle for walks.'

Daisy nods, seriously, and then says, 'And I could go on the trampoline before school. But I don't think probably Granny should.'

Blake leaves on Monday afternoon for a Tuesday morning start; Kate feels odd in her old bedroom at first, with its single bed and the posters that she hadn't cared enough to take down when she moved out. Daisy, used to sleepovers with Granny, settles in immediately. Kate comes down from putting her to bed and watches *University Challenge* with her mum; it's an Oxford college against a Cambridge one. Richenda gets seven questions right, Kate three. Afterwards, Kate remarks that she might have missed Oxford but she doesn't think she ever would have been on the quiz team; Richenda laughs and then asks, 'Do you think about it? What it could have been?'

Kate sighs. 'Sort of. I know I have a degree now, but there's a lot I didn't have.'

Richenda nods. 'There are always paths not taken.'

'Yes.' And there's the memory of Spencer, always waiting for an opportunity to come to the front of her mind, to make Kate think of what else she might have been doing now. Well, she doesn't need to think about that this week. Because she would always have been taking care of her mother.

Richenda is an easy patient; Daisy runs around in the garden, and plays on the trampoline, and they eat meals from the freezer. Kate fetches and carries for her mother, answers the door, pops to the shop for groceries and the chemist for Daisy's new prescription. She has an excuse to hurry home after school drop-off, though Wendy stops her one day with a cake she's made for Richenda, and Kate watches Spencer comes out into the playground as they're talking; he seems to physically recoil when he sees Kate, and retreats into the classroom. Kate's heart shakes in her chest all the way back to her mother's.

On Wednesday, the physiotherapist, Zhu, arrives, and takes Richenda through some exercises and movements to strengthen her muscles. Kate watches, fascinated; she asks for the reasons behind the number of repetitions: which muscles are being worked, how they support each other, bones, body.

'Kate's thinking about a career in physio.' Richenda lies back in her chair at the end of the session, grey-faced with tiredness.

'I thought as much! People aren't usually this interested.' Zhu smiles at Kate, encouragement in her eyes.

'I was. Things have changed,' Kate says.

'The thing is, though, things always change. If I'd waited until I had time to do this, I'd still be picking up after my ex. There's never a perfect time.' Zhu shrugs and starts making notes on an iPad.

'You see?' Richenda asks.

'I know,' Kate says.

After Zhu has gone, leaving her card and an invitation for Kate to get in touch and shadow her for a day if she wants to, Richenda says, 'I didn't put her up to saying that. Honestly.'

Kate laughs. 'I wouldn't put it past you to throw yourself off a trampoline and orchestrate this whole thing to get her and me in the same room.'

'I don't need to. You'll be fine, Kate. You'll find a way.'

And suddenly, Kate feels as though she doesn't even have the emotional power to stand up. 'When?' she says. 'When will I be fine?'

Richenda reaches out a hand, and Kate goes to her, sits carefully next to her. 'How about now? Think how sorted you are compared to when Daisy was born. Compared to a year ago, even. You haven't seen how far you've come.'

'It's only really because of you, though, isn't it? Your help. Your money. The way you've always been there for us.'

It's as though Richenda hasn't heard. 'If you don't want to study any more for a while, that's fine. You don't have to decide anything for now. But don't ever think that you can't get qualified. It might be work and it might be hard going, but you can do it.'

'I'd need so much help,' Kate says.

'Well, yes. But look at me. We all need help.'

'Not—' Kate almost says, *not the kind of help that Daisy needs*, but she closes her mouth because she doesn't need to say that to her mother. And Richenda is right. She can do it. She never would have believed her nineteen-year-old self could have got this far. All she needs to do is begin. Daisy's birth forced one beginning on her; now she has to choose another.

'Why don't you arrange to spend some time with Zhu? We can figure something out with Daisy. And next year, won't she be able to do after school clubs? And why don't we have a look through all of your information about courses?' Richenda indicates her foot, propped on the sofa, slightly swollen toes peeping from the end of the aircast. 'I haven't got anything else to do.'

Kate has that feeling again, as though she is running very rapidly downhill, and her feet are going faster than she thought they would, and her urge is to put on the brakes: to say, *it's not possible, it's too complicated, what if Daisy gets ill?* But she knows the answers. It is possible; it is complicated, but that doesn't mean she shouldn't try. And if Daisy gets ill, Kate will keep on being the best mother she can. She goes to get her laptop and her diary, takes a breath, and sits down next to her mother. And she begins the next part of her life.

Chapter 26

Mid-July

THE NEW KATE, WHO IS, if not happy, at least able to sleep at night, decided not to volunteer to help at the school fete. She didn't want to be pulled into meetings and complicated planning; she didn't want to be in the school building more than she had to be, either. She trusts herself around Spencer now, feels as though things are, if not easy, at least bearable; since the wedding there has been quiet sadness in her, and whatever healing started with her weekend with Melissa has continued. There is so much more to her, she reminds herself every day, than whether she is half of a couple. And there is more to her than Daisy, too. That's allowed. That's OK. More and more, Kate is realising that her life is not, actually, a test that the universe has set her, and simultaneously rigged for her to fail. She isn't Sisyphus. She's just a woman doing her best. She won't be perfect, but she'll try.

She and Zhu are becoming friends; after Kate got in touch to ask for advice, Zhu asked her over for dinner, and what started as a slightly stilted conversation ended up with Zhu telling Kate about the places she has travelled and the plans she has to set up her own practice one day. Kate had come away feeling inspired, excited, and had woken the next morning full of something that she identified, after a moment, as hope. She has university open days in her diary for September, and Daisy is going to have a sleepover at Amelia's during the summer holidays – the first time Kate has trusted her daughter with anyone except Richenda or Melissa overnight. Her dad has offered her the flat for another year, as he's taking on another long-term project, this one in Scotland. Things are happening. Kate is living her life. She's excited, for the first time in a long time. And she knows – knows with an ache – that there may well be a point in the future, if Daisy's health changes for the worse, when she looks back on these years as though they were her luckiest and her best.

But even if she had been tempted to answer the call to arms on the flyer that Daisy brought home – 'Your School Fete Needs You!' – she does not trust herself to smile at Mrs Piper, if she has to be in the same room with her; and from what she knows of her, it's very unlikely that she will be trusting the PTA to organise anything unchaperoned. Kate wants the lowest possible amount of contact with someone who seems to be little more than a small-minded bully, no matter how the children she teaches love her, or the parents admire her for her firm hand.

Even being in the school playground makes Kate feel a little sick, in case Mrs Piper should come bustling through. Although Spencer is the one she should be angry with (and she doesn't know whether she is, really, anymore), at least he acted out of fear, out of a sense of self-preservation, rather than outright malice, which is the only real reason Kate can see for Bridget Piper's behaviour. Especially as Bridget knows nothing about Amanda, about Elise, about the story that could be constructed about Spencer. If she had known, she'd have made the most of it. What a field day she would have had then: ending Spencer's career, ruining his life, because she felt uncomfortable with a man doing what she thought was a woman's job.

On the day of the fair, Daisy is bouncing with excitement. When Kate drops her off in the morning – the slightest of nods at Spencer, no eye contact – Daisy's last words are, 'Remember! Bring my pocket-money purse when you come back!'

'I will,' Kate promises.

And after a day of ordering anatomy books and doing some desultory cleaning, she's back. She's changed her top, put on lipstick, is wearing the cowgirl boots even though it's really too warm for them. She doesn't think about why she has done any of these things, just walks to the school gate and stands amongst the depleted parents – those manning stalls are already in position. Jo waves from behind the tombola on the school field; Kate waves back.

Daisy makes a beeline for the Whac-A-Mole, and gives it her all, before joining the queue for the tuck shop. Kate stands back, just a little, and looks around the school yard at the rest of the fete: there's a guess-the-marbles-in-the-jar, a lucky dip, a bouncy castle, a face painter churning out butterflies, pandas and spider-men as quickly as she possibly can. How little things change. The school fairs Kate came to here as a child were much the same.

Later, Year One will perform a dance, followed by singing from the Year Two choir: Jo's son Jack will be part of that, and Daisy is excited to see him. And then they will slip away. When Kate was at school herself, she was always the outsider, too studious to be popular. Then, she wished things could be different. Now, she suspects they will never be. But she's not sure she minds. This seems to be her place, on the edge of things, looking in. Better to be a little lonely than to be part of a group like the one Serena, Sarah and Cara are huddled in now.

'Mummy!' Daisy bounces into view. 'I got you a lolly too! Shall we eat them straight away?'

'Yes. Thank you, sweetheart.' Kate unwraps it – it's a hard, red ball that smells warmly of synthetic strawberry – and puts it in her mouth, where it sits uncomfortably in her cheek. She takes it out again. 'Where next? Shall we go to the tombola and see if we can win something?'

Daisy rushes ahead, and Kate looks around for a bin, to dispose of the lollipop. Walking back towards the tombola, she sees Daisy has stopped, and is talking to Spencer, gesturing around the school field to various stalls – Kate can imagine that Spencer asked her how she is enjoying the fair, and is getting a more in-depth answer than he was prepared for. She pauses, watching, and then hears Daisy's name close to her, sees, ahead of her and turned away, Mrs Piper and her teaching assistant, looking towards Daisy. They clearly have no idea that Kate is behind them. 'Of course it's all supposed to be resolved now' – Mrs Piper makes air-quotes around the word 'resolved' – 'but I don't buy it. There's no smoke without fire, is there? Even without the child being – a special case. And interesting that *Miss* Micklethwaite dropped him like a hot brick when it all came to light.'

Kate stops. She's not sure whether she wants to hear more, whether she wants to be discovered, or whether she should walk up to Bridget Piper and confront her. She stands still, breathes. There's sticky red residue on her finger, which she sucks at.

'Which tells you a lot. And yet there he is, talking to that vulnerable little girl, in the middle of all this.' Mrs Piper turns her head, a little, enough for Kate to see the corner of her face, the raised eyebrow. 'Shameless.'

There's a route Kate could take, round to the other side of the tombola, so Mrs Piper will not know she has been heard. She takes a step in that direction, but then she sees the looks on Spencer's and Daisy's faces, and the sheer unjustness of what Mrs Piper has said becomes something that cannot go unchallenged. Daisy deserves better than this, and Spencer does, too. Kate remembers what it's like, to always feel under attack. Why should she, and he, skulk around as though they have done something wrong? So what if she was stupid, once, with Mike, and afterwards, with Spencer, she let her heart run away with her?

Kate takes a breath. She wipes the last of the residual stickiness on her finger onto the tissue in her pocket. 'What makes you think you know what you are talking about?' she asks. She sees the two teachers stiffen, sees that they plan to walk away as though they haven't heard. She speaks more loudly. 'Mrs Piper? I was just asking. Perhaps you didn't hear. What makes you think it's acceptable to spread malicious gossip like that?'

When Mrs Piper turns, Kate is satisfied to see that she looks pale, maybe even nervous, for a second, before recovering herself. 'I'm not sure what you think you heard, Miss Micklethwaite, but it was a private conversation—'

Kate hears herself snort. 'No one has a private conversation in the middle of a school fair. And what I heard you say was that' – she keeps her voice deliberately loud, even though heads are turning. She will not be ashamed – 'you think the relationship between Mr Swanson and I ended because there was something inappropriate in his behaviour. And that was not the case. Spencer is a good man. Sometimes things don't work out; not for lack of love, not because someone is a danger. Just because life is like that. Things aren't always as simple as we'd like them to be. As I'm sure you know.'

Mrs Piper can't seem to look Kate in the eye. 'Are you quite finished, Miss Micklethwaite?'

'Yes,' Kate says, then, as she sees that Mrs Piper is about to walk away, 'Actually, no. If I ever hear you talk about my daughter in the tone you just used again, I'll be making an official complaint against you. And it's Ms, not Miss.'

Mrs Piper opens her mouth, closes it again, and starts to turn in the direction of the school building. Kate thinks two things, one fast after the other. First, that if Melissa was here, she would now say something like, 'I don't think I gave you permission to walk away.' And secondly, what a good thing it is that Bridget Piper never found out about Amanda and Elise. She notices the way that other parents are looking at her, with surprise, with admiration, too, and that Mrs Piper is making her way into the school building, as though she has remembered something important. Kate watches her retreat, breathing deeply, not sure if she wants to laugh or cry. She looks for Daisy.

Daisy has moved on to the tombola, and is opening her tickets, one by one, solemnly putting them in a pile. She obviously hasn't noticed anything; from the look on Jo's face, glancing up as Kate approaches, Jo has seen, if not heard, that something has happened.

'Here's Mummy,' she says to Daisy, then to Kate, 'Is everything all right?'

Kate nods, though she couldn't say for sure.

Daisy looks up; freckles are spreading across her nose, the tops of her cheeks, as summer comes. 'I have to look for a zero or a five on the end, but not a zero or a five in the middle or at the beginning,' she says. 'I'm nearly finished.'

'Take your time, sweetheart.' Kate stands next to her, and closes her eyes, letting the sun warm her. She's gone cold, fingertips and face, and she wants nothing more than to be at home. Her speeding heart is slowing.

'I have one with a five,' Daisy announces, and Jo passes over a plastic bottle of bubble bath that Daisy immediately clutches to her chest. 'Thank you!'

'See you later,' Kate says to Jo, and asks Daisy, 'How about getting your face painted?'

When they turn away, Spencer is standing in front of her.

'Hey,' he says. 'Are you OK?'

'I'm fine,' she says, though she can feel that there are tears at the corners of her eyes. 'We're going to the face painting.'

'I heard what happened,' he says.

'News travels fast.' Kate slips on her sunglasses, straightens her spine. It's strange, to have him next to her, and not to automatically reach out a hand to find his, waiting.

*

On the way home, Daisy says, 'Amelia said you shouted at Mrs Piper.'

Kate smiles. 'I didn't shout, sweetheart. I just – I had to talk loudly, because there was lots of noise.'

'But why did you have to say anything?'

'She had said something she shouldn't have said.'

'What did she say?' Daisy is wearing her most persistent expression.

Kate is too tired to think of a way to dissemble. 'She said Mr Swanson did something that he didn't do.'

Daisy mulls this for the length of a street, and then, as they turn the next corner, says, 'Because if Spencer did something he shouldn't do then you would tell someone about it, wouldn't you? Like phone the police?'

'Sorry?'

'Well' – Daisy gesticulates, an expansive, let-me-lay-out-the-case gesture, and Kate is relieved that the balloon she is holding has a plastic weight on the bottom of the ribbon – 'if someone in my class does something that is not the rules then you have to tell Mrs-Orr-DeMellow-who-used-to-be-called-Miss-Orr. Or if it was you, we could tell Granny. So if it was Mr Swanson, we would tell the police. Or Mrs Hillier. Or his own mummy.'

Kate has a sudden, pure moment of pleasure at the company of this clever, thoughtful little girl, blazing through her life with such curiosity and clear-sightedness.

She laughs. 'Well, yes, I suppose we would. But Spencer hasn't done anything bad, Daisy.'

'But then why isn't he—' Daisy says, and Kate knows that she should answer the question, but she doesn't trust herself not to cry. Instead she interrupts with, 'Race you!' hoping that Daisy will forget this train of thought before she gets home.

Chapter 27

DAISY HAS A TANTRUM when the new bubble bath causes some of her face paint to smudge; it gets worse when Kate says it would have come off on her pillow, anyway, so her face needed to be washed. Kate does two things she wouldn't usually – lets Daisy fall asleep in front of the TV, and puts her to bed without cleaning her teeth. She can make up for it tomorrow. She's done with trying to be perfect. It's enough that she's standing. And she did a good thing today: she fought her and Daisy's corner. Spencer's corner, too. She didn't have to. But she did.

After she has scooped Daisy into bed, tucked her in, kissed her forehead, Kate breaks another rule: no drinking alone on a school night. There's a bottle of white wine she unpacked from the supermarket shop but didn't put in the fridge. There's ice in the freezer, though. She sends a photo to Melissa – the tumbler, the ice cube, the wine – with a plaintive, *Tell me things will get better*. Melissa responds with a picture of a sink filled with dirty mugs and plates, another of an almost-empty fridge, and the words *It could be that you're winning*. But Kate knows she isn't. The heart that she thought she had so carefully mended is not healed at all. Yes, she knows now that she does not need a man to complete her happiness. Yes, she is making steps towards a fulfilling life, a life of her own. And yes, she will define herself in more than the terms the world defines her in. All of these things are true. But they don't exclude the longing for Spencer that is in her bones. She closes her eyes, tries to think of anything except him. She pours another glass of wine. Perhaps tonight is the night to finally delete the rest of the photographs of the two of them from her phone.

She's scrolling through the images of their time together – selfies in the hospital garden, wobbly photos taken by Daisy on a Sunday walk, the view from their ill-fated country-house hotel. A family group photo, with John and Sally. Looking at the images has the comforting pain of biting down on a sore tooth, knowing what is coming.

The knock at the door makes Kate jump. It's almost nine, though the midsummer sky is barely dimming.

It's Spencer. It's almost as though her longing has conjured—before Kate can finish the thought, she pulls herself together. 'Hello.' She makes her voice neutral, or thinks she does.

Spencer nods. 'I came to say thank you. For today.' There's a question in his voice that she doesn't know how to answer.

'You said thank you. At the fair.'

'I know. That was before I got the full – information. One of the mothers said you had stuck up for me, so I came over. But afterwards, Bridget's teaching assistant – the one she was talking to – told me all about it. She said she was sorry for being part of what's happened. So I thought I should come and say thank you, again.'

'You didn't need to.'

But Kate notices that she hasn't slammed the door in his face, either. She steps back to let him in.

He's brought a packet of the Italian aniseed biscotti that Kate likes and he doesn't. Either he's made a special trip into Marsham to get them, or he had them at home for her. Wherever they came from, the sight of them makes her happy, and sad. 'Thank you,' she says, when he hands them over. Their fingers touch as she takes the biscuits but she cannot look into his face.

'I had them at home,' he says. 'I was never going to eat them. I suppose I could have kept them, in case I need something to seal up a hole in a wall.'

Kate can still taste wine in her throat; it seems important to be sober, now, so she puts the glass in the sink. 'Would you like a coffee?' she asks. 'And you could watch me eat them.'

He looks surprised; she imagines him making excuses, leaving. But of course, he wouldn't. If he was going to run at the possibility of coffee, he never would have come over to begin with. He could have texted her, or not said anything at all.

'Sounds good,' he says.

Kate thinks making the drinks gives her the chance to steady her hands, calm her heart. But Spencer is sitting on the sofa, saying nothing, watching. His attention makes her drop the spoon, pour a little coffee onto the worktop, wipe it up, turn the tap on too strongly so the water splashes. She could laugh, or cry. She chooses laughter. Spencer has always made laughing easy. 'Fun day, hey,' she says.

'None but the brave deserve the fair. Everyone's favourite afternoon,' he says. He's laughing too, shaking his head. 'I swear the only time I've ever seen Jane Hillier really lose it is after a meeting with the PTA committee about organising this.' The mention of the Head is enough to dampen them both; the smile drops from Spencer's face and he looks away. Kate pushes her hair behind her ear. Maybe she will have it cut short for the holidays. A change is as good as a rest. She imagines warm air on her neck, lifts the hair from her nape to see what the lack of weight would feel like. Spencer is watching. She feels herself blush; picks up the coffees.

Kate sits down opposite him. He holds out the opened packet of biscotti. 'Here, gnaw one of these.'

'Thanks.' The cellophane rustles as she takes one.

Kate doesn't want to try to unscramble what this means – the coffee, the sitting close to each other, the companionship she feels. She's tired; there's nothing left. *This is probably what life is like for divorced couples*, she thinks: *the sweet leftovers of something, and the need for getting on with it. Except divorced couples probably don't get self-conscious when their ex is watching them make a coffee.* Kate remembers the first time Spencer came round; how embarrassed she was, in her pyjamas and the ratty old cardigan that she still wears sometimes. At least tonight she is dressed; she's still in what she wore to the fair. Apart from her feet, naked now, her boots on the rack by the door. Her toes curl in on themselves, self-conscious.

'You didn't have to do that, today. I wouldn't have blamed you if you'd let them say what they liked.' His voice is gentle, grateful.

'They were saying things that weren't true.' She tries to shrug but her shoulders won't move. Her mind goes back, once more, to the first time he came to the flat, and she told him what she'd withheld from everyone else about the day at the hospital. She takes a mouthful of coffee, then slides her biscotti into the liquid in the cup to soften it.

'You're a good person, Kate,' he says. 'I want you to know that I know that. Not just for what you did today, for me, but for all you do for Daisy. I got to see that. All the things that no one else sees. You fight so many battles. I was lucky to see that and I was a fool, too.' He shakes his head, and repeats, 'You're a good person.'

He looks at her while he says this, and as soon as he stops speaking, his gaze drops to the coffee cup in his hands. Kate wants to say 'thank you' and 'I know': in the space where she's deciding which, something else escapes.

'So are you,' she says.

He looks up, startled. Kate bites into her biscotti, which has gone too soft now. It's pulp in her mouth.

'I really am,' Spencer says, seriously. It's as though he's at a job interview, except his eyes say that there is so much more at stake. 'I think. I mean, I was stupid, over Amanda, and I did the wrong thing, but there is nothing more – sinister than that. I knew it wouldn't look that way. That's why I didn't tell you.'

'I know,' she says. And as the words come out – Spencer blinks, once, twice, at the sound of them – she realises how true they are.

And everything might have changed, in theory, since they broke up, but in practice nothing feels different at all. Kate had thought that Amanda altered everything but, sitting here, she can't believe that Spencer is full of anything except love, and good intentions. She thinks of how she distracted Daisy from finishing her thought this afternoon.

Spencer is watching her. He isn't saying anything. He's just looking at her. Waiting. As though she has said half of a sentence; as though he has asked a question.

Then, Kate understands. If she wants him, it's up to her. No one is rescuing her, coming for her, sweeping her up as though she is something to be claimed. She gets to choose – to move, if she wants to. She takes a breath. She'd like to think she's deciding, but actually it's already decided. If it wasn't, she wouldn't still be dreaming of him, crying about him, wishing for his touch. 'Spencer, I can understand why you didn't tell me about Amanda. When I look at you I—' She fumbles for a word, finds it, and it's easy and true: 'I know. I just know. I should have—'

And she falters because of all the things she should have done.

'I should have told you, at the beginning,' he says. 'Then you might have judged me but at least you wouldn't have felt as though I'd – as though I'd tricked you.'

She nods. This is it; this is it exactly. 'I need things to be true,' she says. And she does. She needs to be sure of everything. Firm foundations are the only way she can cope when the world rocks: when Daisy is acutely unwell, or when her stats fall off a percentile, or when she grows and changes and Kate must understand a new landscape. And, Kate has come to understand, in these last quiet weeks, as she has planned her future, that it's OK for her to take steps, too. A foundation is good, but it's only a foundation. Can Spencer be both part of her foundation, and part of her adventure? His face says he's hers if she wants him. Her heart agrees.

He made a mistake. She knows what that's like.

There aren't words now, only the possibility of moving, forwards or back, onwards or nowhere new. She stands. She waits for him to move, to take a step towards her, like he did on that first night. But he doesn't. She realises that he still doesn't know whether she's welcoming or dismissing him. That his love is there for her taking. But he won't know that she wants him, unless she tells him. This is her decision, her moment to tell him that the possible world they talked about once could be theirs. That she wants it, still.

She steps around the table, sits next to him, takes his hand.

And then his arms are around her, holding her waist, tight, and hers are around him, his neck, and her face is turned to his shoulder but she hears every word. 'I didn't know what love was until I loved you,' he says, and she smiles, and she feels him smile too.

'I need this to be slow,' she says. 'I don't think I want to – settle down. I want adventures. As much as I can. I don't think I've ever had much fun.'

'We'll have all the adventures you want,' he says, 'though not on school nights.'

They both laugh, quiet sounds that are a little afraid. Kate hadn't realised how much she'd missed laughing with him, until now.

'Tell me everything you want to do,' Spencer says.

She stretches her legs across his lap, still holding his hand. 'Highway 66,' she says, 'and I want to do some wildlife volunteering. Wild camping. Turtles. Did I ever tell you that before I got pregnant with Daisy I was going to go and save some turtles?'

'You did. You told me everything.' The sadness on his face tells her that he knows – really knows – what toll his silence about Amanda took on her. And Kate doesn't want to think about that anymore. She sticks out her tongue, just to make him smile.

He laughs and reaches for the side of her face, her hair, cradles her head. 'If I said camper van, would you laugh?'

She does. 'Would you fit? Couldn't we get a caravan?' She can see it now: beaches, fish and chips, wandering around old castles and racing Daisy along towpaths in the twilight of a different place.

'We could,' he says. Then, seriously, 'Are you sure?'

'Yes,' and Kate is.

'And the other things?'

She thinks for a minute that he means Amanda, Elise, and she shakes her head. 'It doesn't matter now. I wish you'd told me. But I understand.'

He puts his lips to her forehead; his face might be damp. 'I meant,' he says, 'your life. Physiotherapy. Whatever you want to do next.'

'I've got ideas,' she says. 'And I can't – everything can't change depending on whether we're together. There's more to me than you. I mean—' Kate knows what she means, that she should never have been as diminished as she was when things between them ended, that she should not have lost her plans, her future, in the way she did. That there is so much more to her than Spencer. But he knows that, now. He said as much, at the wedding.

Spencer pulls her towards him and curls an arm around her shoulders. 'I understand. Look. It's two weeks until the end of term,' he says. 'We've got six weeks of summer, and then when school starts Daisy will be in Miss Ingram's class, and I'll have a whole new class of parents to wrangle. None of them will be you. Everything will be easier from here. And we don't need to decide anything big. Not for a while.'

'It's not that simple,' she says.

'I know. But it kind of is. Now that we're here, I mean.' He moves his shoulders, settling further back. 'I'm not explaining myself very well.'

Kate puts her head on his chest. 'I know what you mean,' she says.

She closes her eyes, and lets time pass. It isn't sleep, exactly, but it's peace. And she knows it's real because, not ten minutes later, there's the click of Daisy's door and the gentle shuffle of bare, sleepy feet. Kate sits up, as Spencer says, 'Hello, Daisy.' And Kate feels no panic, no worry, no shame. Her mind doesn't jump to how she will explain this away, smooth it over, how she should never have put herself in this position. It's just – it's fine. It's right.

Daisy is wearing her butterfly pyjamas. Her hair is tousled by sleep but her eyes are wide awake as she studies the two of them. Kate waits another moment to make sure she isn't going to feel tense, caught out, for her heart or mind to tell her that she's making a mistake.

But all she feels is happy. She smiles, reaches out a hand. Daisy makes her way towards them, and stops when she is close enough to touch Kate's leg. She leans on her mother, palms flat against her thigh. 'Mummy,' she asks, 'are you and me and Spencer going to be our own family again?'

Spencer's hand tenses, at her waist, but there's no tension in Kate. She isn't fool enough to think that things are going to be easy from now on, but there's some part of her that knows she's doing the right thing. 'Yes, we are,' she says.

Acknowledgements

There's nothing like writing a novel to show you how little you know about how the world works. Thank you to the many, many people who answered my questions about the experience of cystic fibrosis, in all its forms. I spoke to parents, children, nurses, doctors, adults with CF, and teachers. I also sought advice from those who have studied with the Open University, taught in primary schools, worked in trades unions, and single-parented, as well as parents of children with special educational needs. I've been blessed with beta-readers who gave insightful advice on my scratchy drafts and helped make the finished novel far better. I'm hugely grateful to all those who advised me. Any and all errors are my own. Honourable mentions to: Fiona Black, Sarah Collins, Julie Cordiner, David Pringle, Elizabeth Rowan, and Dannielle, Wayne and Finley Shoults.

I've been working with my agent, Oli Munson at A.M. Heath, for upward of a decade now, and am ever more grateful for his wise counsel and steadfast friendship. Thank you. The team at A.M. Heath is all-round amazing, too.

At Zaffre, my editor, Sarah Bauer, is kind and clever and embraced this novel with love. Thank you, Sarah. Thanks, too, to Margaret Stead and Katie Lumsden for editorial input, and to the talented people who make up the design, sales, production, publicity and marketing teams.

I'm lucky to have three fellow novelist friends who I can trust with anything, and who all read a painfully early draft of this and were encouraging and positive when I needed them most – Carys Bray, Sarah Franklin, Shelley Harris: you know.

Kate's friend Melissa is named for Melissa Conville, as a gift from her sister Katrina Taee, as part of the auction to raise funds for FareShare (fareshare.org.uk), the UK's national network of charitable food redistributors. Belated Merry Christmas, Melissa!

Last but not least, thank you to the friends and family who are always supportive: my parents, Helen and Michael; my children, Ned and Joy; my husband, Alan; my friends, especially Louise, Eli, Rebecca, Jude, Scarlet, Kym and Emily. And last-but-not-least of all, beloved Auntie Susan, to whom this novel is dedicated.